A
Harlequin
Romance

OTHER
Harlequin Romances
by SARA SEALE

Many of these titles are available at your local bookseller, or through the Harlequin Reader Service.

For a free catalogue listing all available Harlequin Romances, send your name and address to:

HARLEQUIN READER SERVICE,
M.P.O. Box 707, Niagara Falls, N.Y. 14302
Canadian address: Stratford, Ontario, Canada N5A 6W4

or use coupon at back of books.

CLOUD CASTLE

by

SARA SEALE

Harlequin Books

TORONTO • LONDON • NEW YORK • AMSTERDAM • SYDNEY • WINNIPEG

Original hard cover edition published in 1960
by Mills & Boon Limited

SBN 373-01096-6

Harlequin edition published March, 1967
Reprinted 1970
1972
1975
1976

Printed in Canada

CHAPTER ONE

I

"THIS ONE," Marcia said, with a laugh that was almost a giggle, picking a letter from the small pile on Raff's desk. "She signs herself Poppy Piper and is prepared to do anything. She will clearly keep Noel amused."

"Heaven defend!" her brother retorted, snatching at the next letter. "I'll settle for this one—she sounds class. *Her* name is Gwendoline de Vere, if she can be believed."

"I have decided on Judith Ware," said Raff, and his voice shared none of the ribald amusement of the other two.

"Why?" asked Marcia with interest. Raff had been against the idea from the beginning.

"She writes a legible hand, can apparently spell correctly and is a sensible age," he replied reasonably, and the girl made a small grimace.

"Probably one of those efficient automatons who'll order us all around and look down her prim English nose at our feckless Irish way of life," she said, and he smiled for the first time. She had no drop of Irish blood in her, but she could, like her brother, be more Irish than the Irish when it suited her.

"I thought efficiency was what we were aiming at," he replied mildly. "A secretary who doesn't know her job wouldn't be very much use to us."

"Well, darling, you'll have to work with her," Marcia said, and rose to her feet, stretching with her lazy cat-like grace.

Raff watched her reflectively. She boasted all the traditional dark beauty of the blood she could not claim and something more besides. It had been Noel's idea to turn Castle Slyne, Raff's elegant but decaying home in the west of Ireland, into a guest house to ease the drain on his dwindling income, but he suspected that Marcia, with her greater driving force, had probably conceived the notion in the first place and, once her brother was established as manager, had offered her services as receptionist with no thought of being refused. It was indeed, he thought, not easy to refuse Marcia when she had set her heart on something.

It had worked admirably. Raff had been shrewd enough to see that it was the two Maules, with their preposterous good looks and equally preposterous charm, who brought in the customers. He himself might be officially the owner and proprietor, but he knew from experience that his manner had none of the expected warmth and easiness of the popular notion of an Irish landlord, nor did he care very much what his unwanted guests might think of him.

He did not like his home filled with paying guests, who left cigarette burns on the carpets and cocktail stains on the mellow patina of period furniture, but it was better, he supposed, than seeing it all go. There had been O'Raffertys at Slyne since Cromwell's time, but he was the last of them, with no wife and no heirs to perpetuate this gently crumbling inheritance.

"You're looking feudal and king-of-the-castle, Raff. A penny for them," Marcia said idly.

"Most likely he's wondering how he's going to pay for the conversion of the cocktail bar," her brother laughed, and saw the quick look of distaste on Raff's thin, ugly face.

"A cocktail bar at Slyne!" he snorted, and Noel hunched his long, elegant body farther into his deep chair.

"Don't be stuffy, old boy, it's been the making of this place. Let's face it, the first demand your rich American clientele will make is for the bar."

"Sorry," Raff said. "If one's going to commercialise one's sole asset one can scarcely afford to be touchy, I suppose."

"All the Irish are touchy," Noel retorted, "but not to worry, me boyo. The guests expect a trace of *grand seigneur* to lend colour to the background. Of course they expect a display of the national warmth and proverbial wit, too, but I'll supply that."

Marcia did not add any contribution of her own, but sat regarding Raff through her lashes, wondering what it was about him that stirred her. He was lean and bony, like her brother but without Noel's elegance, and perhaps that in itself was an attraction. There was a toughness about the

6

loose, angular lines of his frame that appealed to her, accustomed as she was to men who were part of their clothes, rather than their clothes being part of them, and she liked the touch of arrogance that could put them all in their places, if he chose. His face, she supposed, was ugly, compared with the smooth, familiar handsomeness of Noel's, but she liked the long Irish upper lip, the equally long nose with the hint of a break, the grey that was beginning to fleck his dark, rather untidy hair. Grey in the middle thirties? But he was, of course, quite a bit older than Noel, then his grey, ineffably cool eyes met hers for a moment and she knew that this was his attraction for her, that odd reserve which she, despite her own vicarious experience of men, had never been able to break down.

"You look thoughtful, Marcia," he said. "Doesn't my choice of a secretary meet with your approval?"

"Secretary?" Her thoughts had been so unrelated to the subject which had brought them together in Raff's study this mild February afternoon that she could not, for the moment, adjust herself. "Oh, yes—you have chosen Judith Somebody because she writes a legible hand and can spell correctly. What will you do? Engage her on trial?"

"I suppose so. It's scarcely worth paying the return fare over for an interview."

"You don't sound enthusiastic. It was your idea to put an advertisement in the English newspapers. You could have picked someone up over here, probably more cheaply."

"I daresay, but the results of our first advertisement in the Irish press were scarcely reassuring, were they?"

She began to laugh.

"No, darling, not exactly, but I think you frightened most of them off. They probably thought from their interviews that you would be a slave-driver."

"I?"

"Yes, you! You are deliciously vague and remote when it suits you, but you have an abrupt way with you sometimes that might strike qualms in the stoutest breast."

"But not yours?"

Her eyes were soft and fleetingly coquettish as they met his.

"No, darling, not mine," she said lazily, and caught her brother's appreciative grin.

An answering grin creased the rather forbidding lines of Raff's face to unfamiliar softness, bringing back his youth, and he flung himself into one of the shabby chairs and reached for a well-worn pipe.

They sat in companionable silence for a while, listening to the accustomed sounds from outside; sounds woven among the multifarious other sounds which made up the familiar pattern of Slyne and which none but himself, perhaps, noticed. He caught Marcia hiding a yawn and knew that she was bored.

"We'd better get this letter off to Miss Judith Ware," he said. "There's one thing, Marcia, her coming will relieve you of the paper work."

"Praise the pigs for that!" she said, sitting down at the typewriter and finding the ribbon had jammed. "I can only type with one finger and I don't think I'm cut out for a secretary, anyway."

He smiled as he watched her wrestling with the machine. Marcia was cut out for a hostess, a job she filled with admirable ease and elegance; it had been her idea, in the first place, that a full-time secretary should be employed.

"I wish," she said with a grin, "you had chosen Poppy Piper. Noel is going to be awfully bored with your English paragon."

"It remains to be seen whether she turns out a paragon or not, and I might remind you that the girl is scarcely being employed for Noel's amusement," he replied a little dryly, and she turned down the corners of her charming mouth in mock acceptance of a rebuke she clearly did not take seriously.

"Girl indeed!" she observed, slamming paper into the typewriter. "She admits to twenty-seven, which means she's probably well over thirty. A sensible age, you say!"

"Well, what do we care?" asked Noel lazily.

"You will, darling," she retorted with an edge to her voice that made Raff glance at her curiously.

He did not find it strange that the Maules should now so plainly regard Slyne as their home. Meeting Noel again after so many years had been a reminder of old times rather than a mutual delight for, in the past, their ways had seldom led along the same lines, but the younger man's plans for Slyne had proved a fillip after a period of apathy and his viewpoint was refreshing.

"Let's face it, old man," he had said, "we're all on our beam ends, so why not get together and capitalise your principal asset?"

Raff had not bargained for Marcia, whose type was unfamiliar to him. She was different from Kathy who had been young and naïve, and quite without sophistication, but Kathy, he supposed, would never have managed difficult guests as Marcia did, and he was grateful for, and still a little puzzled by, her willingness to stay.

"*Dear Miss Ware,*" he began suddenly, aware that it was slightly ridiculous to be dictating a letter to Marcia when he could quite well have written it himself, "*In reply to your letter of the 10th inst. . . .*"

II

In the days that followed, Raff went about his policies already regretting the engagement of Miss Judith Ware, that unknown young woman from London who, as Marcia had suggested, would most probably look down her prim English nose at their lax methods and hanker after a cosy little flat in Streatham; not that there was anything lax about Marcia, or Noel either, when it came to hard cash. The guests who came to Slyne paid handsomely for their privileges and, when they irked him, Raff had learnt to think in terms of the benefits they brought; restoration to the panelling in the drawing-room, fresh plumbing, and the employment of more labour to keep the parkland from falling into complete neglect. Coming back from his frequent tours of inspection, he would often pause to regard the house rising grey and gracious above its terraced lawns which met the water's edge, and know that the strangers within his gates were unimportant, a bearable pest like flies, or the gentle stench of rotting vegetation in warm weather, but a pest, without which continuance at Slyne would have been barely possible. The love of his land was in his bones, and for Slyne he would bear much, even the indignity of paying guests.

Sometimes, but not often now, he would think of Kathy, remembering her youth and her joy in living, seeing again the ghost of a naïve young girl running to him across the lawns, hearing her laughter or, perhaps, seeing the tears she would have shed that there should be strangers now where once only she had visited. Then he would look towards Slieve Rury, its tapering summit rising in cloud beyond the lough; to the wild stretches of country which cut Slyne off in the splendid isolation of the west, and experience that strange pride and love for his unfruitful acres, an affection which the years of fighting and racketing on foreign soil had only served to strengthen.

"You have a one-track mind, haven't you, darling?" Marcia would say when she observed him regarding his property with that familiar inward look. "Have you only eyes for stone and mortar and the not very fruitful soil of your ancestors?"

His reply would be evasive as usual, but she knew that once there had been Kathy to turn his thoughts to flesh and blood, and that now Slyne had become a protective barrier between him and the rest of the world.

The new secretary was to arrive at the end of the week and Marcia had a little difficulty in persuading the so-called staff that the innovation was for the benefit of Slyne. The permanent servants consisted of Mary Kate, the cook, who, in her youth, had been a nursery-maid to Raff's nanny, finally taken her place, and stopped on ever since, and Timsy, one-time boot-boy who stepped sourly into most capacities required of him, aided by a middle-aged niece and young Rosie Boyle from the farm. The frequently changing complement of girls from the tenants' cottages and the half-trained youths who waited at table in the season were, in their scornful eyes, unqualified to rank as members of the household.

"For what would himself be troubling with a secretary? Are you too grand to type out his letters yourself, Miss Maule?" Mary Kate demanded crossly, and was unimpressed when it was explained to her that Marcia had other duties.

10

"Another to make trouble with the girls who mislike waiting on paid employees they consider no better than themselves," Mary Kate grumbled.

"Well, they'll have to make the best of it," Marcia replied a little sharply. "We'd better give her the Oak Room—it has plumbing of a sort and that will save cans of hot water."

"Ah, sure the old nursery's good enough for the likes of her, and if she wants hot water then she can fetch it herself from the sink at the end of the passage."

"There's only a cold tap."

"Then if she wants it hot she can go down to Timsy's pantry and boil it herself on that new contraption Mr Noel persuaded the poor master to put in there when the furnace was good enough in the old days till Timsy got too grand or too lazy to stoke. You'll not find Miss Doyle traipsing up and down them stairs with cans."

"Really!" Marcia complained to Raff, "your valued retainers can be very pig-headed when they choose. Prim Miss Ware is going to find it hard to please. Mary Kate clearly considers her no better than a servant."

"Most Irish servants of the old school are snobs at heart," Raff replied absently. "'The quality never soil their hands with work' was a familiar saying, even in my parents' time."

"Very right and proper if one's income would allow it," Noel grinned. "Are you going to meet the train, Raff?"

"What train?"

"Miss Judith Ware's train which we trust is bringing her to Knockferry. Really, Raff, don't be so vague!"

Raff frowned.

"You go," he said shortly. "I'm going to have a day on the lough now that we only have a few perishing guests billeted on us. At the moment I don't need the services of a well-trained secretary at all."

"But you will, darling, when the season begins and rich Americans start applying," Marcia said with amusement. "Perhaps she won't stay, anyway. Mary Kate is putting her in the old nursery which reeks of damp, and she must heat her own hot water on the contraption you put in Timsy's pantry."

"I'm beginning to feel quite sorry for poor unsuspecting Miss Ware," said Noel lazily as Raff left the room. "How am I to recognize the lady at the station?"

"Easy," his sister replied promptly, "hardly anyone gets off that train and the English stand out from the others like sore thumbs. She will be stiff and neat with large feet and her hair in a bun—probably glasses, too."

"Horn-rims? You have a prejudiced attitude towards the conventional secretary, my sweet. Can it be wishful thinking?"

"Hardly necessary, would you say?" she answered demurely, "and I can't say I envy the wretched girl if she has to work with Raff when he's in one of his king-of-the-castle moods. Well, I'd better go and see that someone at least thinks of lighting a fire in the nursery, and you, my lamb, should be setting out on that dreary drive into Knockferry."

Noel did not hurry. He was often as bored as Marcia between seasons when their guests were few and sometimes dull, but he did not, any more than his sister, look forward to rewarding company in the shape of Raff's new secretary. He only hoped, when the Land Rover sprang a puncture halfway to Knockferry and made him late, that she would have had the sense to remain on the platform and not have gone seeking the Englishwoman's solace of a cup of tea in the town.

The platform was deserted. The refuse of market day blew on to the line in careless abandon, and there was no nervous arrival waiting beside a pile of luggage. Noel wandered over to the stationmaster's little office where a shot of the "crayture" could always be anticipated, and there he found the only passenger left from the train from Dublin. She was perched on the stationmaster's table, sipping doubtfully at a glass of whisky, and old Mick, the stationmaster, and Patsy Kelly, the solitary porter, were grouped around her, like glasses in their hands.

"Well," said Noel, letting the door slam behind him, "you seem to be having a party—or is it a wake? May I join you?"

"Sure, sure," said Mick, foraging for another glass. "You're late, me boyo, but so was the train. You shouldn't

12

be keeping a lady waiting, though, and she crossing the Irish Sea and sick to her stomach, no doubt. *Was* you sick, miss?"

"No." the girl replied. "But it was cold, and I find the times of your trains confusing."

"There!" the stationmaster exclaimed, as though she had paid him a compliment. "A fine, mislocated country we are, fit to astonish the English!"

"You astonish me all right," she said, lifting her glass to him. "Never before have I been given comfort like this at a station. Slainte!"

"Slainte," echoed Mick and Patsy Kelly in unison, and Noel took a long look at the girl, and his mouth curved upwards in amusement. Was this the prim, efficient secretary of their imaginings? She was younger, far, than the twenty-seven years she had claimed, her face was ingenuous and slightly freckled and her hair, wind-blown and untidy, was a warm but aggressive red.

"Could you possibly be Miss Judith Ware?" he asked with malicious politeness.

"Yes, I'm Judy," she replied with comfortable assurance, then her eyes widened, and she slipped off the table, standing awkwardly before him.

"Are you—are you, by any chance, Mr O'Rafferty?" she faltered suddenly.

He appraised her silently before replying. She was thin and wiry under the nondescript clothes she had travelled in, he saw; but her eyes were green and wide and inquiring and there was a generous, innocent curve to her wide mouth.

"No, I'm not O'Rafferty," he said, wondering what Marcia would think of her. "I'm Noel Maule, the guest house manager. Shall we go, or would you like another drink?"

Her eyes went to the stationmaster with serious challenge.

"Is he who he says?" she asked, and old Mick grinned.

"Sure he is," he said. "You'd not be expecting the O'Rafferty to meet you, would you, and he, like as not, fishing his own waters or doing the polite to those fancy guests they have up at the castle?"

"No—no, I suppose not," she replied uncertainly and, becoming conscious of Noel's ill-concealed look of assessment, she raised her chin and banged down her empty glass simultaneously.

"Hadn't we better be going, Mr Maule?" she said, and he was aware of a flicker in her green eyes which promised to enliven the duller moments at Slyne.

Both Mick and the porter hastened out to the car with her spare luggage and caught the largesse which Noel tossed to them with eager hands.

"Does that pay for my whisky?" Miss Judith Ware asked coldly, as she perched herself awkwardly on the Land Rover's high seat. "I'd thought it was Irish hospitality—the kind you read about in books."

"The kind you read about in books is usually a figment of the author's imagination, and even Irish hospitality has to be paid for," Noel observed indulgently.

Judy said: "Oh!" with a sharp little inflection as if the explanation had disappointed her, and Noel, letting in the clutch and moving away into the main street of the town, gave her a sidelong glance.

"Don't start off with romantic ideas about the Irish — you'll be disappointed," he said softly, and saw that in profile her nose had an upward tilt and that she was holding her head high enough to exaggerate the long clean lines of throat and neck.

"You'll be a surprise at Slyne," he added, wondering, even then, what possibilities of amusement she might hold for him.

"Why?"

"Well—your letter didn't give much indication of what you're really like, did it? How old are you, to be truthful?"

"Twenty. This is my first job, you see, and—and I thought I'd stand more chance if I was older. . . ."

"But twenty-seven! Weren't you overdoing it a bit?"

"Seven's my lucky number—I simply added it," she said with a touch of defiance. "Besides, it's a sensible, safe-sounding age. Does it matter how old a secretary is?"

"Not so long as you're efficient, I suppose. *Are* you efficient, Miss Judy Ware?"

14

"Very. I had a higher speed in typing than anyone else who took the course and I can spell correctly."

Her hair streamed behind her in the wind as the Land Rover bucked its way over the bumps and stones, and she craned her neck to gaze upon the lough and not miss a single aspect of its beauty. Only when they reached the gates of Slyne did her enthusiasm falter.

"But," she said, as her eyes beheld the sprawling, indefinite lines of the house which almost met the water's edge, and the unfenced, neglected boundaries of the parkland, "I thought it was a castle, with a moat and a drawbridge and—and everything."

"Almost every small estate calls itself a castle in Ireland," he answered carelessly. "Were you expecting liveried flunkies as well?"

"Of course not! You must think me a greenhorn, Mr Maule."

He had pulled up in the drive to let her have her first sight of Slyne and, for him, it was an automatic reflex to let his arm slide along the back of the seat behind her shoulders.

"A greenhorn with possibilities, I would say. Slyne can be very tedious in the off-season, you know," he said.

She studied his ridiculously handsome face with unembarrassed curiosity. He was, she thought, almost too good to be true, with his film-star features and black curly hair.

"Are you a wolf, Mr Maule?" she inquired seriously.

He raised one eyebrow and replied indulgently, "What experience have you of wolves, Miss Ware?"

"Quite a bit," she answered calmly. "Girls alone in London have plenty of opportunity to study the species. I don't care very much for wolves."

"Don't you, indeed? I wonder what Mr O'Rafferty is going to make of you."

"Why? Is *he* a wolf?"

"No—oh, dear me no! Raff's wolf days are over, if he ever had any. You'll be quite safe; he won't notice much difference between you and your typewriter."

"Oh! He doesn't sound very cosy."

"Cosy! No, I wouldn't describe our king of the castle as that. But you've just told me you don't care for wolves."

15

"It's quite different," she retorted with some asperity. "There should, after all, be a certain sympathy between employer and employee—don't you agree? Besides, I don't find wolves cosy."

He experienced that sudden attraction which novelty could always hold for him. She might be fun, he thought, this uninhibited little redhead who expected such unlikely results from her first job.

"I don't know about the sympathy," he replied lazily. "But when Raff can spare you, you can always do some typing for me, then we'll find out, won't we?"

"I don't think so," she said, giving him a very cool stare from under her lashes. "Hadn't we better be getting to the house? I should like a cup of tea."

III

If he himself had appeared to make little impression on Judy, Marcia had the opposite effect. Noel was amused to observe the momentary shyness which descended on the girl when she was confronted with his sister's experienced graciousness. Marcia gave a perfect example of the practised hostess putting a raw young employee at her ease, and the fact that Judy became *gauche* and almost tongue-tied would he knew, please Marcia, who did not care for feminine competition.

"Not a very sparkling companion, and perhaps that's just as well," the older girl observed after she had taken Judy to her room.

"Don't you believe it!" her brother retorted. "I was treated to several rather unusual observations on the way home. You made her shy, my sweet, with all that womanly charm and sophistication."

"Did I? Well, she probably felt a bit travel-stained, poor dear, and certainly looked it. I doubt if Raff will keep her."

"Oh, why?"

"Well, she's not what he was expecting, is she? Too young for a start, and that red hair."

His eyebrows rose.

16

"Red hair isn't a monoply," he said, "and she tells me she's efficient. Raff likes efficiency."

"And you, my beloved brother, rather like the new secretary," she laughed. "Well, there's no accounting for tastes. At least she won't be Raff's cup of tea."

"No? There was a certain familiarity of type, I thought."

"Oh, you mean Kathy," she said with a little yawn. "But that was long ago, and one grows out of a taste for naïveness. Raff is thirty-six now, and has progressed out of adolescence, one hopes."

"Who has progressed out of adolescence?" Raff's voice asked from the doorway. He stood in his rough tweeds and sweater, peering into the uncertain gloom which the late February afternoon made in the shadowy, high-raftered hall in which they had remained sitting.

"You," said Marcia, blowing smoke rings lazily above her head. "We were talking of your new secretary, darling —not at all what we expected, young and rather *gauche*, and her mother's milk not yet dry behind her ears, I shouldn't wonder."

He frowned.

"Twenty-seven is a mature age," he said.

"Actually she's twenty and this is her first job."

"Oh, lord! I'm no wet-nurse to unfledged novices! We'd better get rid of her."

"Not without an interview, darling. Here she is. Be tolerant, now!"

Judy came down the shallow, graceful staircase, pausing every so often in uncertainty.

Marcia looked up inquiringly. The girl had changed, she saw, into a dark frock which made her look very slender, and her hair was brushed and burnished into a thick, gleaming halo which curved back from her ears in childish fronds.

"Come along, Miss Ware," Marcia said kindly. "This is Mr O'Rafferty for whom you will work."

She watched with idle curiosity the first meeting between these two and felt a fleeting sympathy for the girl, for Raff did not come forward to shake hands and make her welcome, but stood by the fireplace, his hands in his pockets, observing in silence her slow progress across the vast expanse of polished floor to meet him.

"How do you do, Mr O'Rafferty?" she said, holding out a hand.

In the dusk his face appeared blurred and inscrutable, but she had an impression of sudden hostility in the lean, crooked features. Although he took her proffered hand for a moment and murmured some sort of greeting she was aware first of surprise then of a puzzling antagonism in him, and she looked a little uncertainly towards Noel lying back in his chair in the shadows.

Judy blinked at Raff inquiringly, seeing clearly now the not unattractive ugliness of his face, the unexpected grey in his hair and the coldness of his appraising eyes. Cosy . . . she thought with a hastily suppressed grin . . . no, he would never be that! There was no warmth in him, no welcome, even. Well, better that way, perhaps than the rather obvious intentions of someone like Mr Maule.

"You have red hair" Raff said suddenly, and made it sound like an accusation.

Judy flushed slightly; her hair had always been a sore point, earning for her, in younger days, the inevitable soubriquets of "carrots" and "ginger", but she thought it rude of Mr O'Rafferty to comment so bluntly in front of strangers.

"The colour of my hair won't, you will find, affect my efficiency, Mr O'Rafferty," she retorted, and saw him smile faintly.

"Good for you!" Noel laughed, and Marcia rose to her feet and moved with cat-like elegance across the hall.

"You aren't exactly making Miss Ware feel at home, darling," she observed to Raff. "I'll go and see about some tea. Mary Kate remembers the guests if they ring the bell enough times, but she's apt to forget us. Sit down, Miss Ware, and forget about Raff's ill humour."

The two men talked idly, forgetting her, and presently Marcia returned, pushing a tea-trolley.

"Really!" she remarked, sounding a little exasperated, "I do think you might train your servants better, Raff. Timsy hadn't even the grace to wheel the trolley in for me."

"He probably wasn't dressed for company," Raff replied imperturbably. "Timsy has a great sense of fitness."

"He also has a great sense of idleness, and a taste for the bottle!" said Marcia shortly. "Do the daily girls usually go home so early as this?"

"I don't know. That, surely, is your province," he answered pleasantly, and caught his prospective secretary's eyes fixed upon him in a green, unwavering stare.

"You must be thinking this is a very inefficiently run guest house, Miss Ware," he observed, "but our visitors are properly catered for, I assure you."

"In there?" asked Judy with interest, inclining her head towards one of the closed doors, behind which the desultory murmur of voices could occasionally be heard. The apparent absence of guests had begun to worry her.

"In there," he answered, and she heard the faint distaste in his voice. "Fortunately we have only a handful to contend with just now, but later, according to Mr Maule, there will be rich Americans, wealthy industrialists from the Midlands, even authors and playwrights and jaded film stars discovering the quaint delights of romantic Ireland."

"Why," asked Judy, her mouth full of one of Mary Kate's buttered baps, "do you run a guest house if you think so little of the customers?"

Raff did not trouble to answer, or perhaps he was considering a suitable reply, but Noel said with faint relish:

"L.S.D., my dear Miss Ware. The stately homes of Ireland, though running to decay more obviously than the English variety, need keeping up just the same."

"Oh! Oh, I see," she said, conscious that her inquiry might have sounded impertinent, and was made to feel no happier when Raff observed with an edge to his voice:

"I doubt if you do, my dear young lady. Sometimes I wonder myself if the preservation of one's home is worth the constant irritation of strangers perpetually under one's feet."

The passing glance he gave her seemed to include her in the same category, and she was grateful to Marcia who remarked gently:

"You've got a chip on your shoulder today, darling. Poor Miss Ware will be regretting her trip across the channel."

"I'm sorry," he replied quickly, and Judy observed with surprise the little smile which suddenly lent his ugly face a fleeting tenderness. "I'm being a grouch. I've had a few complaints that are usually reserved for you, I imagine — bath water not hot, beds not properly made—trivial irritations. Now, you'd better come to the study with me, Miss Ware, and answer some questions."

Judy rose obediently, but remarked with reasonable, though ill-judged surprise:

"I answered all your questions when I wrote, Mr O'Rafferty."

His eyes rested on her with sudden unsmiling scrutiny.

"You told me one lie, there may have been others," he replied with rather alarming asperity, and she followed him across the hall to the door of his study, feeling all at once that she was back at school receiving a summons from the headmistress.

"Poor child!" Marcia murmured as the door closed on them. "Raff seems definitely anti, doesn't he? I wonder why?"

"Must be the hair," her brother observed lazily. "I told you there was something vaguely reminiscent about the brat."

"Nonsense!" said Marcia quite sharply. "Kathy was soft and cuddly like a kitten, and very pretty and adoring, from all accounts. This girl is a bag of bones and could, I'm beginning to suspect, speak her mind if pushed to it. She'll not last long with O'Rafferty if the two get across one another."

Judy was beginning to reach the same conclusion as she faced her prospective employer across the littered desk. He sat down himself but did not offer her a chair, and she stood, twisting her fingers together in nervous anticipation while he fiddled aimlessly with the papers on his desk.

"Why did you lie about your age?" he demanded suddenly, and she answered as she had replied to Noel:

"Seven's my lucky number. I just added it on."

"So you're only twenty. What other—er—mis-statements were there in your letter?"

"None, I think."

"But you didn't see fit to mention that this was your first job."

"You didn't ask me. You asked for references, and mine from the secretarial college were very good."

"Possibly, but you have no experience."

"You didn't ask that either. What experience do I need, apart from efficiency in my work and ability to keep myself in the background?"

He smiled faintly.

"I'm beginning to think that's an ability you may not possess to any high degree," he said, and she answered a little forlornly:

"I can learn."

"Can you? Well, let's see what your speed's like. There's the typewriter."

"Yes, pretty fair," he admitted when she handed him the finished letter. "You kept up with me, too. Marcia always says I go too fast. Pity—you might have been useful."

"What do you mean, a pity?" she asked, puzzled again by his manner.

"You won't do, that's all. Naturally I'll add a bonus to your return fare to compensate for your lost time, but I'm afraid you won't suit Slyne."

She was, as yet, too inexperienced not to argue.

"But why—why?" she demanded. "It doesn't make sense to waste all that money on a fare from England and not even give me a trial. You said yourself I was good, and on my own machine I'd do better. This thing must have come out of the ark!"

His eyebrows rose.

"You see!" he observed mildly. "You answer back. I'm sure the college must have warned you that wouldn't do at all."

"I've a right to know where I've failed," she persisted stubbornly, and felt suddenly very near to tears. There was something altogether perplexing about this man's attitude.

"Why do you dislike me, Mr O'Rafferty?" she continued more quietly, and saw a look of uncertainty, or perhaps it was simply weariness, cross his ugly features.

"How should I dislike you on such short acquaintance, Miss Ware?" he replied evasively, and her green eyes stretched wide in an effort to keep back the tears.

"One can dislike anyone on sight. You haven't made such a good impression yourself, if it comes to that," she retorted unthinkingly, and saw the first hint of interest in his cold eyes.

"No, I imagine not," he admitted quite pleasantly. "I've nothing personal against you, my dear."

Judy was tired and bitterly disappointed, and with disappointment came sudden anger. What right had he to look at her with that chilly appraisal and address her as "my dear", as if she were a child?

"Oh, yes, you have!" she cried. "You didn't like the colour of my hair, which I don't either, but can't do anything about short of dying it black, but that's no logical reason for a grown man to give, is it—*is* it?"

"I suppose not. You seem to have a temper that matches your hair, if I may say so."

"I'm sorry. I didn't mean to be rude."

"I'm sure you didn't. Well, now, can I write a letter recommending you, to help you with the next job?"

"How can you recommend me when you haven't given me a trial?" she protested crossly, and he noticed for perhaps the first time the tiredness in her face and the struggle she was having to keep back tears.

"Had you set your heart on this?" he asked with a renewed flicker of interest.

"Yes—yes, I had. I wanted to see Ireland."

He smiled, then asked with a curiosity he had no desire to feel about her:

"What will you do when you get back to England? I mean, where do you live and who are your family?"

She lowered her lashes, not wanting to satisfy an interest which could only be passing.

"I have no family," she said. "I lived in a rather dreary hostel in North London. We had to be in by ten and no men in the bedrooms."

"Very proper, I don't doubt, but hardly home."

"No, it wasn't home," she said, and he saw her wide green gaze begin to travel with unconscious nostalgia over the miscellaneous but comfortable appointments of the one room at Slyne he could honestly call his own.

"We share a mutual need," he told her with faint irony. "It doesn't please me to be obliged to turn my home into a guest house, you know."

"It's better than living in other people's," she replied gently, and he got to his feet with sudden impatience.

"Perhaps," he said brusquely. "Well, Miss Ware, you can stay here for a week, if you would care to—as my guest, of course. A holiday at Slyne with all the trimmings might be a small compensation for your return to the dreary hostel. What do you say?"

Judy had risen also. He was not, she thought, at all like the usual employer, offering a week's expensive holiday in lieu of dismissal as a sop, but he was still a disappointment.

"Thank you, Mr O'Rafferty, I would like to stay, as my room at the hostel is taken, but I wouldn't care for those terms," she replied politely. "I would prefer to do such secretarial work as you need until you can find someone more suitable."

He looked down at her curiously, observing the tension in the slight lines of her narrow frame which, at twenty, he thought vaguely, should not have seemed so brittle and hungry-looking. The reproach in her clear eyes was probably unconscious, but he did not care for the uneasy feeling it gave him.

"You're an odd mixture, Miss Ware," he told her dryly. "Had you been the twenty-seven you claimed, with the large feet and neat bun of Marcia's imagination, things might have been different."

"Can—can I really stay for a week—on my own terms?" she asked hesitantly.

"I suppose so," he answered, rubbing the aggresive bump in his broken nose with an irritable forefinger, "though I can't think what I'll find for you to do."

"Why, then, did you advertise for a secretary?" she retorted with reasonable logic, but he seemed tired of the interview and wandered towards the door.

"It was Marcia's idea," he replied vaguely. "She can't contend with the paper work, she says, and I, of course,

23

can only type with one finger. Typical Irish fecklessness, you see, my dear Miss Ware. I was probably never meant to run a successful business."

He went out of the room, leaving her standing there in slight bemusement. She covered the typewriter, straightened the papers on his desk, and turned the light out.

Through the uncurtained window she could see the still waters of the lough stretching away quiet and solitary in the twilight. Beyond were the mountain peaks, shadowy and indefinite, and a deserted ribbon of road wound through the rough parkland.

She turned her back on that brief glimpse of the unfamiliar, and shook the heavy hair out of her eyes. Tomorrow, the next day and the next, she would store up memories to be taken back to England and a new, depressing hostel, and the unrewarding routine of a London office. She was, she supposed, as her father had often told her, sadly unfitted for the chill demands of city life. Well, one learned; one learned, as her father had also told her, by one's own mistakes and the unfulfilled promises of others.

Michael O'Rafferty's promise had been implied rather than given, she had to admit, and she herself had built too much on a chance which had seemed to be golden and assured. All the same, it was strange and a little insulting, she thought resentfully, to be turned down because of the unfortunate colour of one's hair.

CHAPTER TWO

I

SHE awoke the next morning to find Marcia standing by her bed with a tray laid with early morning tea. Struggling up among her pillows from the deep sleep of exhaustion, she felt embarrassed at finding her elegant hostess of the day before waiting on her.

"Please, Miss Maule, I'm not used to this," she protested, wondering if she had overslept, but Marcia set the tray down with an encouraging smile, and seated herself on the side of the bed.

"I thought your first morning—and it wouldn't have occurred to the servants, I'm afraid," she said. "The guests, of course, have to be afforded the niceties, but the rest of us——" she shrugged, intimating that Judy might already count herself as one of the household.

"Our staff problems are somewhat acute here," Marcia went on. "Once the season starts, of course, we'll have to take on extra hands, but I'm sure, in the meantime, you won't mind mucking in with the rest of us, Miss Ware."

Judy reached for the teapot. The worn silver and the thin bread and butter made her feel cherished and important, but she said regretfully:

"I won't be stopping, I'm afraid, Mr—Mr O'Rafferty doesn't think I will do."

"Nonsense!" Marcia replied. "Raff was in a mood, that's all. It's a pity you had to have red hair."

"Why? A man surely doesn't pick his secretary for the colour of her hair!"

"No, of course not, but Raff hasn't the normal approach to business matters. There was once a girl he had been going to marry, you see."

"And she had red hair?"

"I believe so. I never knew her."

Judy munched her bread and butter with relish.

"If he was so sensitive on that score, he should have stated in his advertisement that no red-haired applicants need apply," she said logically. "Why didn't he marry her?"

"She died," said Marcia, and watched, with a certaain amusement, the girl's expression of slight indignation change swiftly to one of pity.

"Oh . . ." she said softly. "Oh, I'm sorry."

"Why should you be? Raff was rather rude to you last night. How were you to know the colour of your hair might have unfortunate associations?"

"And he still cares?" Judy asked, her eyes wide and very green, and Marcia gave a little shrug of impatience.

"I wouldn't know," she replied shortly. "She was very young, and it was all a long time ago, anyway. Listen, my dear, I want you to stay. My brother and I are getting this place on its feet again, but we need help. You seem a nice, uncomplicated sort of girl, and a job like this won't be exacting—quite good to cut your teeth on, don't you think? My brother, you know, was quite taken with you."

It was the wrong approach, she saw at once, observing the comprehensive flicker in the girl's eyes as she answered with sudden stiff politeness:

"Mr O'Rafferty, on the other hand, was clearly not taken with me, and he, I imagine, has the final word."

"Of course," Marcia agreed gracefully, but she withdrew a little into herself. Miss Judy Ware, though young and sufficiently ingenuous to be no stumbling-block to her own plans, was evidently not to be blandished by implied compliments. She wondered idly whether Noel had already tried his charms on the girl and been rebuffed, but looking at Judy, sitting up in bed, drinking her tea and eating her bread and butter with such frank enjoyment, she smiled a little sceptically. Neither her brother or Michael O'Rafferty would be stirred by such adolescent charms, she thought, and the girl was just what they needed; too inexperienced to feel put upon, and too anxious to hold down her first job to resent the hundred-and-one little chores which could be shifted on to her shoulders.

"You'd like to stay with us, wouldn't you, Judy? I hope you don't mind if I call you that, but I feel you and I could be friends," Marcia said softly, and knew of old that she was hard to resist when she made an effort to be beguiling. The faint colour which crept under the girl's clear skin, with its light, rather charming dusting of freckles, told her that her small effort had borne fruit. Judy's surprised pleasure was only too evident as she replied a little shyly:

"Thank you, Miss Maule. I would like to stay very much, but Mr O'Rafferty——"

"Leave Raff to me," Marcia replied with a conspiratorial smile. "He may be the boss, but he can generally be handled if he's tackled in the right way. Now, get dressed and come down to breakfast."

Judy went down to breakfast, glad to be spared another meeting so early in the morning, and threaded her way through the separate and for the most part unoccupied tables in the dining-room, aware of the curious glances of guests. Judy had not served her apprenticeship in the college without coming to recognise the types among her elders who would want to make use of her. The elderly spinster with the floating scarves and violently blued hair already had a speculative gleam behind her pince-nez as she passed and smiled good morning, the military-looking gentleman with the bald head asked peremptorily for more coffee, no doubt mistaking her for a new waitress, and a harassed-looking married couple at a window table exchanged meaning glances, doubtless hoping that here was someone who might relieve them from time to time of the responsibilities of their two unruly offspring.

The Maules sat at a table in another window recess, and Noel rose with exaggerated courtesy and pulled out a chair for her. The admiring glance he bestowed on her was, she was sure, quite automatic, but it was pleasant to be treated as a guest and to contemplate with delight the kind of breakfast which had never been provided by the hostel.

"Heavens!" Marcia exclaimed, watching her wade with gusto through porridge and cream, bacon and eggs and sausage, finishing up with Mary Kate's lamentable efforts at toast that was always thick and hard as leather. "How can you stomach all that at this hour of the morning?"

"I'm hungry," Judy replied simply. "Besides, we never got food like this at the hostel."

"That's what you should be putting in your stomach, Miss Maule," Timsy said, breathing heavily down Judy's neck. "All that orange juice and heathen grapefruit will turn the bile on you. It's slimmin' you are, I suspicion, and where's the sense of that if it turns you sour?"

Marcia looked annoyed for a moment, but she was used, as Judy was not, to the deplorable habit privileged Irish servants had of joining in the conversation.

"Where's Raff gone?" she asked, dismissing the subject for the moment.

"Over to the other side to fetch in extra provisions from Casey's. Knockferry doesn't deliver till tomorrow and there's another couple expected tonight."

"Yes, I'd forgotten. The honeymoon pair go today, don't they? I wonder if Mary Kate's remembered to pack up the usual butter to take home. I'd better go and see."

Marcia stubbed out her half-smoked cigarette with an irritable gesture and went out of the room.

"Do we puzzle you?" Noel asked, cocking an eyebrow at Judy, who had sat listening to them both in silence.

"No," she replied, seriously considering his rather idle question. "There must be a lot to contend with in running a successful guest house—but—does Mr O'Rafferty leave everything to you two?"

His eyes narrowed, wiping, for an instant, the careless good nature from his face, then the casual, half-impudent charm was back again as he flipped his fingers against her cheek.

"Don't get ideas about our status here," he said, a little mockingly. "Raff may not be particularly interested in the project, but he's still the boss."

"Of course," she said, not understanding, but feeling that in some way she had trespassed. "Only it seemed queer——"

"What seems queer?"

"I don't know. I have no experience of these things, of course."

"No, you haven't, have you? You will work along with us all very happily if you just stick to your job—remember that."

Judy frowned, puzzled by the hint of a warning behind his casual remark.

"I haven't got the job—didn't you know?" she said, sounding a little forlorn.

"Oh, I think you have," he replied with faint amusement. "You took Raff by surprise last night, you know, but Marcia will fix that. Now, when I've attended to my usual duties, I'll show you round. Slyne, though rather falling to bits, is quite an eyeful for urban visitors."

But she did not wait for Noel to be free. She wanted to explore for herself and take back the gleanings of her brief visit unconfused by the flippant nonsense of a stranger. She wandered through the big rooms, examining with interest the fine collection of period furniture which was housed there, then slipped out into the softly falling rain to enjoy her first experience of a new country.

She ran down to the little wooden jetty on the shore of the lough, and saw, too late, the boat pulling in with Michael O'Rafferty standing in her bows, getting ready to make her fast to her moorings. It would have seemed rude to withdraw, she thought, and walked to the end of the jetty to wait for him.

"Hullo!" he shouted, and stiffened momentarily as he saw her standing there, her face lifted towards him in a once familiar attitude of expectancy, her red hair darkened by the rain.

"Hullo, Mr O'Rafferty!" she shouted back. "Can I help you?"

"I doubt if you'd know much about boats," he replied, "but you can help with the provisions. Here—catch!"

He tossed a package to her across the narrowing strip of water wich she caught with difficulty. The next fell in the lough and promptly sank and they both began to laugh.

"Better wait till I've tied up the boat," he said. "Our lodgers wouldn't be pleased if their case of whisky went to the bottom."

II

He seemed quite different this morning, she thought, watching him unload the boat, or perhaps, like her, he was able to forget his prejudices away from the guest house. In his rough fisherman's jersey and trousers, he presented no preconceived notion of the master of Slyne. Noel, with his casual but studied elegance, looked more the part.

"Well, what do you think of your first glimpse of the Emerald Isle?" he asked lightly, and was unprepared for her bright look of happiness.

"It's lovely and strange and different," she said softly, and he felt irritated for no reason by her frank delight.

"It's the back of beyond, as Noel and Marcia would doubtless tell you," he answered shortly. "You'd very soon get tired of our lack of civilisation, my dear—no dances, no cinema, no cosy elevenses in ye olde tea-shoppes."

"What a strange life you must think I've led, Mr O'Rafferty," she said demurely. "I don't care for gossiping in tea-shops, even if there had been time, and dances

29

don't come your way very much unless you have a special young man lined up."

"And hadn't you?"

"No—but I'm not very romantic, you see."

"Aren't you?" he said, and looked quite startled. "But surely all young girls—anyway, you seem to have built up the usual sentimental conception of my country."

He made it sound like an accusation as he had over the colour of her hair, but she only smiled and shook her head.

"Oh, no," she said. "That kind of romantic conception doesn't have to be sentimental. I think you must have suffered unduly from the tourists who probably come here looking for local colour—leprechauns, banshees—that sort of thing."

"Perhaps you're right," he conceded, giving her a quick, puzzled glance. "Well, let's make a start to the house with some of this provender."

They went back to the jetty for the last load, and Raff paused suddenly to look down at his somewhat breathless companion and observe that it was hardly the act of a considerate host to make his guest do navvy's work.

"I enjoyed it," she said. "Besides, if you remember, Mr O'Rafferty, I was to be a guest on my own terms. So far, you haven't found any work for me."

He smiled reluctantly.

"I suspect you have a stubborn streak in you, Miss Ware," he remarked with a certain severity. "How would you like to see something of the countryside this afternoon? We mustn't send you back to England with only the rather bare policies of Slyne to remember."

"With you?" she asked in surprise.

"Unless you'd rather Noel obliged. He'd probably be better company for you."

"Oh, no, I shouldn't—I shouldn't at all," she answered with decision, and his eyebrows rose in surprise."

"Don't you like Noel?" he asked curiously. "He's said to be quite a ladies' man."

"I don't care for ladies' men," she replied, her nose a little in the air, and he grinned and, picking up the case of whisky, swung it with ease on to his shoulder.

"I'll take you through the Pass of Slyne and show you the view," he said. "The rain's stopping and it's going to clear. We'll even pause at the Wishing Well in proper tourist fashion, if you like."

"Do they come true—the wishes, I mean?" she asked, following him back to the house.

"I shouldn't think so. You're rather absurd, aren't you, Miss Judith Ware?" he answered with the impatient indulgence he might have used to a child.

"My friends call me Judy," she said, but he did not reply to that and only shifted the heavy case he was shouldering into a more secure position.

Noel was already behind the bar in the Small Saloon ready to serve pre-luncheon drinks when Raff deposited the case of whisky on the floor. It was, he explained to Judy, Raff's job in the evenings to make the point that, though not often visible, he was in fact the proprietor, but trade was slack at this time of the year.

"I'll mix you one of my 'specials'," he said, reaching for bottles and a shaker. "You'll need a snifter after all that fetching and carrying. I was watching you both out of the window."

"You might have come and given a hand instead of watching," Raff observed mildly, and Noel grinned.

"My dear chap, I'm all togged up as the barman! It wouldn't have done my best suit a bit of good to hump damp parcels about in the rain. Judy, you look rather dank, my child; here's your 'special'—drink it with caution."

Marcia joined them now, demanding a champagne cocktail. She looked put out and insisted rather sharply on paying for her own drink, saying when Raff protested:

"My dear man, you can't have your employees drinking all the profits." She looked rather meaningly at Judy's half-empty glass and Raff said pleasantly:

"Miss Ware is our guest, if you remember."

"So she is. Well, if you're going to be obstinate and refuse to employ her, darling, we'd better start going through the whole dreary business of advertising again, for I can't and won't cope with the paper work that's piling up."

"Is there so much?"

"If you troubled to look at your mail each morning instead of leaving it to me, you'd soon find out," she retorted, and her brother made a small grimace across the bar at her.

"Not the way to break down the famous O'Rafferty resistance, my sweet," he told her. "What's upset you?"

"Oh, everything. The servants have been particularly tiresome, and the honeymoon couple took offence because Raff wasn't there to say good-bye when they went this morning, and all those *letters!* Really, Raff, I'll have to leave if you can't settle something about a secretary. I can be pleasant to your guests and run your house, but I *cannot* cope with the office work as well."

Judy had been feeling uncomfortable ever since Marcia had joined them. She did not wish Raff to be embarrassed on her account, neither did she want to become involved in their domestic wrangles, for, as a guest, she could scarcely be expected to voice opinions on the running of the business. She had finished her drink and started wandering round the room, admiring the elegant furniture which graced it. She touched the smooth surface of veneer and delicate inlay with loving fingers, dwelling on what treasures this house must have held for generations, and as she worked her way back to the bar, she said with delighted pleasure:

"What lovely things you have here, Mr O'Rafferty. It's a pity the only reproduction hasn't been better done. It can't stand up to the others, can it—this chest, I mean?"

The three at the bar suddenly froze. The chink of ice as Noel began mixing another drink sounded sharp and unfriendly, then Raff said with polite indulgence:

"There are no reproductions at Slyne, Miss Ware. The stuff has been in the family for generations."

"Oh, but——" Judy was too much a stickler for accuracy to consider whether or not she was being tactless, ". . . you can see for yourself! Compare the linenfold pattern with the carving on the box chair—it's been clumsily done. This chest must have been made quite recently."

"Then you must be wrong," Raff replied with a slightly raised eyebrow. "I've bought no furniture since the place came into my posession. There's been no need."

Judy felt the colour mounting under her skin. The other two were looking at her with curious expressions, and although Raff had spoken pleasantly enough, the way he turned back to the bar, dismissing the subject and her, made her feel that she had committed a breach of good manners. She cast another surreptitious look at the chest; it *was* a fake, and not a very good one at that.

"There's another drink waiting for you," Noel called to her, and when she shook her head in refusal said, with a hint of laughter in his voice, "Oh, come on, don't be stuffy! Anyone can make a mistake."

Raff's eye on the third "special" was disapproving, she thought, but she was not going to let Noel Maule think she was sulking like a child.

"Very well," she said, resuming her seat on the high stool. "Thank you—and I didn't make a mistake."

"Really, my dear, what can you possibly know about old furniture?" Marcia asked, and the smile she gave Raff implied all too plainly that the young thought it smart to air their knowledge.

"I know a little. My father used to keep an antique shop, you see," said Judy gently.

There was another small silence, and she was aware that the two Maules exchanged significant glances and that Michael O'Rafferty stood looking down at her with a flash of amused interest.

"You seem to be an unusual young woman, Miss Ware," he said. "Wouldn't you rather have gone into the antique business yourself than have taken a secretarial course which I would have presumed to be rather dull by comparison?"

"Of course," Judy replied with her wide, sudden smile, "but one has to live. Father had no business to leave to me, and you don't get paid very much working in junk-shops. Thank you for my drinks. What time do you want to start after lunch, Mr O'Rafferty?"

She spoke casually, because she knew that for some reason or other the Maules were ganged up against her, but as Raff hesitated, she experienced a sudden doubt. She had insulted him about his furniture and he had an objection to red hair. Might he not already be regretting his invitation to show her the view from the Pass of Slyne?

"About two-thirty," he replied, then, aware of Marcia's suddenly inquiring gaze, "There's nothing to keep me here, is there, Marcia?"

III

Judy set out with her host after luncheon, still unsure of the effect of her company on him. He had been uncommunicative during the meal and the Maules, too, had been a little withdrawn, so that Judy, still young enough to be appalled by an unintentional *gaffe,* experienced shame at her unthinking outspokenness in the bar. It was a common enough thing, she knew, for impoverished landowners to sell their more valuable pieces and replace them with good reproductions, but Raff had denied that anything had been sold or bought, though the chest, a bad copy of a thirteenth-century Gothic, had certainly only been made in the last year or so. Well, it was none of her business, either way, but the small puzzle nagged and persisted until halfway round the lough road which led to the mountains she felt impelled to say:

"Mr O'Rafferty, that chest—I'm sorry if I shouldn't have drawn attention to it, but I wasn't wrong, you know. My father was particularly interested in linenfold carving and you can't mistake the real thing."

He glanced down at her with a faint look of surprise.

"What a persistent young woman you are," he observed with slight impatience. "My father might have bought it for all I know."

"How long ago would that be?"

"Well, the old man died ten years ago and since he lived for some seventy-five years before that, it might have been at any time," he replied a little dryly.

"Then it couldn't have been him. That chest isn't more than a couple of years old," she said, and his brief laugh held a hint of exasperation which warned her that, for him, the subject was both tedious and unimportant.

"Well, what in hell does it matter?" he exclaimed. "All the stuff's been moved around a lot since we turned the

34

place into a guest house. I expect it was tucked away some-where else and nobody noticed. Now, for heaven's sake pay attention to the quaint Irish sights you were so anxious to behold or I'll turn the car round and take you back."

She laughed a little apologetically, aware that she had been persistent almost to the point of impertinence. His explanation could be right, of course, and she herself could have been wrong as to the age of the chest. She gave herself up willingly to enjoyment of the landmarks he pointed out, asked innumerable excited questions and, when they entered the Pass of Slyne, fell silent from sheer wonder at the wild strangeness of the rocks which towered on either side with little streams gushing from the crevices where the roots of thorn and rowan still managed to thrive in the stony ground.

"There's your view, Miss Curiosity. That's something to take back across the Channel, isn't it?" he said, and she heard the ring of pride which he could not quite keep out of his voice and knew that he loved the place with a love that sprang from his very bones.

"We are behind Slieve Rury now," he said, speaking a little harshly. "You can just see Slyne the other side of the lough. When the fuschia is out there's a wonderful splash of colour, it grows wild all over the place in this part of the world."

She turned to look at him, sensing that he was talking to rid himself of unwelcome thoughts, and she knew instinctively that he had come here often with the girl who had died and that once again the colour of her own hair had disturbed him.

"Mr O'Rafferty——" she said, "you can find a reminder anywhere you choose to look for it. It shouldn't upset you."

"What do you mean?"

"My hair—it upsets you. It's even made you dislike me."

"On the contrary, I think I could like you very much," he answered, regarding her strangely.

"Is that what you're afraid of, then?"

"Afraid!" He rubbed the bridge of his nose with the same irritable gesture she remembered from the night before and she thought he was about to snub her severely for tres-

35

passing on such short acquaintance, but he only smiled and said quite mildly:

"What an unexpected girl you are! So they told you about Kathy, did they?"

"Yes. You used to bring her here, usen't you?"

"Often. She never lost her sense of wonder. Each time was a fresh experience. You share that quality too with her, I think."

"Tell me about her," she said. Up here, above the pass with the wind and the wild stretches of moorland and mountain isolating them from reality, it did not seem strange that she could venture on intimate matters after barely forty-eight hours' acquaintance.

"There's little to tell," he replied with equal lack of restraint. "We were to have married, but she contracted polio—heaven knows how—and died. For her it was a mercy, perhaps. She couldn't have borne to be crippled and I would have found it hard to see her so. When you are very young, Judy, you take so much for granted."

He spoke quite unemotionally, and probably had not even realised he had used her Christian name for the first time.

"It was best and kindest for both of you," Judy said, conscious at the same time that the observation must sound banal. "And you mustn't let the colour of my hair prejudice you in consequence. One doesn't forget, but one remembers with increasing tolerance."

"You're very wise, Miss Judy Ware," he said. "Tell me more about yourself."

"Well," she said, delighted, as always, to talk about a childhood which had been happy and was, clearly, still not very far behind her "as I told you, we had an antique shop—a little shop in one of the suburbs where there's almond and cherry blossom in the spring, and fields and woods a bus ride away. We used to take a bus into the country every Sunday. It wasn't like this, of course, but it was all we had to hand and we liked it.

"We had a flat over the shop, very makeshift and inconvenient, and I kept house when I wasn't at school. My mother, you see, died when I was quite small, so there were just the two of us. We never had much money because

36

of my father's impractical way of conducting his business, but it didn't seem to matter, and he must have saved a little from the wreck when the business finally folded up, because there were a few hundred for me when he died and I used some of it on the secretarial course on the advice of our lawyer. Whether you're plain or pretty, ambitious or the opposite, he said, you can't fail to find a living of sorts with that behind you."

"And are you ambitious?" he inquired, but she shook her head sadly.

"I'm afraid not," she said. "Of course, like everyone else I used to have dreams of grandeur—turning into a famous actress, writing a book that got banned—even stopping a runaway horse in Hyde Park and being given a medal; none of it at all practical, though."

He laughed again.

"How absurd you are! But why did writing a book that got banned rank among your ambitions?"

"I don't really know. Because it sounded important and madly worldly, I expect—but I don't suppose it would have done, really; if nobody was allowed to read it they'd simply think it was pornographic or something, wouldn't they?"

"Very possibly. So you settled for the typewriter being put to more prosaic use. Do you want me to give you a trial?"

Her face became lit, for a moment, with an extra-ordinary transparency, so that he could clearly see the powdering of childish freckles on her skin, then her expression changed to graveness.

"I think, Mr O'Rafferty, you owe me that," she said.

"And apparently I owe it to Marcia, too," he replied, his gravity suddenly matching hers. "I've evidently taken her routine duties too much for granted, and Slyne would come to a sorry pass as a guest house if she were to leave. She provides the grace the rest of us lack."

"Have they been with you long, the Maules?" she asked.

"Noel a couple of years, Marcia a little less," he replied.

"And it was Mr Maule's idea to turn Slyne into a guest house?"

"I suppose it was. Actually, I ran across him again in Dublin when he was just out of hospital and for old time's sake invited him to Slyne to convalesce, since he didn't seem to have anywhere to go. He'd no job, the place was going downhill, and the idea must have grown out of the combination of the two."

She looked up at him with a puzzled frown.

"It sounds an awfully chancy beginning for a prosperous business," she said, wondering how much capital between them the Maules had put into the venture, but his change of expression warned her that he was no longer prepared to talk on equal terms.

"We can scarcely be called prosperous yet," he retorted a little dryly. "We'd better be getting back, Miss Ware, if you've had your fill of our local beauty spot; and let me give you a word of warning. Don't offer too many criticisms on the running of the business or the authenticity of the furniture alike. Marcia, for one, won't take kindly to uninvited opinions."

On their return the motley pack of dogs rushed out of the house to greet them noisily. Raff admonished them mildly; they were not, he said, supposed to come into the house, so Marcia must evidently be out.

"Doesn't she like dogs?" Judy inquired, regaining her spirits at the indiscriminate canine welcome being showered upon her, but reflecting again that the beautiful Miss Maule appeared to have rather more authority than her position would warrant in ordering the affairs of the house.

"They bring dirt in and annoy the lodgers," he answered indirectly. "Are you by any chance sentimental over animals, Miss Ware?"

"I'm not sentimental over anything," she answered, detecting faint cynicism in the question, "but I like dogs."

She followed him into the house, but there was no one about and he suggested that she might care to check the office work which had accumulated in his study and see what she could make of it. She sorted through piles of bills and unanswered letters, glad of something familiar to do, but his lack of system appalled her. Accounts were certainly kept neatly and methodically in his own writing, but there were several discrepancies, items did not always tally with those in Noel's ledgers, and bills which had been crossed off as paid by Raff had come in again with the latest batch for settlement. There seemed to be little co-operation between them, for though Raff's paper work was orderly and clear enough, Noel's was careless, the items often illegible, and he was either slipshod or just a bad mathematician when it came to adding up columns of figures.

Raff watched her moodily as she worked, sucking at his pipe and answering her inquiries with slight irritability.

"But don't you really *know* what the outgoings are here?" she asked at last, feeling that she must be dealing with a child or a lunatic.

"I know what Noel produces in the way of statements each month. I just sign the cheques," he replied.

"But don't you check up together? You have some of these accounts already down as paid."

"Noel sometimes forgets to send them in, I imagine, or thinks I've done it. I haven't much head for business, as you will doubtless have gathered. I leave the major part to him."

"Then he's been rather careless," Judy said with a prim expression that made him smile.

"I can see," he said with a twinkling gravity, "that we did indeed need a secretary, despite my own reluctance. You seem very efficient, Miss Ware. I think you'll keep us all in order."

She glanced up at him a little helplessly. Did he really think he could run a successful business in this haphazard fashion and treat his subordinates as if they were children to be humoured?

"You look disapproving," he said, wondering vaguely what it was going to be like working day after day with a young woman whose green eyes presented an unconscious challenge and who, for all her tender years, appeared to have a better grasp of business than he himself.

"I haven't," she said, "any experience of running a business, Mr O'Rafferty, but books are books, and figures are figures. There are so many discrepancies."

"Very likely," he answered indifferently, then slumped into a chair on the farther side of the desk and eyed her speculatively.

"What," he asked, "did you expect to find here, apart, of course, from a misconceived notion of Irish country life?"

But he found then, as he was to find later, that, on duty, she was seldom to be lured into irrelevant digressions.

"I came to do a job," she countered briskly. "Now that we've got these accounts into some sort of order for further checking, I would suggest you dictate replies to some of these unanswered letters. You must be losing clients every day."

"Very well," he replied, beginning to rub the bridge of his nose again with the remembered gesture of impatience. "But we can't take them all."

"There are very few as it is, and every little helps," she said severely, and he grinned.

"True," he said. "You and the Maules should get on."

"The Maules?"

"They're always ready to take in every Tom, Dick and Harry who knocks on the door."

"And you're not?"

"No," he said, his bony face suddenly assuming the expression she first remembered, the cold, slightly distasteful expression of a man unused to modern trends. "Slyne is my home, after all."

"Then why——" she began, lured, in spite of herself, into starting one of those eager discussions, of which she had as yet had not time to cure herself, but his mood had changed. He offered no concession to her half-formulated question and, for the next couple of hours, she took down his dictation, sealed and stamped envelopes, and when that was done, found no surprise at being dismissed with peremptory relief.

"Where did you take our little guest?" Marcia asked idly, as she and Raff sat drinking in the bar before dinner, and when Raff told her through the pass and up into the country behind Slieve Rury, her fine eyebrows rose.

"Really? I thought you would never take tourists there yourself," she said.

"Miss Ware is not a tourist in the accepted sense, neither is she any longer a guest," he replied. "I've taken your advice and engaged her."

"I don't think," Marcia said carefully, "that it's a very good idea, after all, to do that."

"For heaven's sake!" Raff exclaimed. "How inconsistent can women get? Only this morning you were threatening to leave if I didn't keep her."

"Is that why you changed your mind, darling? I'm flattered, even though I've come to the conclusion it's a mistake."

"Why—don't you like her?"

She shrugged, tracing a pattern on the bar counter in the tiny puddle her slopped gin-and-tonic had made.

"I'm afraid I find her too negative to have very definite opinions about, though she seems a nice child, if a little too sure of herself," she said.

"We've done an afternoon's work, and she appears to me to have an excellent grasp of essentials," Raff said mildly. "What's troubling you, Marcia—that fleeting resemblance to Kathy? They're not really alike, you know. It won't disturb me."

She saw Judy standing at the door waiting for them and frowned thoughtfully. The Pass of Slyne, usually forbidden territory when Raff was escort . . . red hair . . . a disconcerting flair for truth and naïve enjoyment . . . they all added up.

"And you're making two and two equal five," Noel murmured wickedly in her ear as they all filed out for dinner.

CHAPTER THREE

I

FOR the first week Judy awoke each morning to the pleasant anticipation of a new day. The view from her window was seldom the same. One day the mountains were

41

a dark, irregular line, reflecting themselves in the water with startling clarity, on another both the lough and the far shore would be shrouded in mist which, even as she gazed, would sometimes break for a moment to reveal the tapering summit of Slieve Rury piercing through the clouds before they closed again.

No one had brought early tea to the nursery after that first morning, and Judy had learnt for herself that in order to wash, she must fetch water from the sink at the end of the passage. She had not, as yet, had the temerity to invade Timsy's pantry in search of water that was hot; at that hour of the morning the servants were sketchily clad and uncertain of temper, filling cans for the guests.

Once Judy unexpectedly came face to face with Raff while she filled her can at the end of the passage.

"Don't they bring you hot water?" he demanded with a frown. "What room have they given you, anyway?"

She found it odd that he should not know, but presumed the arrangement had been Marcia's. His frown deepened, however, when she told him she slept in the nursery.

"The room hasn't been used for years; it must be as damp as the cellars! I must speak to Marcia," he said, but when she started to protest that the nursery was much to her liking, he gave her a look which made her very conscious that she must present an unattractive appearance, straight out of bed and that her ancient red dressing-gown accorded ill with the colour of her hair.

She thought he would have forgotten by the time they met again for breakfast, but just as he had finished and was preparing to leave the dining-room, he inquired quite aggressively of Marcia why his new secretary had been relegated to the nursery wing when there were, at present, several empty guest-rooms which boasted more comfort, and had easier access to the hot water supply.

Marcia looked as surprised as she felt. Raff had never before concerned himself with the amenities of the bedrooms, even for an important guest.

"Mary Kate is the one you should take to task, my dear. I had suggested the Oak Room, but Mary Kate seemed to have the opinion that the nursery was good enough for a

42

little English employee who would scarcely expect a choice of one of the best rooms."

"She would expect a room with reasonable warmth and comfort, and a bed without broken springs," Raff retorted, and Judy, having finished her breakfast, without interruption, became aware that she was being discussed.

"I like the nursery," she said. "I like making up stories about the children who've slept and played there. Was it your nursery, Mr O'Rafferty?"

"Yes." His eyes dwelt on her absently for a moment, then he got up from the table without further comment and left the room.

Marcia lit a cigarette and sat back, surveying Judy thoughtfully.

"I shouldn't try to make trouble so early on in your employment here, if I were you," she said gently. "Your services can always be dispensed with in favour of someone older and—shall we say, more tactful."

"I haven't been complaining, Miss Maule," Judy answered cheerfully. "Mr O'Rafferty happened to come along when I was filling my can at the landing sink. He didn't seem to know where I was sleeping and seemed surprised when I told him."

"Well now, hadn't you better be getting down to the morning's mail?" Marcia asked impatiently, and Judy, who had not liked to make the first move to leave the table, scrambled to her feet a little awkwardly. Marcia watched her walk the length of the dining-room, observing the coltish grace of limbs not yet quite disciplined to adult control, and knew the first qualms of uneasiness. No one could call the girl pretty, she thought irritably, although she possessed an annoying kind of candour which, to another woman, could be exasperating, but to a certain type of man might prove endearing; that red hair could continue to remain an unconscious reminder, and that tiresome curiosity might prove a danger in another quarter.

"Oh, hell!" Marcia muttered, riled by her own ill-judged insistence in the matter of Raff's secretary, and, stubbing out her half-smoked cigarette, went in search of her brother.

Most mornings Raff went through his mail with Judy, dealt with such letters as required his personal attention, then left her to answer the rest as she saw fit and leave them for his signature. He was, she thought, still slightly embarrassed at having to work with her, and she could sense the relief with which he vaguely outlined her routine for the morning, then took himself out of the house to find his accustomed jobs around the policies.

The correspondence, she thought, could well have been dealt with by either of the Maules, for once the arrears had been cleared up there was little in a morning's work to justify the added expense of a secretary. Marcia, she soon came to realise, was only concerned with the social side of her employment, although she ran the house efficiently, but Judy sometimes wondered what Noel did with his time, apart from making out bills and being a decorative asset to the bar.

She learnt very quickly, however not to offer opinions or suggestions of her own. As Marcia pointed out, she was paid to do a job for which a modicum of efficiency was called, and nothing more, but Raff must have put his own queries to his manager, for the books tallied for a while and the weekly bills received rather more prompt attention.

By the end of February, Raff had lost his reluctance to work with her. It had, he admitted to Marcia, turned out a good idea to employ a secretary, and the Ware child appeared to be doing all right. He did not, of course, notice the many extra uses to which Judy was put, and she for her part was glad to be of help so long as it was understood that her immediate employer had first call upon her services.

"Really!" Marcia exclaimed to her brother, "she guards Raff's interests like a dog with a bone! Do you suppose she's getting a crush on him?"

"It's always possible, I suppose," Noel replied with a grin. "But that shouldn't worry you my dear."

His sister sent him a look of distaste. He took, she was aware, an almost feminine delight in making mischief when he was bored, and she knew better than to rise to the bait; all the same both Miss Judy Ware and her rather too lively perceptions could bear watching.

Judy, for her part, had her own reservations about the Maules. Noel she had come to tolerate without illusion, for he could usually make her laugh. He might be the wolf of her first impressions, but she felt at ease with him, whereas with Marcia she was frequently on her guard.

Her reservations, she supposed, extended to Raff too, but for different reasons, for she was still unsure of his possible liking for her. There were times when he observed her with an inquiring eye as if he would have liked to venture into personalities, but for the most part he was brusque and abstracted. He regarded her, she thought a little wryly, as something of a cross between an observant child and the efficient machine which never completely failed to surprise him. If he remembered those small, mutual revelations between them on her first day at Slyne, he made no direct reference to them, neither did he suggest a further expedition to show her the sights of the countryside on a free afternoon.

Not that there were many free afternoons just now, for once Raff had finished with her services Marcia found innumerable jobs for her; taking the Lucases' unattractive children for long walks to get them out of the house, doing crossword puzzles with Miss Botley and answering her endless questions, and making inquiries among Raff's tenants on behalf of the American ladies who were trying to trace an Irish ancestor. It seemed unlikely that the mythical ancestor would be located among Raff's tenants, but it gave her the chance to find out for herself the sort of life that was lived within the castle's precincts.

She discovered Granny Malone and, after a session of fortune-telling, was forced to the uncomfortable conclusion that the old woman might after all be a witch. Her clay pipe and old cloth cap were only such as any old woman would adopt in these parts, but her skill with the tea-leaves, and the eldritch cackles with which she foretold disaster proclaimed, if not the powers of darkness, a shrewd summing-up of the weaknesses of others. Judy preferred old Paddy-the-Sheep with his mild, vacant expression and his delight in small presents. He did well out of the tourists, she suspected, with his tales of sheep stolen by the Little People, and the sale of home-made charms to ward off the evil eye.

"Are you happy here, Judy?" Raff asked her suddenly one evening, and she appeared surprised by the sudden question.

"Of course," she answered.

"Not necessarily," he retorted. "Slyne can be dull, I'm told, and you haven't seen much of the country yet, have you? How about both of us playing truant tomorrow? It's market day in Knockferry—always an amusement to English eyes—and we can come back by the Plain of Cluny and stop for tea at the little inn by Lough Creagh that serves trout and lobster and Dublin Bay prawns, which the English dish up as *scampi*, any hour of the day you like to call."

"It sounds lovely," Judy said, and wondered if the inn too had been one of the places which he and the dead Kathy had loved and visited.

The little knot of new guests began to disperse for an early night, tired after their long day's sport, and Marcia brought her nightcap over to their corner.

"You're looking very nice tonight, Judy. Is that a new frock?" she drawled.

"No," said Judy, knowing that Marcia was perfectly well aware that the dress was one that she wore most evenings, but she added obligingly, because it was obviously expected of her: "Yours is new, isn't it?"

"My last extravagance from that expensive little shop in Knightsbridge for some time, I'm afraid," Marcia replied, smoothing the sleek lines of the dress over her hips with a provocative gesture. "Do you like it, Raff?"

"Very nice," he answered absently, and Judy, seeing the disappointment in Marcia's eyes, thought impatiently: *Why can't she see he's not that kind of man?* The dress was clearly expensive and very becoming, but Raff, she knew instinctively, would scarcely define the difference between that and her own cheap frock.

"Timsy tells me that chap Grogan has been around again. Did you see him, Marcia?" he asked, and she shrugged and grimaced at Judy, relinquishing her efforts to focus his attention on herself.

"No," she said. "Did you see him, Judy?"

"That odd little man with the dark skin and a great flow of conversation? He was here this afternoon, wandering through the rooms, making notes about the furniture. I asked him what he wanted, but he said he had the run of the place and you all knew him," Judy replied, and was aware that Marcia was annoyed by the remark.

"Infernal cheek!" Raff exclaimed. "I've shown him the door more than once. If you see him again, Judy, send him packing with my compliments."

"Who is he?" she asked, wondering how far her authority would carry with the persistent stranger in the absence of the master of the house.

"The Irish equivalent of a wide boy, I suspect," Raff answered shortly. "Interested in antiques and anything he can turn into money on the side. He's tried to buy from me on several occasions and apparently won't take no for an answer. You shouldn't encourage him, Marcia."

"I?" Marcia's lovely eyes opened wide in surprise a split second after they had sought Judy's in veiled inquiry. "It's prim Miss Doyle who encourages him. He treats her to the most outrageous blarney and the poor soul laps it up, convinced, I feel sure, that her last chance of a husband hasn't quite slipped by."

"Agnes is forty if she's a day, and a confessed man-hater since she was by her own account, crossed in love!"

"That could be to save her pride. When a woman's nearing middle age she tends to regret her lost opportunities —and that goes for a man, too."

Marcia had risen as she spoke. Although her words were light enough, her eyes dwelt a little mockingly on Raff, and Judy felt herself stiffen. Whatever her feelings, she thought, Marcia should not chide him so openly, or flaunt her own beauty with such indifferent assurance in front of another woman.

Raff had risen also out of politeness, and he stood now, regarding her with a curious expression, while he began absently to explore the bridge of his nose with a finger. Judy felt suddenly embarrassed and wished she could

47

escape. She had the impression that had they been alone, he would either have taken Marcia in his arms or slapped her soundly. Whichever way it was she felt herself to be an eavesdropper, and she slid out of her chair and bade them both goodnight.

"Tomorrow, Mr O'Rafferty?" she said tentatively, because, like a child, she wanted to be sure of his promise and cherish the anticipation of her treat as she fell asleep.

He nodded in brief acquiescence, but when the next day came, either unexpected duties arose, or he had just forgotten. It was Marcia who, later in the afternoon, he drove to Knockferry for some unspecified shopping, and neither of them returned for dinner.

Noel took her to the town on market day in the end, not, she felt, because he wished to, but because his sister wanted them out of the way in order that she might pacify Raff, who she said was showing an unhealthy interest in the receipted bill which Mrs Van Hoop had unwillingly paid on departure only that morning.

Judy had no means of knowing whether the Americans had been grossly overcharged, for the making out of accounts was the manager's province, but Mrs Van Hoop clearly was not satisfied, and there had been a small scene.

"You get confused with the rate of exchange, dear lady —pounds into dollars, dollars into pounds—very headache-making for all of us, but not to worry!" Noel had told her airily.

"Wa-al, I don't know," the woman replied doubtfully. "Elmer—that's my husband—will say we haven't gotten our money's worth—no central heating, cold bath water, and vurry, vurry doubtful hygiene as regards the plumbing. Do you reckon, young man, you have a right to charge this rate?"

"You knew our terms before you came, Mrs Van Hoop," Noel replied with smiling suaveness.

"If I may say so, Mr Maule, your brochure is vurry misleading, and I shall say so when I get back to the States," she retorted waspishly. "All these extra charges— what are they supposed to be for, I should like to know?"

"Well, my dear lady, you can't expect a setting like this without the privilege of paying for it, can you? Antiques

48

have to be maintained and the cost of restoration is expensive," Noel said smoothly, and saw, with relief, his sister and Judy coming down the stairs. "Marcia, will you try to explain to these ladies that our charges are high because of the unusual background offered?"

Marcia took over with an ease and charm which won Judy's admiration.

"Of course," she said, her voice soft and pleasant but her manner subtly very much the lady of the house, "our visitors from the New World frequently don't understand the privileges of the Old which, alas, like all good things, have to be paid for. Where else will you find a genuine Irish castle dating from the days of Cromwell?"

"Gen-u-ine Irish castle my foot!" exclaimed Mrs Van Hoop vulgarly, shrewd enough to know when she was being high-hatted.

Mrs Van Hoop's companion, who seldom spoke except to agree with her friend's pronouncements, remarked in a timid voice that perhaps they had better see the proprietor.

"Certainly, Mame, it was what I was about to suggest myself," Mrs Van Hoop snapped with annoyance. "Kindly send for him, young man."

Noel shrugged, then tugged at his black curly hair with a gesture which he knew to be boyish, wondering whether to turn on the slight brogue which usually could capture the transatlantic visitors, but his sister forestalled him.

"Go and see if you can find Raff, Judy," she said, and following the girl a little way down the hall, added in a low voice: "If you *do* find him, keep him busy. He hates a scene of this kind. Noel and I will get the matter straightened out between us."

Judy went, rather glad to be out of any further argument. She had been led to believe from the beginning that the richer the customer the more they objected to paying, and it seemed to be true. She found Raff eventually in the old gun-room, seldom used now, except for his own purpose. He was cleaning a shotgun and she stood and watched him, seeing that he would be occupied for some time without the necessity of any intervention to distract him.

Eventually he looked up and asked casually:

"Have those American women gone yet? I ought to do my stuff, I suppose, and wish them God-speed."

She started a little guiltily at the reminder that she had entirely forgotten her reason for being in the gun-room.

"I think they must have gone by now," she said, speaking rather quickly. "They were having a little argument about their bill, but I expect it's all settled now."

"Had they asked to see me?" he inquired sharply.

"Well, yes—but Miss Maule said you hated those sort of scenes and they would settle it between them."

"So you were sent to keep me out of the way, were you?" he said on a curious inflection." "I'd better go and find out what's been happening."

He walked out of the room with that long swinging stride she had come to associate with his loosely built frame. His tweed jacket, she noticed, needed another patch of leather just below the elbow. She followed him back to the hall and the open door of the manager's office, but to her relief brother and sister were alone, and Noel, catching sight of her over Raff's shoulder, gave her a wink.

"What was this trouble over the American's bill?" Raff asked, and Marcia, busy filing her nails in an idle moment, said, opening her eyes wide:

"Didn't Judy find you in time? Well, never mind, it's all settled now and they've gone. Rather an impossible woman really."

"Had you overcharged?" Raff asked, and Noel shrugged.

"Only the usual little frills we pile on for the Yanks. And we always cock it on for the Sarsfield Suite—after all, it's got the lot—four-posters, gloomy tapestries, and even gloomier Irish history! It's even got plumbing of a sort," he said.

"You're too fond of sticking on extras when you think the currency will trip them up," Raff said with surprising brusqueness. "You'd better let me see the bills."

"How can I? They've gone off with them, all nicely receipted as they should be."

"You presumably keep duplicates in the ledger."

Noel shrugged again.

"I don't always bother—just write down the total," he said. "Anyway, I got rid of these two by handsomely knocking something off, so not to worry."

The overworked phrase irritated Raff.

"You're a little too casual over these matters, Noel," he said. "Can't you see that by reducing the bill to end an argument you're only admitting you've overcharged?"

"Dar-*ling!*" Marcia said silkily, shaping one nail with exquisite care, "you're making awfully heavy weather. Poor Noel's only trying to make money for you. Let's leave it all now, shall we? After lunch you and I will go through the details quietly together. I saw the bills, so even if the poor sweet hasn't kept duplicates I can probably remember. We'll write it all down in a ledger so that we'll know for another time what extras are permissible and what are not. Shall we all go and have a drink? It's nearly lunchtime and Noel ought to be behind the bar."

So Judy found herself driving to Knockferry with Noel on some unspecified errand of his sister's, and although she wished that Raff had kept his earlier promise and taken her himself, her interest and pleasure soon became independent of her escort. To Noel the market was a familiar sight and one to be avoided if one wished to effect one's personal business quickly, but to Judy's English eyes the town presented a scene of colourful chaos, very different from like proceedings in an orderly market square. Stalls were set up in every street, and beasts roamed at will on to the pavements and even into the shops, while their owners gathered in the drink-shops or argued excitedly at the street corners. Rosy-cheeked men with long upper lips and round eyes and snub noses all looked alike to her, wearing the extraordinary hats of their race, desiccated felts like puddings, and bowlers green with age with flattened brim and battered crown.

"I've never *seen* such hats!" she told Noel, staring in frank amazement, so much so that one mildly inebriated gentleman chucked her under the chin and observed, with rich appreciation:

"Is it the face on me that takes your fancy, me doty? Sure, you're a lovely gurrl, a lovely gurrl. . . ."

"Do you think he meant it?" Judy asked, her face pink and her green eyes shining, but Noel was already bored, and had not been paying attention. The little redhead's naïveness had amused him at first, but now he wanted to get out of this smelly mob and go home; Marcia should have succeeded in smoothing down Raff by now, and he was tired of doing nursemaid.

While he was putting away the car, back at Slyne, she wandered down to the jetty and, still mindful of the compliment which had been paid her by a stranger, knelt down on the end of the jetty and gazed into the water, trying to see in her wavering reflection the promise of a beauty not before suspected.

She heard a step on the wooden planks behind her, and, thinking it was Noel, did not move until Raff's voice asked suddenly:

"What on earth are you doing?"

"Looking to see if I was pretty," she answered, without stopping to think, and he squatted down beside her and began peering into the water too.

"O-ho!" he said. "So you're vain, after all, Miss Ware! What do you see in your watery mirror—Cinderella transformed, Beauty awakened, duckling into swan?"

"You're laughing at me!" she said, suddenly a little shy. "I'm not really vain, only—well, a man in the town called me a lovely girl, and no one ever has before. Of course he was a bit drunk, so that probably explains it."

He glanced at her with amused affection.

"It's a common expression in Ireland and can apply to almost anything," he told her, then laughed gently at her crestfallen face. "How do you know he wasn't what you would call a wolf?"

"One can tell," she said.

"How?"

"I don't know. Wolves are wolves and nice men are nice men—it's quite simple, really. It's an instinct one's provided with, I suppose."

"Very convenient," he retorted a little dryly. "Do your labels never come unstuck?"

"Not so far—but then," she added honestly, "I haven't very much experience."

52

"How would you label me?" he asked her suddenly, and she gave him a little sidelong glance.

"Not a wolf anyway," she said, and his ugly face registered mock regret.

"How disappointing! Wolves have the best of it, I imagine," he said, and she frowned.

"Not in the long run, would you think?" she replied quite seriously. "I mean there are fundamental things they miss —things like roots."

"Ah, yes, roots—how serious we are becoming!" he said. "Did you enjoy yourself today?"

"Yes, but I wish you'd taken me."

"Why—didn't Noel come up to standard?"

"It's hardly Mr Maule's idea of an afternoon's entertainment, I imagine. Why are you talking to me like a child, Mr O'Rafferty?"

He raised his eyebrows as they turned to walk back along the jetty.

"I wasn't aware of it," he said, sounding surprised. "Now I'll ask *you* one! Why do you resent your youth, Miss Ware?"

"I don't," she replied sedately. "I only resent being talked down to. Twenty, after all, is quite a responsible age."

"Dear me!" he exclaimed, glancing at her a little wryly. "What a terrible indictment! I'd no idea I sounded such a prig."

She slipped a hand through his arm, quite unconscious of the familiarity.

"You could never be that," she told him fondly.

Marcia herself came out of the house at that moment, and stood under the porch, watching them, observing the unconscious ease with which Judy was hanging on to Raff's arm, and the quick response he made to her eager questions.

"Well," she said as they reached her, "you work fast, I must say, Judy! I thought Noel was your escort for the afternoon."

"We've just got back," Judy said, trying to withdraw her hand, knowing very well that Marcia was displeased by the gesture, but Raff unexpectedly anchored her hand firmly under his arm, then put the other carelessly round Marcia's shoulders.

"Come on!" he said. "Let's go in and see what Mary Kate's got for tea."

II

March was a month to be remembered for events which annually stirred their small community and, indeed, the whole of the country. St Patrick's Day with its holiday air, its shamrock and its drunks: the Grand National and the Irish horse which nearly won, and the football games, and the dog tracks and the horse fairs and all the hundred-and-one brief happenings that lent colour to the days and seemed to crowd together following the wild inconsequence of the weather. The Atlantic storms broke over the mountains which sheltered Slyne and lashed the quiet waters of the lough to an angry sea of turbulence so that miniature waves beat on the shore and the north side was hidden in a mist of spray.

Sometimes it was too rough to take the boat across to the other side for provisions and Noel or Marcia would send Judy in the Land Rover to Knockferry for supplies. She was not an expert driver, having had little opportunity in England for practice, and she found difficulty in mastering the Land Rover's unfamiliar gears, but she enjoyed bumping over the rough south road in the wind and rain, blissfully unaware, in her ignorance, of its perils. Visitors and tourists, she knew, used the north road which lay on the other side of the lough past Casey's, and was properly macadamed, but it was a long way round and no one at Slyne ever thought of taking it.

It was Raff who put an untimely stop to these jaunts, and by so doing did not further Marcia's liking for the girl.

"You must be crazy, sending her on the south road alone!" he snapped at Noel when, one day, he discovered the cause of his secretary's absence at a moment when he needed her services. "Those twists and bends are most dangerous unless you know them, and for someone inexperienced they're murder! What on earth possessed you?"

"My dear chap, it isn't the first time!" Noel protested

mildly. "The girl has her wits about her even if she does crash the gears. Who else is there to send if Marcia or I are busy?"

"One of the farmhands—or myself, if necessary. It's not to happen again, do you understand, Noel? I won't have the child risking her neck and limbs on that road."

"You let Marcia use it," Noel said, too interested in such a definite reaction to turn sulky at being reprimanded.

"That's different. Marcia can look after herself," he retorted, and then found she had joined them in Noel's office and was standing at his elbow.

"How ungallant! In what way am I supposed to look after myself?" she said lightly, but her eyes were suddenly watchful.

"You and Noel have been sending Judy on errands to Knockferry without warning her to take the north road. Apart from the fact that she should take such instructions from me, I will not shoulder that kind of responsibility for an inexperienced girl who hasn't the sense to realise the danger. You should both of you have known better."

"*We-ll. . . .*" Marcia drawled when he had slammed out of the office. "What an extraordinary to-do about a very ordinary matter! The girl *can* drive, can't she?"

"She gets there and back each time, so I imagine she can, but don't air those remarks to Raff or he'll flay you again for not making sure," her brother said with a grin.

"And I don't matter, taking this dangerous south road— *I* can look after myself," she said with narrowed eyes. "If that's to be simple little Miss Ware's line, I'll think up a few rather more subtle approaches myself, to spike her guns."

"I don't honestly think she's got a line," Noel submitted regretfully. "She's just a nice, uninhibited young girl, anxious to please."

"Have you fallen for it, too?" asked his sister scornfully.

"No, she's not really my cup of tea—besides, she's up to the tricks of wolves, so she tells me."

"Another line, I shouldn't be surprised! Oh, don't think I underrate her, darling. Even I can see there's a sort of coltish charm, coupled with that ghastly passion for truth and honesty."

Noel began to laugh.

"You sound quite human when you're jealous, my sweet."

"What do you mean, I sound quite human?" she asked.

"Just what I say. You've been putting on the elegant sophisticate act for so long that you've probably forgotten about the milk of human kindness that's supposed to spring up in us all."

"I think you're nuts!" she said. "Since when have you discovered the milk of human kindness in yourself?"

"Not often, it's true," he replied cheerfully, "but I haven't needed it. In your case you might find it an asset—if you still want to land old Raff, that is. He's one of the Romantics, I suspect, and Kathy pandered to it. He's very simple, really—too simple for you, sweet. You'd get bored."

"Do you think so? You don't know as much about me as you think you do, darling, and I'm sick and tired of Kathy's wholesome little ghost always popping up to my disadvantage. He can't still be hankering after her!"

"Oh, I shouldn't think so. She's probably just a sweet, nostalgic memory of his own youth."

"She'd have been my age now if she'd lived, and he'd have been tired to death of her. Sweetness can cloy."

"But not youth—not the untapped capacity of inexperience to give and be grateful," he said, not because he really believed it but because he never could resist sowing seeds of mischief and watching for results.

"Are you thinking of Judy, by any chance?" she asked with a sudden dangerous calm.

"Aren't you?"

"That red hair! But of course it's ridiculous!"

"Yes, isn't it?"

But he knew it was not.

When Judy returned, ignorant of the small stir her absence had caused, she was unprepared for Raff's reception.

"I employed you as a secretary, and not to go gallivanting into the town with no specific orders from me," he snapped when she joined him in his study. "There's a pile of work to get through."

"I'm sorry," she said, pausing uncertainly before she sat down at her typewriter. "They said you were out, and things were wanted from Knockferry."

"They—if you mean the Maules—had no business to send you. In future, you will take your orders from me—understand?"

"Yes, Mr O'Rafferty," she said, and sat down opposite him to await his instructions, wondering what had caused such sharp displeasure in him.

It was the first taste she had had of what Marcia called his king-of-the-castle mood and she was at a loss to understand how she could have provoked it. Already her duties had begun to exceed those usual to a secretary and she countered the errands to Knockferry as one of the more pleasant of them.

"Are you afraid I'll damage your car?" she asked, thinking a little guiltily of the hazards she had met with on the south road, the twists and turns that she had negotiated by a miracle, the sheep that seemed to appear from nowhere, causing her to brake with such suddenness that she stalled the engine.

"I'm more concerned that you might damage yourself," he said then, and the disfavour had gone from his voice. "The south road is not suitable for the novice driver, as Noel should have known, and whole limbs are more important to me than a broken back axle. Remember, will you?"

She looked at him with sudden understanding. He had been thinking, of course, of Kathy, whose limbs had been crippled by disease, with whom he was sometimes bound to compare her because she was young and whole and had red hair.

"I'm not a very good driver, but I'm safe," she said, wishing to reassure him, but he suddenly switched on the desk-light, dispelling what illusions he might have had, and answered briskly:

"Safe or not, you'll ask permission from me before you take either of the cars out again. Now, we'd better get on with some work."

He kept her hard at it for several days, seeming suddenly to have shed his old indifference in regard to the running of the place. Noel was several times called upon to explain discrepancies which were beginning to creep back into his own ledgers, and an awkward little scene over their bill with the departing Lucas family only served as an unfortunate reminder of the recent trouble with the two Americans.

"You might have known you were sticking it on too much for people like that to swallow," Marcia told her brother impatiently. "That type always check their bills with care and raise a stink if they've been overcharged, and it's too soon after that business with the Yanks. Why couldn't you have put things right without bringing Raff into it?"

"Because, my dearly beloved sister, they insisted on seeing the proprietor, thanks to that halfwit Judy's interference," he replied sulkily.

"Judy? What had she got to do with it?"

"Simply that I'd wangle a nice bit of surcharge for her services baby-sitting which, if you remember, was Ma Lucas's own suggestion, and I suppose I piled it on too thick."

"Well?"

"Well, I tried to get out of it by saying the money went into Judy's pocket in lieu of a tip, and the wretched girl let me down. Said she'd never had it."

"Oh, you're a fool! Why didn't you prime her first?"

"Didn't get the chance. Anyway she'd probably have been suspicious after that other affair."

"And what pretty tales has she cooked up for Raff?"

"God knows! He swept her off to his study like a delinquent pupil and she's in there with him now."

Judy herself felt not unlike a delinquent pupil as she sat at her typewriter listening to Raff's terse comments. She had been acutely embarrassed by the scene in Noel's office and had realised, too late, that she should have held her tongue when appealed to by Mrs Lucas. Even so, she could not let what she at first took to be a genuine mistake pass without trying to correct it. Raff had dealt with the matter with such chilly courtesy that the Lucases almost found themselves apologising, and it was not until she was alone with him that Judy realised he might have misunderstood the whole incident.

"Is Noel in the habit of putting a surcharge on the bill for your services for the guests?" he asked, and she looked unhappy.

"I don't know," she said.

"Now let this be plainly understood between us, Judy," he said. "You are employed here as secretary first and foremost, and if you choose to do extra chores for my guests that's entirely a matter for your own good nature and nothing more. You might have known that I wouldn't countenance a charge on the bill for unlisted courtesies, and neither will I permit anyone on my staff to take money, other than the servants who would naturally expect their tips. If the wage I pay you is not sufficient, then you should say so and not scrounge perks with Noel's misguided connivance."

She listened, at first dismayed by the unexpected turn of his conclusions, then her temper began to rise.

"The wage you pay me is perfectly sufficient, and I'm not a scrounger, Mr O'Rafferty," she said, and her eyes looked suddenly very green.

"I'm sure you're not by nature," he replied more pacifically, "but you're inexperienced, rather naturally, in this type of post. If guests choose to make you a present on leaving, that's a different matter, but you must never make private charges that are outside the tariff I draw up and send out. What sort of reputation do you imagine that would get us?"

She said, following her own line of thought, unconscious at that moment that it was she herself who was being found fault with:

"You should keep an eye on everything a great deal more than you do. You don't see the bills when visitors check out. How do you know if they tally with the books?"

He raised his eyebrows.

"The presenting of bills is the manager's job. Have you any further suggestions for the running of my business?" he observed dryly, and saw her flush.

"I'm sorry," she said. "That wasn't meant as an imper-tinence. Do you want me to go?"

"Certainly not. We have some work to do."

"I didn't mean now. I meant do you want me to leave your employment?"

He reached automatically for his pipe and his face became frankly puzzled.

"Now why on earth should you imagine that?" he asked. "I'm not prepared to sack you every time I have to haul you over the coals."

She blinked at him dumbly, confused by this odd habit he had of addressing her at times with the indulgence he might have shown to an argumentative child. He had, she thought, no conception of when maturity in a woman began.

"You label us, don't you?" she said, and, had she known it, equally confused him by the sudden voicing of her private thoughts.

"Who do you mean—secretaries in general?" he asked, frowning.

'No, young girls. Under twenty we're sort of half-baked fledglings—after twenty-five we blossom into woman-hood—if we're lucky."

"What very extraordinary things you say! I wouldn't have set you down as a half-baked fledgling, if that's any comfort to you, but I don't imagine I'd be far wrong in saying that you're a most unusual secretary."

"Am I? Perhaps I haven't learnt to conform," she said, sounding suddenly humble, and he smiled, his ugly face creasing into those lines and wrinkles that were expectedly endearing.

"Then don't try," he said. "I, no doubt, haven't learnt to conform as an employer and, as I've never had a secretary before, we'll just have to make a guess at the right relationship. Let's get down to some work."

III

The Maules' attitude changed slightly after that incident. Noel, though he shrugged the whole affair off and only laughed at Judy's endeavours to avoid him, took pleasure in a form of teasing that was not always kindly, and Marcia, after a few sharp words, made it her business to exclude Judy as much as possible from the routine business of the guest house.

"Leave such matters as bills and accounts to Noel. That's what he's here for," she said.

"But I have to check the accounts when they come in for Mr O'Rafferty's final O.K.," Judy said, and Marcia gave one of her conspiratorial smiles and patted Judy lightly on the cheek.

"Of course," she said humorously, "but you don't have to dot your i's and cross your t's quite so thoroughly, do you? Your conscientiousness is very praiseworthy, my dear child, but it can become an awful bore if carried to extremes."

"I'm paid to be conscientious—and accurate," Judy replied stubbornly, and Marcia yawned.

"Of course," she said again. "But your job is to transscribe what's set before you, not to question methods which you couldn't be expected to understand."

"Yes, Miss Maule," said Judy dutifully, and Marcia threw her a look of impatient tolerance.

"Oh, for heaven's sake, call us by our Christian names!" she exclaimed. "We should be friends, you and I and Noel, Judy. We're all three employed here in minor and lesser degrees."

"But you and your brother have money in the business, haven't you? That would make you partners."

"What gave you that idea?" Marcia laughed. "We are paid for our services, the same as you are, so that puts us on an equal footing, doesn't it? Perhaps you'll understand now, my dear, that any little perks on the side are a quite justifiable license. Noel and I were flat broke when we came here."

Judy understood, but not in the way Marcia had intended. She had thought, all along, that the Maules had money in the business; neither of them behaved like subordinates, and the fact that the friendship between the two men appeared to be of long standing had given her the wrong impression. Marcia, for some reason of her own, was evidently trying to establish a new relationship with the latest member of the staff, but Judy thought she preferred the old one. It was not pleasant to be tentatively included in methods of taking advantage of a tolerant employer.

She did not find it easy at first to address either of them by their Christian names, but since Marcia seemed to become irritated by a more formal approach, the habit grew. They were forced, the four of them, very much into one another's company by virtue of the fact that Raff's study was the one private place left to them when the house was full, but the hours spent there were often uncomfortable for Judy. Marcia, lying back in a chair, smoking her interminable cigarettes and watching Raff through half-closed eyes, made it plain that she wanted to be alone with him, and Raff himself would sometimes lean over the back of the chair, between restless pacing about the room, as if he also was impatient of the presence of the other two. Often Noel would lounge and chatter as if he enjoyed the fact that his company was unwanted, but sometimes he would make the excuse that the bar needed him and leave the room with studied casualness, taking Judy with him.

"I don't want to sit in the bar for the rest of the evening," she said on the first occasion, and he slapped her carelessly on the behind.

"Then go to your room, Miss Gooseberry," he said. "Don't you know when you're not wanted?"

She spent many evenings in the nursery after that, looking at the books which had been Raff's as a child, and wondering, as she had at the beginning, whether Marcia's undoubted beauty was succeeding in effacing the ghost of that early love. She had no knowledge herself of affairs of the heart, but she did not believe, from the little she knew of him, that a man of Raff's temperament would be content to remain celibate for the sake of a memory that must, by now, be a little dimmed; but Marcia . . . what had she to offer in exchange? Beauty, poise, the natural makings of a good *châtelaine,* the accomplished façade of a woman most men would be proud to claim as wife; but underneath all that . . . was there a core to be touched that was not self-seeking, was there some deeper quality which was not apparent in the brother?

It's none of my business, Judy told herself, crossly, at the end of these speculations. Raff was old enough to look after his own interests, both personal and financial. If he was being cheated by the handsome couple who depended on him for a living, it was not her affair, neither were Marcia's future intentions; it was merely a little unfortunate that Michael O'Rafferty was beginning to stir feelings in herself that were not altogether impersonal.

"What would you say to a drive across the Plain of Cluny and that promised tea at the inn by Lough Creagh —I did promise, didn't I?" he said, one afternoon.

So he had remembered after all!

"I would say thank you very much, Mr O'Rafferty," she replied at once, and he smiled.

"Can't it be Raff?" he asked unexpectedly. "I'm not a great deal older than Noel and Marcia, you know."

"You're my employer, and that's quite different," she answered, whereupon he told her a little brusquely to go and get ready and not to keep him waiting.

She perched beside him in the Land Rover which he had chosen today instead of the shooting-brake he usually drove, and was dismayed when he bade her take the wheel and show him what she could do. He was soon, however, uttering soft imprecations, and after she had stalled the engine for the third time avoiding the sheep and the unattended donkeys which to her seemed to populate the roads of Ireland, he ordered her to change over again.

"Never in all my born days!" he exclaimed, conscious, with a sudden jolt of memory, how he had endeavoured to teach Kathy to drive all those years ago. But Kathy had dissolved in tears under his instruction and had to be comforted; this girl simply gave him a wide smile and observed tranquilly that she was afraid she had not got the hang of the gears.

"You certainly haven't—or the hang of our roads or an eye for judgement," he retorted. "You'll not drive, even on the more civilised north road, without further lessons from me."

"Very well, Mr O'Rafferty," she replied obediently, but she did not think he would be a very patient teacher, neither did she imagine he would remember, or find time to instruct her.

"I've ceased to be your employer for the afternoon," he said, and added, at her look of surprise, "I get tired of being addressed with such formality. It makes me feel old."

"Oh, I see. Very well, I will call you Raff for the afternoon, if it would please you," she said with composure. "It's a nice nickname, but Michael is nicer. Does no one call you that?"

Kathy had called him that, and she knew it at once as he answered absently:

"Not for many years. Raff was the obvious abbreviation of my surname, and in the Air Force most of us collected nicknames of sorts. Noel's was Spongy."

"Spongy! Not a very nice nickname to acquire—and did he?"

"Sponge? Quite blatantly, nobody minded. Noel could always charm the shirt off your back."

She was silent, irritated for a moment by his tolerant acceptance of the rights of a young man who could still behave with the unthinking egotism of a spoilt child.

He said gently, glancing at her disapproving profile:

"I haven't any illusions about Noel, you know. He's good at his job, but he's out for what he can get."

"Why do you keep him, then?" she asked, before she could stop herself, and expected an immediate rebuff, but he answered quite mildly:

"I've a sort of fondness for him, I suppose, and I couldn't run the place without him. Besides—there's Marcia."

Of course, Marcia . . . if Noel were to leave Slyne, his sister would go too, presumably . . . it seemed very obvious to Judy now where Raff's interests lay, and the wind blowing in through the unprotected windows of the Land Rover felt suddenly cold.

They had reached the Plain of Cluny, a wild bleak stretch of moorland, broken only by a criss-cross pattern of neglected stone walls and a brilliant patch or two of bog.

Judy looked at it with dubious eyes; it was unfriendly, barren country and she thought of the gentle beauty of the view from the Pass of Slyne and shivered.

"Cold?" Raff asked, and she nodded; but it was a coldness of the spirit rather than of the flesh, she thought, which made her pull the collar of her coat high about her ears.

"Tea will warm you up," he said, negotiating a hump-backed bridge with the ease of one well versed in the peculiarities of the terrain. "The plain is a bit dour for the tourist taste, but Lough Creagh should cheer you up. It's very beautiful."

It was indeed beautiful, smaller than their own lough at Slyne and incredibly blue, with a silver rim of powdery sand encircling its shores. The little inn was empty of visitors at this time of the year and they were welcomed in by the landlord with all the extravagant display of delight and amazement which Judy was becoming used to.

Tea, in the warming comfort of the inn's spare parlour, redolent with the scent of turf and the lingering smell of paraffin, compensated suddenly for the bleakness of the Plain of Cluny and her own disturbed thoughts. There was trout, as Raff had promised, and Dublin Bay prawns, and hot bread from the oven and a pile of richly buttered baps.

"I shall burst," she said, heaping her plate with child-like gusto, and Raff smiled.

"You haven't lost your appetite for adolescent treats," he said, and she looked surprised.

"Do you count this sort of enjoyment as adolescent?" she inquired gravely. "I'm twenty, Mr O'Rafferty—Raff, I mean—but I don't expect my appreciation of the simple pleasures of life to diminish with the years."

"Don't you, indeed? And how would you have satisfied this appreciation if you hadn't come to Slyne?"

"I don't know. Not in this way, of course—but there's always something, isn't there—even in London streets and the rather sad make-believe of the suburbs?"

His eyes were tender as they rested on her bright, shining head, bent so expectantly over her lavishly piled plate.

"I think for you, Judy, there would always be a way." he said softly. "You are perhaps one of the rare ones of the earth."

She glanced up quickly, startled by such a strange tribute, but her mind was still on the delectable morsels she was discovering on her plate.

"Oh, no," she replied, her mouth half full. "I'm very ordinary and rather easily pleased—but there's nothing rare about me."

There had, he supposed, been nothing rare about Kathy, either, except this same endearing zest for living.

"What do you think of Marcia?" he asked suddenly, and, as she carefully laid down her knife and fork and faced him over the rough oak table, he saw that he had dispelled that inconsequent mood of the moment. She looked across at him with eyes that were grave and attentive.

"What do you want me to say?" she asked gently. "Marcia is a very beautiful woman, which in itself is self-evident. I don't really know her as a person, so how can I tell you what I think of her?"

He felt for his pipe, filled and lighted it, the scratch of the match sounding loud and irritable in the little pause. He was, she thought, like her, lost in that same abstraction from time and place which, once before, had fallen between them. On that other occasion it had been Kathy who had filled his thoughts; today it was Marcia, and in either case, Judy knew that once back at Slyne with her typewriter clacking away and the prosaic work of the day to get through, both would be forgotten.

"Do you want her, Raff—permanently in your life, I mean?" she asked, but saw that she had trespassed as soon as she had spoken.

"That's a question for the two most concerned, don't you think?" he said pleasantly, and went out to the kitchen to settle up his bill.

Judy, left alone with the debris of the meal, leaned her elbows on the table and thought how like the empty finish of their conversation it all looked. What right had he to invite opinions, then snub her for her pains in answering? What right had he to bring her here at all and offer half-revelations which could only be disturbing? But when Raff

66

came back, assurance again came with him. A lamp, carried by the landlord's wife, dispelled the shadows and, in its warm glow, his ugly, bony features had a homely attraction that was becoming familiar.

"Does she remind you of anyone?" he asked, his eyes on Judy with an indulgence that was faintly proprietorial.

"Miss Kathy, I suppose you'd be meaning," the woman replied, observing Judy with a curious eye. "The hair's the same, but 'tis common enough in these parts; for the rest, no. Miss Kathy was pretty as a picture and soft as a kitten—no disrespect to you, young miss, for you'll have other things, I'm thinking. Would you be still grieving for her, O'Rafferty?"

"No—no, Mrs Farrell. One doesn't grieve for ever, one just remembers," Raff replied, and although his eyes still rested on her, Judy knew that he was not thinking of her.

"They say the fine young lady you have at the castle is fancied as mistress there. Have you put off the willow, O'Rafferty?"

"I've just told you one doesn't grieve for ever."

"And this young lady here—does she put you in mind of that other one, for all they're not alike at all?"

Judy made a little movement, surprised but not embarrassed that they should be discussing her as if she were not there, and Raff, perhaps because he sensed her restlessness, said, with a return to his more familiar manner:

"Miss Ware is my new secretary. She helps to keep the books straight and the bills in order. She's from over the water."

"There's too many from over the water at Slyne," the woman said with a disapproving glance at Judy. "Secretaries, lady receptionists—grand titles for an O'Rafferty's servants! And what would you be wanting with two women in the house, I'm askin' you?"

"We must go," Raff said with a smile, ignoring the question which, Judy knew, could never be taken as an impertinence, for were not these people, and others like them, once tenants of Slyne with a personal interest in the affairs of the castle?

Judy got up, stretching her young limbs with contented unconcern. She had a restoring suspicion that the elegant Marcia was not well liked in the neighbourhood.

"Thank you for my lovely tea, Mrs Farrell," she said shyly, and the woman's eyes rested on her with fuller attention, observing the planes and angles of her face in the lamplight, the coltish grace of her immature body, and the familiar fall of bright hair which, even to her, stirred an almost forgotten memory.

"Come again, young miss, if himself will bring you. You may be from across the water, but your heart's already in Irish soil, I'm thinkin'," she said with unexpected softness, and, for Judy, the earlier magic of the day returned.

They reached Slyne to hear angry voices raised in the hall. Miss Doyle's plaintive whine, Mary Kate's more robust spate of words and Marcia's polished tones with already an edge to them. The evil smell from Timsy's oil stove was particularly pervasive and the mournful sound of his cornet rose every so often above the babel of voices.

"What on earth's going on?" Raff demanded, and there was immediate irritation in his own voice. "If you must brawl and argue, can't you choose a less public place? It can't be very edifying for the guests."

" 'Tis that Grogan, takin' the furniture away in a van, and he with no permission from the master of the house, as you'll be tellin' them yourself, Mr Michael," Mary Kate said, her fat round face red with temper, and the flouting of her authority.

"Mr Maule gived permission," Miss Doyle stated stubbornly for doubtless the twentieth time.

"I keep telling you, Mary Kate, it's gone to be repaired," Marcia managed to interrupt, and Raff, in very few words, ordered the two servants back to their quarters, without waiting to hear their explanations. It was rather enlightening, Judy thought, how definite and authoritative he could become when he chose.

"Now, Marcia, perhaps you'll explain,"

"It's perfectly simple," Marcia replied, pushing irritable fingers through her dark, disorderly hair. "A bit of the veneer had peeled off a panel of the William and Mary tall-

68

boy in the Grand Saloon and one of the legs was shaky. Grogan has taken it away to repair, that's all."

"Was the damage bad? I hadn't noticed," Raff asked with unusual persistence, and she made a small grimace of amused tolerance at him.

"Oh, darling, but you never notice anything! You've lived with all your lovely pieces much too long to be observant. You take them all for granted," she said, and turned to Judy. "You noticed the damage, Judy, didn't you? You're always prowling round, looking at stuff."

"Yes, I noticed it several days ago," Judy said slowly, aware that Marcia's dark eyes were watching her carefully. "Are you sure this Grogan person knows his job, Marcia? That's a valuable piece and should have expert attention."

"Grogan's very clever," said Marcia glibly. "He's done repairs for us before, hasn't he, Raff?"

"So Noel tells me," he said, "but I would prefer to be consulted another time. I don't care for Grogan, or the way he tries to make a fool of poor Agnes Doyle."

"Then you'd better take the matter up with Noel. I had nothing to do with the arrangements—and for heaven's sake can't you do something about Timsy playing that horrible instrument in the house?" snapped Marcia, suddenly losing patience, and turned on her elegant high heels and left them to relieve her feelings on Timsy in the pantry.

"Well," said Raff wearily, "I'd better go and have a word with Noel. Sometimes he takes a little bit too much upon himself."

He went away in the direction of the manager's office, but Judy continued to stand in the middle of the hall, a slight frown between her eyes, and wondering what, in the small disturbance to which they had both returned, had made her feel uneasy.

CHAPTER FOUR

I

AS March drew to its close with a mildness which heralded an early spring, so Timsy said, Judy felt herself to be an established part of the household. The fact that she was called upon to fulfil many more duties than those for which she had been employed pleased rather than dismayed her, and even the servants had come to accept her. Rosie Boyle, one of the young girls from the vast family at the farm, who came daily to wait in the dining-room, was sent up each morning with an early cup of tea by Mary Kate, and a can of hot water was usually left outside her door to save her the chilly trek to the sink at the end of the passage.

"You're quite the daughter of the house now, aren't you, darling?" Marcia said, but there was an edge to her lazy comment. The servants had never been persuaded to address her as if she belonged there, whereas they called Judy "Miss Judy" with the easy familiarity they accorded to Raff. "They confuse you, of course, with Kathy. Does Raff suffer from the same confusion, I wonder?"

As always, in her dealings with Marcia, Judy was made to feel that, under that indolent, charming manner, the older woman did not really like her.

"I don't think so," she replied, guardedly and, indeed, of late, Raff had afforded her nothing more than the casual consideration of any impersonal employer. The moments in which he had seemed to reach out to her as one human being to another had, she thought now, been moments of nostalgia, even of irritation, at the passing reminder of an affair he would prefer to forget.

"Men are extraordinarily adolescent, aren't they?" Marcia observed, suddenly admitting Judy to a cosy feminine conspiracy. "Raff is nearly thirty-seven—you'd think he would have grown up—but life here is very cut off from reality, I suppose."

"I don't think so," Judy said slowly. "Reality is where your roots are, surely?"

"My dear girl, how very deadly! And who has roots now, with life a hand-to-mouth business at best?"

"But the lucky ones are like Mr O'Rafferty. The old traditions are something to hang on to. I wouldn't find it deadly."

Marcia looked at her with closer attention, assessing the girl's possible attractions. She had, she supposed, some latent charm in the fresh quality of independence of the youth of today, and an inquiring mind which might compensate for a time, a lack of feminine awareness. Her clothes were cheap but well chosen and emphasised her long lines with casual carelessness. Judy, thought Marcia, with sudden shrewdness, would not care whether she was dressed by Balmain or the cute little numbers she picked from the cheap stores and wore with such indifference.

No, she wouldn't find Slyne deadly, or those tiresome roots she had mentioned with such extraordinary solemnity.

"Because, to you, it seems like security," Marcia said a little sharply, not caring for the conclusions she had drawn.

"But don't all women want that—don't you?" Judy asked simply, and Marcia's eyes narrowed.

"Meaning would I marry for just that?" she said with slow deliberation. "Very possibly, my dear, since I'm broke, and you might as well know it now as later, but if we're speaking of Slyne—and I think we are—I wouldn't be content to stagnate here for ever, for all your dreary talk of roots. The place is worth nothing as a decayed inheritance, but the contents are; Raff needs jolting up, that's all."

Judy returned the slightly defiant stare with faint compassion. To her it seemed extraordinary that a woman of Marcia's beauty and worldly knowledge should have such little understanding of the ties of blood and inheritance or the fundamental demands of a man bred to another way of life.

"He would never sell, if that's what you're thinking," she said softly, and saw the little smile of amused tolerance curve the corners of Marcia's mouth and reach her eyes with lazy confidence.

"What can you know of Raff? If a man's enough in love he will do most things," she said. "You may learn that yourself some day, darling. Have you never been in love?"

"No."

"Then you speak without experience, as one would expect. You can make a fool of most men—just once, anyway. You'll learn that, too, Judy—or perhaps you won't, with a temperament like yours."

"But not Raff!" Judy exclaimed with shocked candour, and Marcia's eyebrows rose.

"Raff?" she repeated inquiringly.

"Mr O'Rafferty, I mean. It slipped out."

"I see. Well, in learning the simple arts of feminine wiles which I've been trying to explain, don't set your cap too high, will you?"

It was not a remark, Judy thought afterwards, which either of them could be expected to take seriously. Marcia was too secure in the assessment of her own powers, Judy too ignorant of hers, to join issue on such an unpromising subject, but she knew now that she minded that Raff should be exploited, and that it was probably true that a man enough in love might throw away his beliefs, even though he lived to regret it.

"Could a man live without roots?" she asked Timsy one morning, watching him swill down the yard with the inadequate broom he preferred to the new one which had been provided for his use weeks ago.

"Well now, I wouldn't say that," he replied, leaning on his broom to consider the question, prompt, as always, to seize any excuse for stopping work. "A plant now—you pull it up and it dies. Had you himself in mind, Miss Judy?"

She nodded, unembarrassed by his shrewdness. She had found for herself that when the old man forgot to be what Noel termed a Character, he could be both wise and understanding.

"Ah, well, the master's roots is in Slyne soil, the same as the rest of us," he said, "but you'd not be knowin' what takes a man when the fever comes on him. Miss Kathy, now, would be guided and not set herself up to cry for the moon—for the moon, you see, was right here at Slyne

72

and she wantin' no more than the things she'd known since a child—but that was long ago."

"But he still remembers?"

"We all remember—but a man must put away his dreams and bring comfort to his bed and beget children to follow him."

That was how Raff saw her, taking them unawares as he came unexpectedly into the yard. Swinging on the gate with her red hair flying and the laughter in her eyes, she reminded him, not of Kathy, but of a little girl playing truant from school. Every so often she bit into an apple and, whether she knew it or not, she was flirting outrageously with the old man, safe, no doubt, in the assurance that on him she could innocently practise the least expected of her charms.

She called out something provocative, then arriving at the core of her apple, spat it out with blithe unconcern for the niceties, and saw Raff watching her.

"Oh!" she said, scrambling down from the gate, and looking suddenly guilty. "Did you want me, Mr O'Rafferty? I thought you said you were going to Casey's."

"So I am," he replied, adding unexpectedly: "Would you like to come?"

"Oh, yes!" she cried eagerly. She had not been out in the boat yet, and she had a great curiosity to know what the other shore was like and to see for herself the redoubtable Casey's store which, besides providing for every imaginable contingency, combined the offices of public house, post office, coal and timber merchant and, when the season was right, game and fish openly poached by himself and his cronies.

"I've kept you cooped up too much," Raff said, with an unfamiliar sense of apology at seeing the pleasure in her face, and Timsy paused in his half-hearted labours to remark:

He was still the disreputable figure of fiction, with his short, flying coat-tails and knotted kerchief, an ancient, shapeless hat that had once been Raff's on the back of his head, but his faded eyes had a poet's look for a moment and she regarded him curiously.

"Give her time to play, O'Rafferty, and maybe she'll teach you, too."

Raff's eyebrows rose inquiringly. When Timsy addressed him by his title it usually meant he was disapproving of something.

"I've got past the frolicking stage, Timsy," he said with a grin, but the old man gave him a sour look.

"Och! You've got into their fine ways at the castle now. That Miss Maule, with the two heels of her shoes like grasshoppers' legs, and the per-*fume* she puts behind her ears like they do in the pictures, would never go rollicking with you over the mountains like Miss Kathy did."

For a moment Judy thought from the expression on Raff's face that he was going to administer a sharp reprimand, whether at the reference to Kathy or Marcia, she was not sure, however, but he merely shrugged and turned away.

"It's useless, arguing with you when you're in this mood. Come along, Judy," he said, but saw, out of the tail of his eye, the furtive kiss she blew to the old man as she turned to follow.

"What have you been doing to Timsy?" Raff inquired as they walked down to the jetty.

"We were having a quite serious talk about roots," she said.

"Roots?"

"Belonging somewhere—*you* know. But Marcia thinks roots are deadly."

"And what does Timsy think?" he asked a little grimly, and she was afraid that she had been in danger of becoming indiscreet.

"It wasn't very clear," she answered.

"Well, well! You mustn't demoralise my not very active staff or I shall have to issue a rule for no fraternising."

Her eyes were round and suddenly uncertain as she watched him pull the boat alongside the jetty, afraid that she had annoyed him by gossiping with Timsy in the yard, but looking up, he caught sight of her expression and laughed.

"I was only joking, you silly child! Here, jump in—not like that, you little loon, you'll capsize her!" he said, then, as she hesitated, he picked her up and lowered her firmly on to one of the thwarts, following himself and starting up the engine.

She twisted round excitedly to watch the shore receding and catch a glimpse she had not seen before of Slyne. The house rose above its sloping lawns in muted graciousness, its long mullioned windows sparkling in the sun. Its faded grandeur was, to Judy, made friendly by that gentle hint of decay; the neglected lawns showed bright promise of the new spring grass, and moss grew with a brilliant splash of colour over the ruins of the wing that had been burnt out in the "troubles".

"Not a very edifying advertisement for an expensive guest house, is it? Raff observed, following the direction of her gaze.

"It's lovely," she said softly, and indeed, with the water widening into a clear mirror of ripples which threw back the reflection, Slyne had a beauty enhanced by its decline.

"How could you bear to do it?" she asked.

"Do what?"

"Turn the place into a guest house, with strangers poking about and wanting modern plumbing and cocktail bars and most likely neon signs flashing out across the lough. You'd never have neon signs, would you, Raff?"

"No, Judy," he said gently, "I wouldn't do that—though Marcia has some idea for floodlighting the place. It might look rather effective from the lough."

"And hideously expensive," she retorted. I think the Maules have the wrong idea about this place. Instead of trying to run it as a flash establishment for rich tycoons, it should have been left as it was for people who appreciate the old world, and like lamps because they're homely, and don't mind about the plumbing or want a cocktail bar. You could have made it pay without all this extra expense and upheaval."

"Dear me!" he exclaimed softly, "I'd no idea we'd taken on such a shrewd little critic. Have you voiced these ideas to Noel or Marcia, by any chance?"

"No—I've only just thought about it."

"Then let it remain a thought, my dear. They won't thank you for interference."

"But it's your house—your home. You have the final say, surely?"

"How persistent you are! Yes, I have the final say, but I, no less than you, have little idea of the running of a commercial business."

"I," she said, quite unabashed, "would make it pay."
He grinned.

"Would you, indeed? It's beginning to pay now."

"Not enough. You have to set off all the expense of what Timsy calls contraptions before you can even begin to show a profit."

"By the end of the summer——" he began, starting to sound impatient, then refused to argue any further.

"Ah, may the divil fly away with you!" he exclaimed, just as Timsy might have done, and suddenly began to laugh. "A flash establishment for rich tycoons—Castle Slyne! I shan't forget that one in a hurry!"

"You see? You think as I do," she said with the satisfied smirk of one who has had the last word, then her attention became wholly taken up with the approaching shore of the north side of the lough, and she cried: "Look! Look!" pointing in first one direction and then another until Raff told her brusquely to sit still before she upset the boat.

They climbed the steep path cut into the bank which led to the road, and Judy was aware of sharp disappointment. The cottages which from the other side had seemed a charming huddle of picturesque stone were a mean little straggle of ugly slate and dirty windows, and Casey's store was a tumbledown structure with a galvanised roof and torn posters stuck to the walls. The straight, macadamed highway had none of the wild charm and unexpectedness of the ill-kept south road.

"What's wrong now?" Raff asked, watching her face with amusement. "Ireland isn't a universal beauty spot any more than England is, you know."

"I suppose not, only—well, you see, the other side has tantalised me ever since I've been here. I've always wanted to come across."

"And now you're here you find it was a mirage, like so much else in life. A good example of stopping on your own side of the fence, perhaps. What's on the other side is seldom what you imagine."

She glanced up at him quickly, wondering if his words held a special meaning, but his grey eyes were merely quizzical as they met hers.

"Well," she said, "I'm glad we don't live this side. Ours is much nicer." He smiled, thinking how innocently she assumed an integral part of his household, and went into the store to execute his order.

"And what would you be wantin' all this lot again for, O'Rafferty?" Casey demanded, scanning Marcia's list with a jaundiced eye, and Judy was unsurprised to find, since he dwelt in such ugliness on the north side of the lough, that he was the dour type of Irishman with little warmth and humour. "Didn't Mr Maule come across yesterday with this very same order, and him without the price again for me last account?"

"I wrote a cheque at the beginning of the week—he must have forgotten it," Raff said absently. "I didn't know he'd been across yesterday. Miss Maule must have made a mistake when she sent me over this morning."

" 'Tis the very same list she wrote. I mind the way it read and the corner torn off at the top."

"She must have forgotten, or given me the wrong one. I'd better take back another supply, though, to avoid a wasted journey."

"That's needless extravagance," Judy interposed disapprovingly, and Casey suddenly became affable. He was, it transpired, that rare product of his race, a man careful of his money.

"Now that's common sense," he declared. "Even your fancy guests couldn't have ate all that lot in the time, *or* drunk all the liquor. Come back tomorrow, or the next day, but come yourself, O'Rafferty. Is this the young lady from England who gives an eye to your buks?"

"Miss Ware is my secretary, yes. Why do you tell me to come myself, Casey?"

The little man lifted his shoulders in a shrug and turned down his mouth at the same time.

"I wouldn't be knowin' why. Just a fancy I had, maybe," he said vaguely.

"Well, it won't be convenient. I'll take the stuff now, so get a move on and pack it up, or we shall be late for lunch," Raff replied a little curtly.

"Will you now? And miss that felly Grogan if he's as fly as I think he is?"

Raff frowned.

"What do you mean? He wasn't expected at Slyne this morning, as far as I know."

"He passed here earlier with that van of his, and I know where he was bound for. He always takes the north road for the castle because of the bumps in t'other. Says they'd destroy them gew-gaws he calls his art treasures. You'd not be doin' business with a felly like that, would you now? If you want a price for some of that stuff you have at the castle, there are better men to deal with than Dan Grogan, and I'm tellin' you that as a friend, mind."

Judy watched Raff visibly freeze. It would, she realised with surprise, touch his pride badly to have the district imagine that he was obliged to sell the family treasures because the guest house was not paying as well as it should.

"Thanks, Casey, I'm sure you mean it kindly," he replied stiffly. "Now, if you'll please get on with that order, Miss Ware and I will wait outside."

"You've forgotten," Judy said slowly. "Grogan was probably bringing back the tallboy. Don't you remember? He took it away to repair."

"So he did," said Raff, his face clearing, but Casey leaned across for a final word.

"Funny that felly always visits the castle when you're out of the way," he said with a wink. "Thick as thieves they are, him and Mr Maule. Miss Doyle tells Willie-the-Post, and Willie spreads the tale wherever he delivers the letters—thick as thieves, they all say."

Raff walked out of the store before he had finished speaking, and Judy, after stopping to the end for politeness' sake, joined him to sit on the wall outside and wait, but he offered no further conversation. His earlier mood had completely altered, she saw, and she was careful not to disturb

78

those inward thoughts with idle chatter when they embarked again with the provisions, but all the way back to the south side of the lough her own thoughts plagued her. Had Marcia's repeated order been a genuine mistake, or had she really wanted to get Raff out of the house, and if so, for what purpose?

Then Judy remembered the fake chest in the Small Saloon and her eyes widened as her first suspicions began to crystallise. She could hardly wait for Raff to make fast the boat before springing ashore and running into the house to see if the tallboy had been returned.

II

She ran across the hall and down the long corridor to the Grand Saloon, aware only vaguely of the familiar sounds of the house; Mary Kate's shrill voice somewhere from the kitchen quarters, Rosie's light footsteps pattering backwards and forwards to the dining-room, the clocks striking the hour with varying degrees of accuracy. The Grand Saloon was empty of visitors, and the sunlight, streaming in at the window, caught the faded tapestry and mellow patina of old wood into a hazy Conversation Piece which made her pause, drinking in the beauty of old things of which her father had made her so much aware, then her eyes went round the room, seeking the tallboy.

It was there, but not as she remembered it. The furniture had been shifted and it stood now in a dark corner where any change or discrepancy would not be noticed. *It is a racket*, she told herself fiercely, as she advanced into the room, and was then aware of the click of high heels behind her on the polished floor which could only be Marcia's.

"Grogan's brought it back, as you see. He's made a good job, I think, but of course I haven't your knowledge of antiques," Marcia said, and Judy turned to face her, thinking, even in that moment of distrust and the certainty of what she would find, how well the older woman graced the room. She leaned, with studied effect, on the arm of a high-backed Jacobean chair, smoking one of her inevitable

79

cigarettes, and the smoke rose in a thin, graceful spiral to mingle with the dancing motes in a shaft of sunlight.

"Why have you put it in that dark corner?" Judy demanded, and scarcely knew that her voice was accusing. Marcia gave an imperceptible shrug and tipped her ash with an automatic gesture on to the carpet.

"I like to rearrange things from time to time," she said "Don't you approve, darling?"

The tone was teasing but delicately indicative that a brash young newcomer had no right to doubt or criticise, and Judy turned her back and walked over to the tallboy, aware that both Raff and Noel had suddenly joined them.

"Why are you in here?" Raff asked.

"Judy wants to make sure of the tallboy," Marcia said, with a little ripple of amusement. "She seems upset because we've changed the furniture around."

"Make sure?" Raff repeated, with a frown, and Noel grinned, and began to stroll across the room with the conscious elegance he could adopt so well when he knew he was being watched.

"She imagines there's been some dirty work. Like you, she doesn't think much of poor Grogan and his rather obvious blarney," he said. "Well, Judy—are you satisfied with the job he's done, or do you still think the piece should have been sent to experts in Dublin who would have charged twice as much?"

She was aware of him negligently propped against a cabinet watching her fingers run over the smooth veneer of the tallboy, seeking out flaws that would proclaim it a copy, but her touch faltered and was finally still. It was the genuine article restored very cleverly, she had to admit, and she turned to meet Noel's mocking gaze.

"Satisfied?" he asked, and she nodded, aware now that she had precipitated some minor crisis in their relationships. While Noel's eyes were frankly derisive, and Marcia's smilingly tolerant, Raff's expression was one of barely concealed impatience.

"If Judy has finished giving her opinion on the furniture, we might go in to lunch," he said.

They followed him back to the dining-room, and Marcia slipped an arm round Judy's waist.

"You shouldn't try to make an issue out of something before you're sure, darling," she said softly. "Raff doesn't like atmospheres, you know."

"I haven't," said Judy stubbornly, "been trying to create an atmosphere."

"Haven't you? Well, we'll give you the benefit of the doubt. You're very young, after all, and don't know quite as much as you think you do about old furniture and—and other things."

If it was a warning, Marcia's gracious friendliness gave the lie to it, but there *was* an atmosphere, Judy had to admit, eating her lunch in uneasy silence, and was not surprised when Raff asked suddenly:

"Did you mislay your list this morning, Marcia, that you sent me out with yesterday's? Casey seemed surprised that we needed the identical order again so soon."

Marcia's lovely dark eyes grew wide and bright with apology.

"Oh!" she exclaimed. "That must have been your fault, Noel—you would come and natter while I was trying to give Mary Kate the orders for meals and I must have confused my lists. I'm sorry, Raff darling; now I suppose everything's duplicated."

"I suppose it is. What was on the fresh order that couldn't have waited till next time?"

"How should I remember? Whatever it was, we'll have to make do till the van comes out from Knockferry. I'm sorry if you had a wasted morning, Raff, but Judy will have enjoyed the unexpected jaunt. You did, didn't you, Judy?"

Raff did not give Judy time to reply, but continued quite pleasantly:

"There seem to be some odd rumours going about via Miss Doyle and Willie-the-Post. I really would prefer that you cease dealing with Grogan for repairs and such-like, Noel."

Noel shot his sister a wry little smile.

"You should know by now how rumours circulate in lonely country spots like this, old man," he said airily.

"What are they saying—that Marcia and I are swopping your antiques for reproductions, or that Grogan has ulterior designs on prim Miss Doyle?"

Judy thought she heard Marcia catch her breath for an instant, but her eyes, as well as her brother's, held only affectionate amusement. If the Maules were indeed up to such tricks, then Noel called a very pretty bluff.

"Of course not," Raff replied, with a reluctant smile. "The implication was, I think, that I'm secretly selling my stuff because the guest house doesn't pay. I don't like that sort of rumour, Spongy, or the running up of debts."

"Spongy . . ." Noel repeated, giving him a speculative glance. "You haven't called me that for a long time, Raff. Any connecting thought, would you say? And what's this about running up debts?"

"Casey's account wasn't paid yesterday, and I gave you a cheque a week ago."

"Oh, is that all? I'll take it over next time—not to worry!"

"No," said Raff. "Give it to Judy this afternoon and she'll put it in the post."

"Of course," drawled Noel, a flash of insolent malice in the eyes that rested for a moment on Judy. "That's what she's here for, isn't it—not to stick her charming little nose into affairs that don't concern her?"

"Darling, why drag poor Judy into this?" Marcia said sending a warm woman-to-woman look across the table to Judy. "And Raff—you really shouldn't haul my little brother over the coals in front of your secretary. He is, after all, your manager."

They had all finished their lunch and were sitting, smoking, over their coffee. Judy, feeling distinctly uncomfortable, saw the surprise in Raff's face and could have hit him for his apparent obtuseness.

"I'm sorry," he said mildly. "I wasn't trying to trick anybody off. I simply thought that over hotel matters we all pulled together. What's eating you both?"

"Nothing, darling," said Marcia on a sigh. "I suppose we thought—oh, well let it ride."

Raff got up to leave the table and, in passing behind Marcia's chair, rested both hands on her shoulders for a moment and bent over her. It was an oddly revealing little gesture, Judy thought, both intimate and conciliatory, and Marcia's response was as plain as she slid her own hands over his.

"Come along Judy, we've the morning's work to catch up on," he said, straightening up again and as Judy rose and followed him, Noel called after them:

"Send her along to my office for that cheque. There are one or two others she can deal with, now I come to think of it."

She did not want to go to the manager's office, knowing, if Raff did not, that Noel held her personally to blame for any fault-finding his employer might have done. She was not surprised that he deliberately kept her waiting while he idly searched through files for the missing cheque nor when he looked up suddenly to say softly:

"Don't try to make mischief here, Judy. You haven't been engaged to snoop and tell tales, and it won't get you anywhere."

"I haven't snooped, neither have I told tales," she answered, giving him a level look.

"Haven't you? But you've stirred up a nice lot of trouble."

"Casey's rumours did that. Raff—Mr O'Rafferty is easy-going up to a point, but he's proud, too."

"So it's Raff now, is it? What's your game, my clever little puss?"

"What's yours?" she retorted, and he laughed.

"I have no schemes that could further my own future here," he said. "But you, my dear little Judy, have the advantage of your sex. Can it be possible that you have notions of becoming mistress of Slyne?"

He saw her colour and the angry glint in her eyes, and dashed behind his desk in mock alarm.

"Don't hit me!" he said. "I must admit that you look attractive when you're roused—damned attractive—but you can't hold a candle to Marcia all the same, and she has prior claim in the matrimonial stakes, you know—though why the O'Rafferty should attract a woman of her type and temperament, I wouldn't begin to understand—still, there it is, so be warned."

"If you'll give me Casey's cheque and any others you've mislaid, I'll go back to my work," Judy said, her lips a little white. He presented her with several, and as she turned to go, caught her round the waist and pulled her on to his knee.

"Why not be a bit more forthcoming with me, if Raff won't play?" he asked. "A little gentle dalliance could do neither of us any harm, and I'm beginning to think you have possibilities I've missed until now."

She sat there stiffly, making no attempt to free herself.

"What, not even a struggle! But you aren't very responsive either, are you?" he said.

"One doesn't struggle with wolves—it only makes them more ardent," she replied calmly, and he laughed in spite of himself.

"When you've time to spare for me, Judy, I should like to get on with some work," Raff's icy voice said from the doorway.

Judy sprang to her feet, knowing her sense of guilt must be evident in the wave of colour that rushed to her face. Noel, quite unabashed, observed with his impudent grin:

"Caught in the act by the boss—how compromising! Really, my dear fellow, you might warn us more tactfully of your approach another time. One likes to preserve the conventions when one is under observation."

Raff said nothing, but turned on his heel and walked away, and Judy, picking up the cheques, followed him back to his study. They sat down in icy silence, she at her typewriter, he in his familiar chair on the other side of the desk. She glanced surreptitiously at his face and was astonished to see the anger there. He might justifiably be annoyed by his misinterpretation of the scene he had interrupted when she should have been working, but such frozen displeasure seemed out of proportion. Then she saw the disappointment in his eyes, a disappointment which seemed to refute the anger, and she remembered him then, admitting her to the warmth and intimacy of his half-reluctant confidences those times when he had seemed to want her company; even this morning when she had lectured him absurdly and made him laugh. But the glory of the morning had faded outside, too; the day had lost its brightness and turned to rain.

She sighed. Excuses had never been her way out, but she did not want him to hold her cheaply.

"Mr O'Rafferty . . ." she said, ". . . it wasn't what you thought. I mean——" she stopped, aware of the futility of trying to explain away an incident without attaching the blame elsewhere.

"Your private affairs are no concern of mine, so long as they don't interfere with the efficient running of the guest house," he said in a hard, brittle voice. "You are quite at liberty to join Noel's obliging band of girl-friends if it amuses you, but not in working hours, please. Now, if you're ready, I have some dictation for you to take."

III

It was, she thought afterwards, absurd to care one way or another what he thought of her, for as he had told her, her private affairs were no concern of his; but she did care. She found she minded very much that he should have caught her apparently behaving like any little empty-headed floozie not particular where she bestowed her favours. Judy was no prude, but she began to suspect that he might be; was it not said that the Irish, as a race, were fundamentally chaste? Raff had loved his Kathy, who must have satisfied whatever ideals he might have about women, and perhaps he was beginning to love Marcia, exposing once again a vulnerability in himself that neither of the Maules would understand.

It was this, of course, and not the slight to her integrity that she minded, Judy discovered, lying on her hard bed with the broken spring in the darkness of the nursery. His mistaken opinion of a girl he employed and scarcely knew could not hurt him as it could hurt her, and he would not know, for she had not known herself, that he had become important to her in a way no man had since her father had died. When? That day at the inn by Lough Creagh? The morning's simple trip in the boat to the other side; or even the moment of shock and anger when he had so coldly rebuffed her and she had seen the odd disappointment in his eyes?

Was she falling for the O'Rafferty of Castle Slyne like the girls at the college with their first jobs and their first association with men of a different world? she asked herself scornfully, but she knew that for her the answer could never be quite the same. She had not desired petting parties with the few young men who had found her attractive; she did not now desire the time-honoured convention of the foolish young girl imagining herself to be in love with her boss.

"Damn Ireland! Damn the romantic twaddle than can seep into your very bones!" she exclaimed and, realising that she was cold in her thin nightdress, pulled the curtains to impatiently, shutting out the moonlight, and went back to bed.

With the coming of April parties began arriving from England for the Easter vacation, for the most part university students who liked to hit it up at the local races and who, one and all, fell hard for Marcia.

Judy watched, with reluctant admiration, the ease and skill with which Noel's sister handled a situation to which she was clearly well accustomed. It made no difference that these young men must be several years her junior, and she seemed to blossom, so that even Raff came to watch her with a new, slightly enigmatical expression. Was she doing it, Judy wondered, simply to arouse his interest, or was she one of those women who could not help responding provocatively to male admiration?

Sometimes Judy would watch them all a little enviously. They were young, and probably foolish, and their ways were not really hers, but she knew, had it not been for Marcia, that they would have been glad to pay her idle attention. They shouted "Hiya Judy!" and slapped her on the back, and bought her chocolates, if they remembered, when she dried their wet clothes for them or performed the small services that the servants could not be persuaded to undertake, but they never offered her the courtesies they showered on Marcia, or noticed her clothes or the way she did her hair.

"They make me feel like their kid sister," she said wryly to Raff, who had caught her clearing up the mess left from one of their rowdy parties. "Wouldn't you think just one of them might want to make a date to be shown the sights, or—or for anything?"

"Poor Judy!" he teased. "But I thought you told me once that you didn't care for young men."

"I don't—still, one likes one's sex to be recognised," she answered crossly, and he laughed.

"You can't compete with Marcia when it comes to scalp-hunting," he said lightly. "She's probably been very bored all the winter with only old Colonel Frazer as a permanent victim."

"And you," she said, then coloured slightly at the way in which her remark might be taken, but he only said mildly:

"I don't consider myself to be a victim."

Because you're hooked already, she wanted to retort vulgarly, then her eyes grew gentle.

"Don't you mind?" she asked softly, but his reply sounded suddenly cold and she knew that he did mind.

"Why should I? They're only youngsters infatuated with an older woman. Very natural, Judy, and nothing to make an issue out of. Doesn't Noel satisfy your own inclinations for dalliance?"

"That was unpardonable," she said quietly, and he began to rub the bridge of his nose, that now familiar signal of distress.

"Yes, it was, wasn't it? I'm sorry. Judy——"

"Yes?"

"You're very young. Don't take Noel too seriously, will you? He can't resist making passes at any reasonably attractive girl."

"Oh, Raff, do you think I don't know that?" she said. "He's just a wolf and a bored one at that. He deliberately let you think—he'd pulled me on to his knee that day and was quite annoyed because I didn't struggle."

"And why didn't you struggle—or is that an impertinent question?"

"Of course not. I didn't struggle because that's what he would have liked. There's nothing more deflating to a wolf's ego than a victim who remains passive and just doesn't care."

He gave a reluctant smile, then it reached his eyes, creasing up the corners in the tender expression for which she had begun to watch.

"I misjudged you, Judy, and that was very stupid of me" he said, and she asked with natural curiosity, because now there seemed to be no misunderstanding between them:

"Why were you so angry? It wasn't very serious after all, whatever you thought."

"I think I was disappointed in you," he said slowly. "You had seemed to me different—more like——"

"Kathy, were you going to say?" she interrupted sharply.

"Perhaps I was, but you should take that as a compliment, my child. She was clean and uncomplicated and simple of heart."

"I daresay she was," Judy replied, feeling suddenly cross, "but one doesn't want always to be compared with somebody else. I hope I'm clean, but I doubt if I'm simple of heart."

"How cross you sound," he observed, his eyes twinkling. "And are you sure you know what it means?"

"No, not really. Do you?"

"I think so."

Then, she wanted to say, *don't love Marcia, for she is not simple of heart as you mean it, and she's very, very complicated.*

Judy felt distinctly relieved when the end of their present guests' visit was in sight. It was she who had to pacify the Colonel and Miss Botley who perpetually threatened to leave, and fill the post of receptionist also, when necessary, for Marcia, making the best of the few days left to her, went gaily off with her posse of young men, not even troubling to ask permission. Raff never reminded her, as he had every right to do, that she was a salaried worker like everyone else employed by him, and Judy found herself irked too by his apparent reluctance to assert his authority which must surely spring from his fear of losing her.

"Men!" exclaimed Judy, just as Miss Doyle was passing by with a basketful of her uninviting woollen underwear which she had been washing against orders in one of the guests' bathrooms.

"Ah, you may well say that, young miss," she paused to remark. "It's the divil they are with their false faces and lyin' tongues. Seducers they are, all the lot of them!"

"Oh, no, Miss Doyle!" Judy objected from habit. She was used by now to the indictments uttered by Timsy's star-crossed niece, and often she enjoyed them, but she always felt bound to protest.

"Oh, yes, Miss Judy, and don't you be led away by soft words and promises, like me. There's not a man alive I'd trust and so I'm tellin' you."

"Not even Mr O'Rafferty?"

"Ah, him—that's different—but that fancy housekeeper will get him, you mark my words."

"Do you mean Miss Maule?"

"I do so. And she's no better than a housekeeper for all the fine names she likes to call herself. Thinks to be mistress here and sell the place up. I've heard them talkin', those Maules and Dan Grogan."

"Miss Doyle——" Judy's old suspicions gathered again, making her indiscreet, "why is he always around, when Mr O'Rafferty's not here?"

Miss Doyle looked coy and sly at the same time and her thin body strained against her washing-basket.

"He's around because he fancies me, much good will it do him," she said, with a rather sad preening of herself. "Him and Mr Maule has business, so I believe. You'd better ask him yourself, young miss."

She made off for the kitchen quarters, the basket on her hip, and Judy stood there frowning, remembering the certainty with which she had expected to find a reproduction in place of the returned tallboy. That Noel and Grogan were up to tricks of some kind she was sure, but on that particular day the Maules had very neatly called her bluff. Because she was still so sure, she went to the Grand Saloon and examined the tallboy again, but it was undoubtedly the original piece, and the repair work had been skilfully done. Her eyes went to the piece next to it, a small eighteenth-century kneehole desk in burr elm with ebony mountings, which had always charmed her, and perhaps it was a trick of the light that made her suddenly go on her knees beside it and examine it more closely. It was, she could see now, quite a clever copy of the original, but a copy, nonetheless, and she was convinced this time how the substitution had been managed. The tallboy had been a blind all along to cover the exchange of the desk, either at the time when the damaged piece had been taken or when it was brought back; on both occasions both Raff and Judy had been out of the house.

She was still on her knees beside the desk when she heard footsteps crossing the polished floor and someone switched on the lights.

"What on earth are you doing, Judy?" Raff asked in surprise.

She spoke before she had given due consideration to her words, tumbling them out in confused eagerness.

"This is another copy," she said. "I thought they'd make an exchange on the tallboy, but all the time it was the desk, which was quite clever. Look — can you see how one of the mountings is out of alignment? And the golden colour of the wood hasn't quite the richness of the period."

"What on earth are you talking about?" Raff said, frowning. "Do you imagine you've discovered another fake like the chest in the Small Saloon which has been in the family ever since I can remember?"

"Yes," she asnswered, taking no warning from his sudden reserve. "Raff—don't you understand? Someone's robbing you quite cleverly, and it isn't hard to see that Grogan has a hand in it."

"And who would you suggest is conniving, if that's the right expression?"

The cold smoothness of his voice warned her now, and she set back on her heels, blinking up at him. Suspicion was not, after all, proof, and the Maules, brother and sister, were established here with his trust and his friendship.

"There isn't much choice is there?" she faltered at last, and saw the fleeting look of distaste in his eyes.

"If you are making accusations, which I hope you're

not, I should think again, my dear," he said quietly. "I wouldn't like to have to set you down as a mischief-maker, Judy."

"But you can't get away from facts," she persisted stubbornly. "This piece and the piece in the Small Saloon are reproductions, and if you say they've been in your family ever since you can remember, then the substitution must have been made under your nose!"

"You were sure about the tallboy till you saw it again," he said with controlled patience. "How can you be sure this piece, that's always stood in this dark corner, isn't the same? If it's a copy as you suggest, then it's something we've always had."

"I feel I would have known," she said obstinately, "I feel that the very difference I sensed today proves——"

"It proves nothing, except possibly a too highly developed imagination where antiques are concerned," he replied, and his voice was once more indulgent, and he used the irritating tones of the more experienced adult seeking to humour a well-meaning but misguided child. "Don't try us too highly with these flights of fancy, will you, Judy, or I shall have to think, as Marcia does, that you want to attract attention to yourself."

"Is that what Marcia thinks?"

"Well, she's rather had the monoply with those young guests of ours, hasn't she?"

"And she thinks I'm jealous?"

"Not jealous, perhaps, but left out of things a little, shall we say?"

"I'm sorry," she said, "I may have been wrong about the desk, though I don't think so, and I was *not* wrong over the date of the chest. As to being left out of things — I wouldn't dream of competing with Marcia, even if I could, and she's welcome to her young men."

"Judy——" he said, but she wheeled round quickly, her red hair swinging out in a shining curve as she ran out of the room without waiting to hear what he had to say.

She must not, she realised now, play into Marcia's hands by trying to warn Raff before he was ready to listen, and that same evening she was afforded an unwelcome opportunity for discovering how unlikely he was to listen at all.

Marcia had returned from a day at the races with her escorts who were frankly merry after repeated rounds of the bars on the course. They had flocked immediately to the Small Saloon, of which Judy and Colonel Frazer were the sole occupants, and Raff had refused to serve them. They were decent young men for the most part and, after the first indignant protestations, were prepared to submit sulkily to his ruling, but Marcia, following in their wake, slipped quietly behind the bar and announced that she herself would take their orders.

"Marcia, please——" Judy heard Raff say with an edge to his voice, but she just smiled up at him and began using the shaker.

"Don't be stuffy, darling," she said. "You, an Irishman, to turn prudish at an extra drop of the crayture! I'll mix you one of my brother's specials, boys—that will make your hair curl! Where *is* Noel, by the way?"

He looked so white with anger for a moment that Judy thought Marcia for once had gone too far, but he replied with rigid control:

"He's gone into Knockferry for some fertiliser. Will you please mix yourself a drink and take it over to Judy's table? It's not a question of being stuffy, but we have other guests to consider."

"Where?" asked Marcia innocently. She had already seen Colonel Frazer stump, muttering, from the bar, and Miss Botley did not drink and was probably listening avidly on the other side of the door. She picked up the shaker again and began rapidly filling glasses one after the other.

"On the house—just to show there's no real ill-feeling," she said with her brother's charming insolence.

Raff stood perfectly still without speaking and his silence was reflected suddenly in the three young men who, after shuffling their feet awkwardly, uncertain how to react, sheepishly began to drink their "specials".

Raff waited until they had finished, then said very courteously, but with a hint in his voice that he would stand no more nonsense:

"Gentlemen, this happens to be my home as well as my house, and it is only by my favour that you come here.

Miss Maule is employed by me, as I think you all know, and hasn't the authority to countermand my orders, so I hope you will embarrass neither of us by prolonging this interview. Dinner will be ready in about half an hour. Good evening."

They filed out with muttered apologies and Raff began to rinse out the glasses.

"How dare you, Raff!" Marcia said, but it was plain from the way she looked at him that, angry though she was, he had aroused fresh interest in her. She had, Judy thought shrewdly, been quite deliberately provoking him to find out of what stuff he was made.

"I might say the same to you, my dear," he replied quietly. "I don't care to be made a fool of in my own house in front of a bunch of ill-mannered youngsters."

"Are you jealous?" she asked softly, and Judy, who was just within earshot but out of their line of vision, knew that they had forgotten her.

"Jealous of that lot?" he said, but a little too quickly, and Marcia reached up a hand to stroke his cheek, the soft lines of her body suddenly fluid and inviting.

"Darling—you take such a lot of persuading," she said with a little gurgle of laughter. "Can't you respond—like lesser men?"

To Judy, still sitting over her half-finished tomato juice, it was highly embarrassing. She could not leave the room without crossing directly in front of the bar and, even as she sought vainly for some other means of escape, Raff pulled Marcia roughly into his arms and kissed her.

"Is that what you wanted?" he asked harshly.

"Of course. How slow you've been, darling."

He kissed her again, and this time she wound her arms round his neck and there was satisfied response in every line of her body, and the taut lines of his own relaxed visibly.

Judy slipped to the floor and began to crawl on all fours in the shelter of the bar counter towards the door. She was halfway round when Noel came in and, after a glance at the silent couple behind the bar, stood watching her with interest. She made frantic faces at him, whereupon he began to laugh.

"What on earth do you think you're doing?" he asked, with bland disregard to her signals of distress. "If the Colonel comes in for a snifter he'll think you're drunk, or something."

"He's been and gone," she said, giving up all attempt to escape detection, then, as the absurdity of the situation struck her she sat back on her heels and began to laugh too, as much from embarrassment as amusement.

Marcia peered over the counter, her face betraying satisfaction rather than annoyance.

"I'd forgotten you were still here, darling," she said. "Were you trying to make a tactful exit before Raff was in danger of making a declaration? How sweet!"

Judy stood up rather sheepishly and avoided looking at Raff, who had his back turned to them and was needlessly shifting the bottles on the shelves.

"You might," she observed with as much dignity as she could muster, "have invented some reason for getting me out of the room before—before——"

"That's enough, Judy," Raff said, suddenly turning round. "I'm sorry if we have embarrassed you, you should have knocked over your glass, or something."

"If you're disappointed in me again, it's hardly my fault, Mr O'Rafferty," she said, speaking aloud the thoughts which he could scarcely be expected to follow. All the same, it seemed as if he did, for although he made no reply, his eyes, as they rested on her flushed face, held a curious expression. It could, of course, have been Marcia who had disappointed him this time.

"What's all the double talk in aid of?" Noel asked, and slipped deftly behind the bar to mix himself a drink.

"I wouldn't know, darling, but probably Raff understands," Marcia said, changing places with her brother, smiling and unruffled to put an arm round Judy's waist.

"Let's leave the men to have a little business talk, shall we? In the meantime I'll explain the facts of life to you if you're still left in any doubt," she said, throwing Noel a conspiratorial smile, and gently pushed Judy out of the room.

CHAPTER FIVE

I

JUDY, escaping as soon as she could from Marcia's uncharacteristic desire for confidences, ran out on to the terrace to cool her cheeks before facing them all again for dinner. Mist rose from the lough meeting the growing twilight; soon the soft spring evenings would lengthen into those of early summer, and Raff and Marcia would wander by the water's edge to avoid the latest guests' invasion of their privacy, and the spell of Ireland would deepen about them, and he would kiss her, this time with gentleness.

"Oh, hell!" Judy exclaimed aloud, and turned, as she heard a footstep on the terrace behind her, grateful that it was Noel and not Raff who had followed her out.

"What are you blaspheming about so inelegantly in the damp night air?" he inquired, his eyes mocking her. "Did that unexpected but very workmanlike embrace upset you?"

"It would have been more tactful if they'd waited until they were alone," she answered somewhat tartly.

"Darling, I doubt if either of them were aware at that moment if you even existed," he said a little cruelly. "Well, it looks as though she may have brought him up to scratch at last. Our rather tedious young undergraduates served their purpose, after all. Poor Judy! Do you feel neglected? I'm always ready to oblige, you know, to bolster up your little ego."

"My little ego is in quite good shape, thank you, and you, if I may say so, are rather cheap and boring."

"Boring, am I? Oh, no, my pretty, that's just sour grapes. Still, like Marcia, I go for the ones that are hard to get. You may continue to abuse me, if it amuses you."

"Not very much about you amuses me at the moment," she said, and he grinned.

"You can't be on your dignity after that very funny exhibition in the bar," he said. "What on earth possessed you to go crawling about on all fours?"

"So that I wouldn't be seen, of course."

"They wouldn't have noticed if you'd walked out right past them, my sweet. Love is completely oblivious, didn't you know?"

"Love?" faltered Judy, and he gave a little shrug.

"Call it what you like," he replied. "My beautiful sister wouldn't be above a little light dalliance, but not the O'Rafferty, would you think?"

"No," she said bleakly, and turned to stare out over the water again.

"Have you lost your heart a little, poor innocent?" he asked, and moved up behind her to take her lightly by the shoulders.

"I don't know," she replied, but she did. She had known that day he had misunderstood her relations with Noel; she had known with every small rebuff or coldness, and this evening she had known it with pain and jealousy and a wild, unfamiliar stirring of the heart. Was it only through pain that one learnt these things? she wondered, and said quickly, before she was tempted to ask the question of someone who could have no counsel to give:

"This place must be beautiful in the summer . . . sitting out here, watching the dusk fall . . . that feeling this country gives you that nothing matters today because tomorrow will do. . . ."

"Pretty deadly stagnation, if you want my opinion," Noel answered. "All very well for a holiday; or folk with their heads in the clouds, but give me the bright lights."

"Then why do you stay?"

"I'm broke, my sweet. Until I've built up a little reserve of capital I'm stuck with Castle Slyne."

She moved uneasily, remembering her earlier suspicions.

"Can you build up capital out of a manager's salary alone?" she asked sharply, and felt his hands squeeze her shoulders with a warning pinch.

"Of course not, but there are pickings."

"Such as fiddling the accounts, like the Lucases' and those Americans'?"

"How unwisely curious you are, my sweet. I get a percentage of the takings in addition, if you must know, and there are a hundred ways of collecting perks via tradespeople's commissions and the more unsuspecting guests —all quite legitimate in the hotel racket."

"Is it? It sounds more to me as if your pockets were being lined at Raff's expense. Shouldn't all profits go back into the business?"

"All legitimate profits do, as you can see by the books. Don't pry, my child, into matters that don't concern you."

"And is your business with Grogan one of the matters that shouldn't concern me?" she asked, but he leaned over her shoulder and gave the lobe of her ear a quick nip.

"Take that for impertinence!" he said teasingly. "My business with Grogan, for all you know, may be a matter that concerns Raff's own finances. Have you thought of that?"

She had thought of it, of course, the first time she had drawn attention to the fake chest in the Small Saloon, but Raff had seemed so oblivious of the value of the treasures which his house held that it had seemed only too likely that he was being robbed. If, however, exchanges were being made with his authority, then to draw attention to them was an impertinence and an embarrassment.

She sighed, resting her head for a moment against Noel's breast.

"I've thought of a lot of things, and they confuse me," she said, and Raff's voice behind them spoke suddenly out of the darkness.

"Judy—Noel—they've started dinner. Hadn't you better come in?"

It was difficult to know how long he had been there, for he stood in the window embrasure, a tall, dark figure watching them, and neither of them had heard him come. Judy tried to twist herself free, but Noel held on to her shoulders, quite aware of the interlinked silhouette they must have made against the lighter background of the water.

"Judy was saying that she finds Slyne beautiful—she has a romantic conception of your country, Raff," he said, and Raff stepped slowly on to the terrace. He wore, Judy observed with surprise, the old duffle coat which was a relic of his flying days, and carried a rod and a creel and the ancient haversack which held provisions for a lone expedition.

"It's hardly the moment to indulge in romantic fancies," he observed, looking at them coldly, and Noel replied, with his old impudence:

"Perhaps it's the air. You haven't a monopoly of romantic interludes, me boyo! Where are you off to, anyway, with dinner, you say, already on the table?"

"A spot of night fishing," Raff answered curtly, and Judy, understanding that for him that meant solitude in which to think and, possibly, sort out his immediate problem, if problem it was, said softly:

"I'll leave the side door unbolted, like I always do."

"Don't bother with late offerings—I have my provender with me," he said, his soft voice unusually abrupt, and she became aware, only then, that she was still standing under the light pressure of Noel's hands and that in the gathering darkness they must present the easy unconsciousness of intimacy. She wrenched herself away with a quick little twist of her body, but Raff only smiled, with a quizzical lift of the eyebrows, and walked towards the jetty.

"Well," Noel observed, watching him, "I wouldn't have thought the O'Rafferty would turn dog-in-the-manger."

"What do you mean?"

"If you don't know, I shan't tell you. Really, Judy, you are either unbelievably ingenuous, or just plain simple. Come in to dinner."

The meal was less trying than Judy had expected, thanks, possibly, to Raff's absence, but Marcia wore a look of the cat that had eaten the canary and, for the rest of the evening, made herself charming to her undergraduate admirers, whose last night it was, lavish with drinks on the house to make up, she told them, for their host's earlier inhospitality, and slapping them down with callous indifference when the liquor made them too bold in their advances.

The party broke up suddenly, with Marcia yawning her way to bed, and the young men soon following suit. Judy stayed behind to give Noel a hand with the dirty glasses, but even he seemed weary of the evening and abandoned his chores to make the rounds and seek his own bed.

Judy finished the glasses, conscious of weariness herself, and the sudden silence of the house. Idly she went round the room with a damp cloth, trying to remove stains from the furniture because it still hurt her to find rings and cigarette-burns on the mellowed wood of objects that could have been museum pieces; and the anachronism of a bar in what had once been a gracious retiring-room roused her anger afresh. Slyne was never meant for this, neither, she thought, would such half-and-half measures attract the clientele the Maules were aiming at. Why couldn't they see that the place had its own standards and these would be more acceptable to the right type of visitor than Noel's endeavours to ape a common road-house? How could Raff allow his home to be so abused for the sake of a woman who, once she owned it, would ruthlessly commercialise any article on which she could lay hands?

She carried a tray of coffee and sandwiches to the study and made up the fire, enjoying the bitter-sweet scent of the turfs as they sprang into flame. Timsy must have forgotten the generator again, for the lights burned dimly and might, she knew from past experience, go out at any minute, so she lit the oil lamp which still stood on the mantelshelf and, watching the spreading circle of light, understood the servants' preference for the old ways. She crouched on the hearth to enjoy the comfort of the fire for a moment and must have dozed, for she heard Raff come in, too late to make her escape before he found her.

"You shouldn't have waited up," he said, but he seemed to have forgotten his earlier injunction, for he started at once on the coffee and sandwiches.

"Have some?" he said, and because there was no second cup she tipped the sugar on to the tray and poured her coffee into the bowl.

"Did you catch any fish?" she asked, going back to the hearth and squatting on her heels.

"No, but I put my house in order."

"Did you?"

"Well, not entirely, perhaps. Tomorrow the old problems will probably pile up, but out there on the water, life becomes simple and familiar."

Whatever knots he had been trying to unravel, he had at least achieved relaxation and a return to the old companionship. His dark hair was plastered to his head with the rain, and even as she watched him, he rubbed away the drops which still clung to his bony features.

"It's turning into a stinker of a night," he observed comfortably, flinging himself into his favourite chair. "Have the lights gone again?"

"Just about to. I thought I'd better conserve them in case the guests start shouting for candles in the night. Rosie always forgets to replenish the boxes in the bedrooms."

"What a crazy sort of guest house this is, isn't it?"

"People would like the old ways, if you'd let them—the right sort of people, I mean."

"I remember you told me that in the boat that morning I took you to the other side. I wonder if Marcia could be made to see it."

"Marcia?" she queried tentatively, aware at once of being on dangerous ground.

"Well, she has the running of the place," he answered absently. "And in the future——" he did not finish the sentence, and she supposed, with a fresh little stab of that now familiar pain, that he was thinking of the day when Marcia would have the right to order his house as she chose.

"Couldn't you make her see that business might be better if Slyne was run as a typical Irish country house with no concessions to this day and age?" she said gently, and he sighed, glancing at her with the quickened interest she had found in him when they were out in the country alone together.

"The trouble is she's become imbued with Noel's ideas," he answered, frowning. "He thinks we're all stick-in-the-muds over here."

"You can't alter people," she said, and he replied with sudden sombreness:

"No, and perhaps one has no right to try, but a woman

is more adaptable—a woman can identify herself with someone she cares for—don't you think so, Judy?"

"Some women," she said carefully. "I don't know a lot about these things, but—I would imagine everything would depend on how much she cared."

It was evidently not the answer he wanted, for he moved impatiently and began rubbing the bridge of his nose with a finger.

"Yes. Yes, of course—and that could be the snag, couldn't it?" he said.

"If it's marriage you have in mind," she retorted boldly, "you should at least be sure of that."

He did not answer, but sat observing her through half-closed eyes, aware that she had suddenly come into focus for him. Her face was raised to his and he could see the mature hint of pain in her eyes and wide, unchildlike mouth; he could even see the scattering of freckles standing out clearly in the lamplight which burnished her hair, reminding him again of Kathy.

"You will always be sure, I think, Judy, because you are young and generous and single-hearted, but so much water has gone under the bridge for me," he said then.

"But you are the most single-hearted person I know," she exclaimed with surprise. "For Slyne, for Ireland, and once for Kathy."

"Perhaps, then, I'm just too old," he replied with a smile, and the door opened suddenly to admit Marcia.

"Well!" she observed with a slight edge to her voice, "what a cosy scene! Do you often have midnight feasts, you and your secretary, darling?"

"She kindly made me some coffee for which I was very grateful after an evening's soaking on the lough," Raff replied, rising courteously.

"I can't think what you wanted to dash out in the boat for just as dinner was starting," she said a little crossly, then added, her head on one side: "I would have thought you and I had plenty to discuss in private this evening. Noel told me he'd asked you——"

"It can wait till tomorrow," he interrupted pleasantly but firmly. "I had my own problems to sort out first, and I can never think clearly indoors."

"Can't you, darling? Well, I hope the damp air of your very wet country didn't fail you. I missed you and spent a dull evening in consequence."

Well, really! Judy thought, and nearly spoke aloud. How could she have the effrontery to make such a remark in the presence of someone who had witnessed the evening's capers!

"Did you, Marcia?" he said indulgently, and his expression was inquiring and, uncharacteristically, a little shy as he looked down at her. She stood beside him, a hand tucked through his arm, the long velvet housecoat which she wore as a dressing-gown falling in graceful folds to her feet. Her dark hair was loose about her neck, and her fine eyes were brilliant with the knowledge of her own attractions. Judy grinned as she thought of her own unbecoming but useful red garment which clashed with her hair, and silently saluted Marcia for the appositeness of her effects.

"It *was* dull, Judy, so take that smirk off your face," Marcia said, mistaking the grin. "Being gay with a bunch of hearty undergraduates can be exhausting."

"Very," Raff remarked a little dryly. "But you seemed to be enjoying their attentions when last I saw you."

"Perhaps I was working for an end," she said, fluttering her long lashes at him, and his smile was both quizzical and a little puzzled.

"Were you, Marcia? I'm not really a jealous person, you know."

"You're a most infuriating one! Anyway, it worked, and I, for one, don't believe that jealousy had nothing to do with it."

They were quite exasperating, Judy thought, in their ability to behave as if she were not present, but even as the thought crossed her mind, Marcia turned to her and said:

"Do *you* believe Raff's boast, darling? You would claim, I suppose, that you're above rousing jealousy in anyone, though I bet my little brother was giving you a lesson or two out there on the terrace."

"Your brother and I were simply talking," Judy said stiffly, aware that she was foolish to try to explain as she saw Raff's eyebrows lift in a sceptical quirk and knew that the silhouette she and Noel had presented to him must have told quite a different story.

"He was biting my ear," she said, and knew, even as she spoke, what a ridiculous statement it must sound.

Raff said nothing, but Marcia gave a low gurgle of amusement.

"And what was that a lesson for?" she asked.

"Nothing. Anyway, does it matter?" Judy looked at Raff as she spoke, but it was Marcia who answered.

"Not in the least," she said. "Now, Judy, do show a grain of tact and go to bed. I want to talk to Raff."

Judy scrambled to her feet at once, aware that she must have been in the way of both of them for some time. Raff bade her a grave goodnight, and as the study door closed behind her she heard Marcia say on a note of seductive invitation:

"Now that we've at last got rid of that tiresome girl, come and make love to me, darling."

II

Every day she expected an engagement to be announced, and every day she was cheated of that final stab of pain. Raff seemed to have retired into his familiar absorption with his estate, but Marcia went about the place with fresh confidence, picking sharply on the servants where before she had been conciliatory, and giving orders without consulting Raff, as though she were already mistress of Slyne.

With the departure of the undergraduate party, Slyne had been virtually empty, which allowed the Colonel and old Miss Botley to resume their rather dictatorial ways, but by the end of April bookings began to come in again, and in May, Marcia said, the place would be full.

"We must have staff," she told Raff. "Rosie and the other girls are all right for the casuals, but the American crowd will expect waiters in tuxedos and someone more prepossessing than Timsy to attend to their demands."

"Then they shouldn't pick on Slyne if they want a replica of hotel life in their own country," he retorted mildly, and she gave vent to a small sound of impatience.

"Really, Raff, you're impossible!" she exclaimed. "I arranged those American contacts with a great deal of trouble—people I'd met when Noel and I were running that place that went bust. We're trying to make money for you, darling—can't you understand?"

They were sitting in his study, waiting for Judy who had been sent with a message to the farm, and Marcia had already made chaos out of the neatly stacked morning's mail which had still to be dealt with. She looked delightful in one of the thin, expensive woollen dresses she had been wearing since the weather grew warmer, but Raff's eyes were on Slieve Rury, across the water, noting how its colour had changed with the spring and the approach of summer. He was in one of his abstracted moods, she saw, and told herself wryly that this was the first time she had been obliged to compete with a mountain for a man's attentions.

"Did you hear me, Raff?" she asked, trying to keep the impatience from her voice.

"Yes, I heard," he replied, and turned with reluctance from his contemplations of the mountain. "You know, Marcia, I'm beginning to think Judy's right."

"*Judy!*"

"She's often said that Slyne would pay better if it had been left as it was—an Irish country house run on simple lines, offering something of the old dignity and tradition that is fast dying out. We're attracting the wrong clientele."

"And is that Miss Judith Ware's opinion, too?"

"No, it's mine."

"Well!" said Marcia, her dark eyes angry, "I must say I hardly expected you to take the wafflings of a chit of a girl seriously! What do you imagine she knows about the running of a place like this?"

"She has a sense of values," he said, biting on the stem of his empty pipe.

"Meaning that I haven't?"

"No, I didn't mean that, yours are different, probably. Marcia . . ." he leaned forward suddenly and she became aware that he was at last observing her intently, but the sunlight flooded through the window behind him and she could not read his face, ". . . do you think you would really be happy at Slyne for the rest of your life?"

"Am I to take that for a declaration, or are you just being vague?" she asked with a little smile.

"Was a declaration what you wanted?" he answered, and she glanced at him sharply. He was in many ways a surprising man, she thought, and now that he had given her a direct opening, she scarcely knew how to use it.

"Oh, darling!" she exclaimed with a little laugh. "I've made all the running—I admit it shamelessly. Have I been so easy to resist?" She thought he seemed to withdraw as if she had slightly shocked him, and when he answered it was with a certain stiff formality.

"You are a beautiful woman, Marcia; you should know the answer to that one. If I've seemed backward, you must blame the sort of life I've led at Slyne. We don't, perhaps, understand women like you in this part of the world."

She moved restlessly, telling herself she must be patient. His curious detachment was hardly flattering, but it only served to heighten her desire for him, a desire, she recognised, which might, as Noel had warned her, be slowly extinguished once she had got what she wanted.

"But do you never want to leave here?" she asked curiously, unable to resist further probing.

"I don't think so."

"I believe," she said, softly echoing Judy's words to Timsy, "you don't really know what you want. You've stagnated too long, living with Kathy's memory."

"No, I haven't done that," he replied thoughtfully. "I recognised long ago that one cannot live with a ghost. If she's sometimes in my thoughts it's because of some unexpected association like a place once visited, or little Judy's red hair and youthful wisdom."

"Little Judy's youthful wisdom may land her in trouble before she's much older," she retorted sharply, then bit her lip as she saw his frown of distaste.

"You don't like her?" he said, more as a statement than a question, and she made a small grimace.

"Darling, I don't think about her except when she gets in my hair. It might be fairer to say that she doesn't

105

like me," she said, and he replied absently, dismissing the matter:

"Yes, you are very different."

"You aren't very flattering, darling," she said with a little laugh. "You say I'm a beautiful woman, but how much does that mean to you? Had you been more experienced in affairs of the heart, I would have said you were just being clever and holding me off. What must I do to rouse that spark in you, or are you temperamentally frigid, like so many of your race?"

She was leaning over him and he could feel the softness of her breasts against his shoulder and smell the subtle scent which she always used, and he pulled her down into his arms with a gesture that was both urgent and reluctant.

"No, I'm not frigid," he said with a sudden undertone of roughness. "I've been celibate a long time, Marcia, and never learnt, perhaps, the easy way of passion. We are a chaste race rather than a cold one, and that, I suppose, can have its disadvantages."

She lay passively in his arms, not understanding at all the struggle that was in him. Her mounting desire fought to assert itself, but instinct warned her that it was too soon. It would, she thought, returning his kiss with frank curiosity, be amusing and stimulating to break down a resistance that was still a delightful novelty.

"If marriage frightens you, darling, I'm quite ready to take you as a lover," she murmured drowsily, and knew at once that she had shocked him.

"Do you imagine I would start an affair with a woman under my own roof?" he said.

"No, I suppose not, with your outlook. But others aren't so particular, you know. Take Noel and Judy, for instance."

She felt him stiffen so violently that she slipped off his knee and stood looking down at him curiously.

"You told me you weren't a jealous man," she said slowly, "but there's something very like it in your face now—and on little Judy Ware's account, too! Well, well, well!"

"Aren't you being rather absurd?" he said coldly. "If I'm concerned for Judy it's because she's a young girl in my employ and I feel responsible for her."

"I hope that's all it is," she said. "Or have you been getting up to larks with her on your own account?"

"Oh, really, Marcia!"

"I wouldn't grudge the poor child her fun, even though I don't much care for her, so why should you?" Marcia's eyes narrowed. "Is this absurd reminder of Kathy responsible for something a little more than the kindly interest of a watchful employer?"

He stooped for his pipe which he dropped on the floor and began to fill it. She had, perhaps, gone too far, but at the same time, she was no fool. It did not seem possible that he could have been stirred by Judy, with her own riper charms at hand to tempt him, but there was always the ghost of that tiresome Kathy getting mixed up in their relationships.

"Darling," she said, kneeling down beside him, "I've shocked you about Judy and I'm sorry. I've shocked you about myself too, I'm afraid, but—I want you, Raff. Aren't you ready yet to settle down?"

"I'd like to settle down, yes—raise children—put down roots—but are you?"

"You make it sound a bit dreary, darling," she said, and he gave her a long, questioning look.

"You had better think about it carefully," he said gently. "My terms of partnership mightn't coincide with yours."

"You are expert at evading the issue, aren't you?" she said a little sharply, and he looked surprised.

"Am I?" he said, and added with apparent irrelevance: "Judy had better go."

"But why?" Astonishment made her forget for the moment that she had been sidetracked.

"If she's likely to lose her head over Noel, then I want no responsibility in the matter. He's hardly the marrying kind, I would say," he replied.

"You can't get rid of her yet, Raff," she said reluctantly. "With fresh bookings coming in every day there's a mass of paper-work to be got through which neither I or Noel could begin to cope with—besides, it would cause an upheaval all round. The servants are used to her and won't take kindly to someone new, and she keeps our two chief bores happy when they periodically besiege us with complaints—also she's a good secretary, and you wouldn't easily replace her."

He was frowning, but he listened attentively, nodding his head gravely when she had finished.

"Yes. I see your point," he said. "Well, you'd better speak to Noel—or I will."

"No, no, leave it to me. The whole thing is probably a mare's nest, anyway. She's hardly Noel's cup of tea, now I come to think of it," she said quickly. It was, she thought, too infuriating that the very moment she could have fulfilled her ambition to get rid of the girl she must plead for her to stay.

"Very well. Perhaps I'll drop a hint to the child should the opportunity occur," he said, and she looked at him speculatively.

"I shouldn't do that if I were you, darling. So embarrassing for the poor sweet, don't you think?" she replied casually. "Are you fond of her, Raff?"

"Let's not discuss Judy," he answered a little brusquely, then gave her one of his rare, charming smiles and laid a deprecating hand over hers.

"I'm afraid I've failed you, Marcia. Will you bear with me a little longer?" he said. "I'd not ask a woman to marry me unless I was sure."

"Sure of me, do you mean?"

"No, my dear, of myself."

"Don't worry, darling," she said, getting to her feet again. "We're neither of us children any longer and I'm not at all concerned with romance."

"Aren't you?" She almost thought she detected disappointment in his voice, then he smiled again, this time a little ruefully, and got out of his chair.

"Well, as you rightly say, neither of us are children. Forgive my shortcomings, will you, my dear?" he said a little formally, and, stooping, kissed her gently on the forehead just as Judy burst into the room, afraid that her errand to the farm had delayed her too long for the morning's work.

"Oh!" she said, then added: "Sorry!" in the gruff tones of an awkward schoolgirl.

"Come in, Judy, we've a lot of work to get through," Raff said, and Marcia prepared to leave them.

"I mustn't delay you," she said, adding with a warning glance at Raff: "I'll go and find Noel," and blew him a kiss before she shut the door.

III

Judy, dishevelled and out of breath, sat down at the desk and began to sort out the letters which Marcia had reduced to untidy chaos. They both of them puzzled her. Marcia's expression had plainly shown satisfaction and the triumph of achievement, but there seemed nothing to be learnt from Raff. She was aware, as she took his dictation, that he watched her with more than ordinary attention and that the reflective look in his eyes was not entirely reassuring.

"What is it?" she said at last, made uneasy by an attitude she did not understand.

"I'm not aware that anything is amiss," he replied, gravely. "Am I going too fast for you?"

"No, I'm used to your ways now. It was only that——"

"Only what?" But she was beginning to wish she had remained silent.

"Nothing," she said, and put a fresh piece of paper into her machine. She waited for him to begin his dictation, but he said instead, with a suddenness that took her by surprise:

"Marcia warned me not to speak to you, Judy, but I think I should drop you a hint all the same."

"Has Marcia been making mischief?" she asked before she could stop herself.

"On the contrary. I was, in fact, contemplating sending you back to England. It was Marcia who persuaded me not to," he replied and saw those endearing freckles stand out as the colour drained from her face.

"Send me away!" she echoed. "But *why?* Haven't I worked well—haven't I given satisfaction?"

He moved uneasily, as if already regretting that he had brought the subject up.

"I've nothing to complain of in your work. You do more than the secretarial job you're paid for, as it is."

"Then why do you want to send me away?"

"I've already told you, I'm not sending you away—not yet, at any rate. But you're very young, Judy, and I feel responsible for you so long as you're under my roof. Perhaps we'd better leave it at that."

The colour was coming back to her face and a hint of temper to her eyes.

"Oh, no, we won't," she said. Dropping hints, being vague and rather ridiculously avuncular! You should come right out with your complaints, Raff."

He looked a little surprised.

"Was I being avuncular?" he asked. "Well, I'm a very great deal older than you, so perhaps the habit is un- conscious. I've no complaint, Judy. I had a notion that you were possibly getting a little too fond of Noel, and I don't want you to get hurt, that's all."

"Spongy Maule!" she exclaimed with such genuine mirth and derision that he had to smile. "But he's an *obvious* wolf—I told you that before! Why, I don't even *like* him very much, except in a superficial sort of way. Did you honestly think that I was having an affair with Noel?"

"You've been giving a pretty fair imitation of it, haven't you?" he said. "That day in his office——"

"But I explained that."

". . . the other night on the terrace. I realise you didn't know that you could be seen."

"He was biting my ear—I *told* you!" she said, trying to make fun of it again, but he merely raised sceptical eyebrows and she rushed heedlessly into speech.

"Whatever you think, O'Rafferty," she said, addressing him with unconscious formality by the title his tenants gave him, "what right have you to order my life? Soft words—kisses in the moonlight, perhaps—what do they mean to you?"

"Rather more than they mean to you, evidently," he replied, and she flung back her head in defiance, making the thick red hair swing out in an angry curve.

"And can you and Marcia play games and go unreprimanded?" she demanded. "Shouldn't it be a case of what's sauce for the goose is sauce for the gander?"

"That's a little vulgar, don't you think?" he answered mildly, and she suddenly bowed her head in her hands and wept.

His eyes, as he watched her, held a tenderness tinged with dismay. In the short time he had known her, she had sometimes been near to tears, but he had never seen her weep.

"Judy . . ." he said, reaching across the desk to touch her, ". . . don't cry like that, my dear. I'm—I've probably been clumsy. Marcia warned me——"

"Marcia warned you that I was an unbalanced little schoolgirl with the usual propensity for crushes, I suppose," she gulped, and did not see the puzzled uncertainty in his face.

"No, of course not," he said, and his voice was soft again with the beguiling cadences of his race. "It would never have occurred to me that you would have given me a thought."

"Wouldn't it—wouldn't it, Raff?" she said, and lifted her tear-stained face from her hands to gaze at him.

"No," he answered with sudden brusqueness. "Why should it? Noel is, after all, more your own age, and has an easier way with women than I've ever learnt."

"Oh, no, dear Raff," she said, smiling through her tears. "You have the gifts most women want—integrity, wisdom —tenderness, I think."

He got to his feet with a sudden, clumsy movement, and walked to the window. She could see the outline of his lean, loosely-built frame in dark silhouette against the brightness of the spring sky, and saw, too, the little hunch of discomfort he gave to his shoulders as he thrust his hands into his pockets.

"I think I should tell you that there may be changes at Slyne," he said, and wondered, even as he spoke, exactly what he meant to convey to her.

She sat very still, and surreptitiously brushed the drying tears from her cheeks. She felt her spine stiffen as the

111

minutes ticked away and neither of them spoke, then she said in a voice that was suddenly completely composed:

"How very nice. Do these changes call for congratulations?

He turned then from the window to look at her, but she could not read his expression with the light behind him, and her own was carefully schooled to show only polite interest.

"We are at cross-purposes, I think," he said.

"We often are. You talk in conundrums."

"Do I? I merely thought I might owe you an explanation of some sort. I've run off the course a little, I think," he said, and sounded as though he was appealing for reassurance.

"You owe me nothing, Raff," she replied in a clear, untroubled voice. "How long do you want me to stay on here?"

"Stay on here? Oh, I see. We'll talk about it some other time, shall we?"

"As you like, but I'll need some warning—in order to get another job, you see."

"Yes, of course. I'll give you fair notice, naturally, and a bonus to tide you over while you look for a post in England—also every recommendation."

"Thank you," she said, "but I shall stay in Ireland, if I can, so it may not be necessary—the bonus, I mean."

"Stay here?"

"Well, somewhere in the country. I've taken a liking for it."

His ugly features softened to an unconscious tenderness.

"Mrs. Farrell was right, I think. Your heart's already in Irish soil," he said softly, and she got up abruptly, knocking her row of newly sharpened pencils on to the floor.

"Would you excuse me if I went now, Mr O'Rafferty?" she said, unaware that she had reverted to the old, formal mode of address. "I'll finish the letters this afternoon and get someone to take them to the post."

She went upstairs and saw from the nursery window Raff and the Colonel putting out in the boat to fish the lough, and sighed, envying them their masculine escapes from domestic stress. She watched the boat growing smaller and smaller in the distance, then sat down at her dressing-table and stared distastefully at her reflection in the mirror, aware only then of the dishevelled state of her appearance. With Marcia so poised, so finished as to detail, it was no wonder, she thought, that she herself was treated as a child, a nice, healthy, freckled child with few pretensions to beauty, and hair that could have been an asset had it not served as a disagreeable reminder of another.

What had Kathy been like? she wondered, picking up a brush and attacking the thick red tangle with impatience. Had she really been a person with whom Judy shared some affinity and, if so, how could Raff turn to Marcia who had none of his ways of life? And why, she wondered, frowning, did he escape from his new commitment, if such it was, just as he had escaped the evening when Marcia had provoked him to action in the Small Saloon?

The same question was being asked by Noel, shaking cocktails behind the bar. Since the Colonel was out and the new arrivals had not yet taken up residence, he and Marcia had the place to themselves.

"Not a very enthusiastic suitor, going off fishing on top of a proposal," he said, and Marcia shrugged.

"It wasn't a proposal—only a hint of things to come," she said with a cosy little smile. "He's gone fishing to clear his mind, I shouldn't wonder. He says he can't think indoors."

"Why do you want a chap like that?" her brother asked irritably. "You don't like Slyne, and I can't see you stuck here for the rest of your natural for the sake of a man who, to put it mildly, seems a trifle faint-hearted."

"Darling, it's the faint-heartedness that attracts me," she said. "Maybe I'm peculiar, or maladjusted, or something, but there's a lot of pent-up emotion behind all that façade, I think. Fun to explore his possibilities."

"Then why don't you just have the usual affair and get it out of your system? He's not really your cup of tea, my sweet."

"Oh, I'd be willing but, unfortunately, he's not the man to indulge in such things, and I'm afraid I shocked him.

No, Noel, you may think I'm crazy, but he attracts me and I want him, and if I have to marry to get him, then that's all there is to it. Of course I won't be stuck here for the rest of my life! I will have turned these mouldy antiques to some advantage, once I'm mistress here, and then— well, we'll hit the high spots on the proceeds and settle down, maybe, in a nice little luxury flat within easy call of the bright lights. Isn't that a thought? You can come and stay."

He gave her a sidelong look. She was, he had often thought, extremely stupid for a sophisticated woman, when it came to affairs of the heart.

"It's a thought, certainly," he observed a trifle dryly, "but can you be sure that Raff will share it with you?"

She shrugged and pushed her empty glass forward to be refilled.

"To start with, anyway—and marriage, after all, isn't irrevocable. There's always a way out through the divorce courts."

"And supposing Raff won't play?" he said. "You haven't my experience of the puritanical streak that runs through many of the Irish. The O'Rafferty doesn't strike me as a man who'd care for his dirty linen to be washed in public, my sweet."

She shrugged again, and looked provocative.

"Then perhaps he'll be able to hold me after all," she said. "I'm not sure it isn't that puritanical streak you speak of that attracts me. He's the first man I've ever wanted who's been hard to get."

"Lord, women!" he exclaimed, emptying his own glass at a gulp, and replenishing it. "Why don't you leave the poor devil to his own half-baked conception of womanly virtue? All things being equal, our Judy would make an excellent successor to Kathy."

"*Judy!* Are you mad, Noel?"

"No, I don't think so. Incidentally, he gave me quite a telling off earlier—just his prudish instincts, maybe."

"He feels responsible for her. Actually, he wants to get rid of her."

"Does he, indeed? And what's stopping him?"

114

"I stopped him. She may be a nuisance, but I'm certainly not prepared to cope with the secretarial side just as business looks like booming—neither, I'm sure, are you."

"Oh, well, you know your own affairs best, I suppose," Noel said, "but don't underrate our Judy. She would be prepared to make a burnt offering of herself for your laggard suitor, if he wanted her."

"Don't be ridiculous! He wants to get rid of her, and as soon as it's convenient I'll see that he does. The servants are trouble enough as it is."

"Funny how they've taken to her, isn't it?" he drawled, cocking an eyebrow at her.

"How you love to try and make mischief—even with me," Marcia countered coldly. "As for Judy, she's too familiar with the servants—that's why they like her."

"Maybe. Incidentally, I've rung Grogan, since we can be sure of Raff's absence for the rest of the afternoon."

"Grogan?" she frowned. "Is that wise?"

"Wise or not, he has some accounts to settle with me," he replied. "That smooth little crook isn't going to get away with half my share of our transactions. Better keep Judy out of the way. She's too sharp by half."

His sister's eyes grew wary.

"Very well," she said. "But remember I've had nothing to do with your transactions. I've thought it dangerous ever since that wretched girl started nosing about, knowing more than we'd bargained for about old furniture. She could make trouble for you yet, Noel."

"Then why did you dissuade Raff from getting rid of her?" he retorted sulkily. "Anyway, this is the finish, since you seem to be going to marry into the family and can look after turning the stuff into hard cash rather more legitimately. I simply want to get my just dues out of that little blighter."

The gong sounded for luncheon and they repaired to the dining-room which, deserted but for themselves and Miss Botley and a couple of strangers who were not stopping the night, was waited on with indifferent attention by Timsy, since it was Rosie's day off.

"I suspect the old villain's been tippling again," Noel observed with easy tolerance, but Marcia frowned.

"I don't find Timsy particularly amusing any longer," she said rather shortly. "Neither does Miss Botley, judging by the sour look on her face at this moment. Something must be done about him."

"Timsy's a fixture, like the other antiques, my sweet, but not one that you could work a lucrative fiddle on, unfortunately," he said with gentle malice, and she sent him a warning glance.

"You'll be giving our Judy fresh ideas if you talk that kind of nonsense," she retorted, and began pouring the coffee. "Tepid again! I believe the old fool boils it up on his smelly old stove and then lets it get cold on purpose. I shall have to speak to him again."

As they drank their coffee in a rather uncomfortable silence, Judy thought she could hear *The Mountains of Mourne* being played somewhere in the distance, and grinned as she pictured the incorrigible Timsy registering a final protest in the pantry.

CHAPTER SIX

I

JUDY worked undisturbed in the study all afternoon. She signed the routine correspondence herself now, on Raff's behalf, and when the pile of letters was ready she collected them together and went through the hall intending to find Mick or Pat or one of the Boyles to take them to the post.

The hall was deserted, as were the living-rooms, their doors standing open, but high voices were coming from the manager's office and Judy recognised the rich, exaggerated brogue which Grogan appeared to adopt as part of his stock-in-trade.

"And what d'ye think you can do, me fine boyo?" he was saying, and Judy recognised the source from which Noel's occasional Irishisms must spring. "Is it the O'Rafferty you'll be runnin' to with tales of bein' cheated, and he as innocent a a new-born babe of the dirty tricks you've played him?'

"You know very well the money goes into his own pocket," Noel shouted. "Well—half and half, that is, allowing for my commission."

"Och, that for a likely tale! D'ye think I didn't guess that himself knew nothin' of your shenanigans? I wasn't born yesterday, me fine young bantam cock. If you'll do no more business with poor Dan Grogan, then you can whistle for your money, and so I'm tellin' you."

"That's blackmail!"

"Ay-ah—the harsh way you have with you, Mr Maule! And who's to believe you—tell me that?"

"I can call the Garda."

"The Garda! And what would you be tellin' the Garda? That you've been robbin' your employer and can't get your money? Oh, no, me brave gossoon, you'll not do the like of that, I'll wager. Is it true that pretty sister of yours is to be mistress here?"

"That's got nothing to do with it."

"And it might have at that. You'd not spoil her chances by grudging poor Grogan a bit of a present, would you, now?"

"But you're proposing to take the lot on the last deal," Noel protested shrilly, and Grogan's voice in replying held a well-practised richness which almost became a whine.

"But think of me own expenses, your honour. That chest I did meself, but it was bad work, bad work. The other wan, now, needed an expert craftsman, and I had to pay him. There's been nothin' much in it for any of us, but if you let me take the tallboy, now, we can have a settlin' up that will suit us both. Didn't I get a lovely job done when I had it in for repair, and only waitin' the moment to make the change-over? Come on, now, I have it waitin' in the cyar beyont."

Judy had listened shamelessly, uncaring for the tenets of her upbringing, for in a case of this kind, what did ethics matter? She heard Noel say: "W-ell . . ." on a note of doubt and capitulation, and the scraping of chairs pushed back, and she turned on her heel and sped into the Grand Saloon and, kneeling down in front of the tallboy, began to rub up the handles with her handkerchief. She could not, she thought, do good at this juncture by ad-

117

mitting that she had overheard their conversation, but at least she could prevent them from taking the piece away.

"What are you doing here?" Noel snapped at her, his handsome face like a sulky child's as he discovered her kneeling on the floor. "I thought you were typing in the study."

"So I was," she replied. "But I've finished the letters and was going to look for someone to take them to the post."

"Ah, sure! And on the way you thought you'd put a shine on the handles of that beautiful article of furniture," said Grogan. His voice brimmed over with cajoling *bonhomie*, but his full, dark eyes were not so pleasant.

"The brass soon gets tarnished with the fires. It will be better in summer, I expect," Judy replied calmly, and spat nonchalantly on a corner of her handkerchief and resumed her polishing.

"What a very conscientious young lady," Grogan said. "But shouldn't you be findin' someone to take the letters? The last post goes from the crossroads at six o'clock."

"You could take them yourself, Mr Grogan. You'll be passing that way," Judy said sedately, and his sallow face grew ugly for a moment.

"So I could, then," he replied, apparently forgetting that he always travelled the north road when he carried merchandise in the back of his van. "Give them to me, then, and you can run away and play, or whatever young ladies do when they've finished work."

"I don't think so," she said. "You'll be going by the north road, won't you? The post will have gone from Casey's, so I'll find one of the men."

She sat back on her heels on the floor, and leant against the tallboy, enjoying their discomfiture. Noel said nothing, knowing very well that her bland remarks were far from innocent, but Grogan began to try persuasion again, and Miss Doyle chose that moment to sidle into the room, crying:

"And is it yourself, Mr Grogan, come to do another job for us, and not a word to poor Agnes Doyle!"

"Och, women!" the dealer exclaimed bitterly, and turned on his heel. "Another time it will have to be, Mr

118

Maule, and you mind to have that other little matter cleared up between us. Good day, now." He pushed past Miss Doyle with scant politeness, and Noel, with a very unpleasant glance in Judy's direction, followed him.

"And what's the trouble with them two fine cocks?" Miss Doyle demanded, highly offended. "Mr Maule has the English way with them he thinks of as the lower classes, which he can't help, I don't doubt, the poor heretic, but Dan Grogan is never without a kind word and an admiring glance, and he with the hard livin' to make doin' tinker's work about the country—patchin' up old worrum-eaten stuff like we have here, when a bonfire is all it's good for."

"Is that what he tells you?" said Judy, scrambling to her feet and surveying a fresh ladder in one of her stockings. "Your Mr Grogan is a scoundrel, let me tell you, Miss Doyle, and you should have more sense than to be taken in by him."

"Has he deceived you too, Miss Judy?" Miss Doyle asked, avid, as always, for drama, and already seeing herself as a woman scorned for the second time.

"He's never deceived me for a moment, neither, really, has Mr Maule," Judy said, and grasped the woman's arm with sudden urgency. "Think, Miss Doyle—the day they brought this tallboy back—did anything else go out of the house? That desk, for instance?"

"It's here now, isn't it?" the woman said vaguely. "I misremember what came in and what went out. They was fetchin' and carryin' all the time, but the room looked the same when they'd gone."

Yes, thought Judy grimly, the room looked the same, only one fake piece had been cleverly substituted, and there would have been another today had she not been in the way. She picked up the bunch of letters and ran out of the room and through the hall. The office door was wide open, but Noel was not to be seen, and Judy wondered if Marcia had been diplomatically keeping out of the way all this time and whether she was a party to what had been going on.

"A fine couple of vipers for Raff to nurse in his bosom!" she exclaimed aloud angrily, and a fine start to married life when the deception became known, she thought, for

Grogan, holding the whip-hand so self-confidently, could not muzzle her as he had muzzled Noel.

She went out on to the terrace and looked towards the lough, but there was no sign of the boat as yet; there was no sign, either, of any of the men who worked about the place, so it must be later than she had supposed. Two of the letters were urgent, but Grogan's van had gone, so there was nothing else to do but take one of Raff's cars and go herself.

She chose the shooting-brake because the gears were easier, and set off down the south road, remembering as she encountered the bumps and twists in the road Raff's decree that she should not drive either of the cars until he had given her lessons. It seemed a long way to the crossroads where the only postbox for miles around was situated, and she did not realise that the rather momentous happenings of the day were beginning to catch up with her. She was tired, and the brake was heavy to swing round the bends, and the driving-seat badly adjusted for her to reach the pedals with comfort.

When she had posted the letters, Judy realised that not only had she missed the last collection, but she must reverse the car in order to make the return journey. The crossroads were a misnomer, like many landmarks in the west, being a meeting of ditch-bound tracks with one little-used secondary road leading to Knockferry. You could, thought Judy, racing the engine, very easily run over the edge and into a ditch, and, getting her gear into reverse more quickly than she expected, did that very thing almost immediately. The car seemed to hover for a moment on the brink of an abyss, then tipped backwards and over on to its side with its wheels spinning and a sound of splintering glass.

"Holy St Michael! Holy St Patrick!" Judy groaned, invoking Mary Kate's favourite saints. She struggled with one of the doors, finally clambering out with difficulty, then jumped into a foot of bog water, wrenching her ankle badly on landing.

It was too much. The day's happenings, the shock of overturning and the pain in her ankle mingled together, bringing final defeat, and she sat where she had fallen in the water-logged ditch and burst into tears.

At last she climbed out of the ditch and stood wringing water out of her skirt, while she surveyed the wrecked car with rueful eyes. The rear window was broken, one wing badly dented, and Raff would be furious. Well, he should have given her the promised lessons; he should have left her carefree heart alone; he should have followed his inclination and sacked her this morning; he should never have employed her in the first place; everything, in fact, was his fault.

She looked, not very hopefully, down the Knockferry road, but no one was likely to pass at this hour. She would have to walk; but a very few steps of putting her weight on the damaged ankle persuaded her that this would be an impossibility. She must climb back into the car, if she could, and if necessary spend the night there. It was more difficult to accomplish the feat of getting in than getting out, but she managed it, with disastrous results to her skirt, which caught and tore, and sat huddled in a corner, nursing her aching ankle which was beginning to swell rapidly.

It seemed to her that she sat for hours, watching the daylight begin to fade, and listening to the sounds which Raff had made familiar to her. That was a curlew calling; that sharp, intermittent bark was a hill fox, and somewhere not far distant must be a waterfall, for the rhythm of its tiny splashes over the stones lulled her to drowsiness and finally to sleep.

A blinding light roused her and it took her a moment to realise that it was the headlamps of a car and that someone was hammering on the window above her head and shouting her name.

"Raff . . . Raff . . ." she cried, and struggled up to meet him as he wrenched open the door.

"Are you all right?" he said, and there was the rough edge of fear to his voice as he peered down at her.

"Yes . . . yes . . ." she answered, and began to weep again with the pain and the cold and the sheer relief at seeing him.

"Thank God!" he exclaimed, and then she felt him lift her, and snuggled her face into the warmth of his shoulder, sniffing the scent of turf-smoke and tobacco which always seemed to cling to his clothes.

"It was all your fault," she sobbed. "You never gave me those lessons and you t-took my nice clean heart and squeezed it dry and now it's like a wizened old walnut. It's m-most uncomfortable. . . ."

He thought she was lightheaded, and perhaps she was for the moment, but as he set her on her feet she cried out with the pain in her ankle and he said quickly:

"You're hurt. Can you stand?"

"I t-twisted my ankle, that's all, but it was too bad to walk home. I did try," she said.

"There's blood on your forehead."

"Is there?"

"You must have been cut by the glass. I'll get you into the Land Rover, then we'll see what the damage is."

He lifted her into the other car and told her to sit still while he soaked his hankerchief in the stream. The stream must be part of the waterfall, she reflected, trying to sort out again the different sounds of the night, and then he was back, bathing her forehead, assuring her that the cut was only a small one.

"Now let's see that ankle," he said, and stripped off her torn stocking, and having tested the ankle with gentle, experienced fingers, bound it up tightly with the wet handkerchief. She looked down at his dark, ugly face bent in grave concentration over his job, and remembered how she had wondered what the touch of his fingers would be like to the skin. She had stopped crying, but was beginning to shiver after the long hours of sitting in damp clothes.

"No more than a sprain, I think. Good grief—you're wringing wet!" he exclaimed, touching her skirt.

"I sat in the bog-water for too long, I'm afraid," she said, and he glanced at her sharply.

"Well, take your skirt off."

"Take it off?"

"There's no one to see you but me," he said impatiently. "Here—where does it undo?"

She unfastened the zipper and he pulled the skirt off without ceremony and flung it in the back of the car.

"Here's an old mackintosh you can wrap round your knees to keep warm, and I had the sense to bring a flask of brandy with me," he said, reaching for the flask. "Drink it up, now—a good big swallow. Your hands are like ice."

She drank the brandy obediently, grateful for the warmth and comfort of the spirit trickling down her throat.

"That's better," he said and, dropping the flask on the floor, turned to look at her.

"Well," he said a little grimly, "you see what comes of disobeying orders. What possessed you to take the car out by yourself? The letters could have waited till tomorrow."

"I was delayed or I'd have asked one of the men," she said, then began to talk a little feverishly while he held her icy hands between his own to warm them.

"It was Grogan—Noel and Grogan. I heard them quarrelling and then they were going to change over the tallboy, only they couldn't because I was there. He had it in the van, you see—the other one, I mean—and Noel said he'd call the Garda and Grogan just laughed and said he wouldn't dare, and Noel said you knew about it, but you don't, do you, Raff?"

"You seem a little incoherent," he said. "Shall we leave explanations until we get home?"

"Miss Doyle will tell you. Grogan's been pulling the wool over her eyes for ages."

"Agnes has already told me nearly as garbled a tale as yours, only she seemed obsessed with false promises and male deceivers! But at least she remembered the letters and Granny Malone saw you pass, or we wouldn't have known where you'd gone."

"She put the 'fluence on me—that's why it all happened."

"It happened through your own silly fault and nobody else's," he said, and the anger that can follow hot on the heals of fear and anxiety began to rise in him. "How do you think I felt when I saw the overturned car and you lying there apparently unconscious? Do you imagine my only thought was that I should have the inconvenience of hiring another secretary?" He stopped, for he could not tell her that the sight of her limp young body and the red hair falling over her face had brought an unbearable reminder

123

of Kathy. He could not in any way be blamed for that first small tragedy, but for Judy, whose endearing simplicity he had needed, but stubbornly rejected, he would always feel reproach.

"You are going to sack me, so it wouldn't have been an inconvenience in the end," she said meekly.

"It was not a question of sacking you in the accepted sense, as you know very well," he replied. "In any case that's all in the future, and we'd best be getting home. Willie-the-Post will spread the most fantastic rumours when he finds the car in the morning."

"Will you warm me a little before we go?" she asked, and he took her into his arms and rested his own cold cheek for a moment against hers.

"What did you mean about your nice clean heart?" he said, and felt her hand thrust confidingly into the breast of his jacket.

"It *was* nice and clean—like a slate, a—a piece of fresh paper that's never been written on. I wasn't romantic, you see."

"So you once told me, but I hardly think it's true."

"You remember a lot of things I told you, don't you?"

"Well, it's more than I can say for you, forgetting, even, that I'd told you not to drive!"

"I didn't forget. I haven't forgotten anything you've told me—but I don't think you'd like to be reminded of some things."

"Such as?"

"Oh, no, I couldn't tell you now. You wouldn't have thought them important, anyway. Avuncular, probably," she said sleepily, and he took her chin in his hand and, rasing her face to his, kissed her gently.

"Avuncular is probably what I should remain," he said, and kissed her again, this time with a lingering tenderness that made her slip a hand round his neck.

"Dear Raff . . ." she murmured. "Must you do it?"

"Do what, you irresponsible child?"

"Marry Marcia. And I'm not a child, and I'm not irresponsible, but I don't seem able to make you understand."

His grasp tightened on her for a moment, then slackened.

"What makes you think I mean to marry Marcia?" he asked.

"Oh, everyone thinks so. Besides, you told me this morning there were going to be changes at Slyne. You made it very clear, I thought, that you'd decided to settle down."

"And is that why you cried?"

She drew away from him, aware that she had probably been impertinent and that this conversation could embarrass them both.

"My tears were a matter that need not concern you, and it was unkind to remind me. I don't often do it," she said. "But, Raff—be careful. It's so easy, I imagine, when the time is ripe for oneself, to make a false assessment of another."

"How do you know these things?" he asked.

"I just know. My father was a wise man—but even he couldn't teach me the things one must learn for oneself. I suppose no one can."

"No, Judy, no one can," he said a little sadly and, as if putting a period of finality to the interlude, pressed the self-starter and set the engine running.

"It was all your fault . . . all your fault . . ." she murmured in a kind of chant as they bumped home over the south road.

She was, he thought, driving in silence, a little lightheaded after all, and he cursed himself for having lingered at the crossroads when he should have been getting her home and out of her wet clothes. Presently he thought she slept, her head against his shoulder, and he could see the dark crescents her closed eyelids made and the innocent curve of her mouth. The dried trickle of blood on her temple and the streaks of dirt gave her face the look of a chidden child's. It would be better for him, for all of them, he thought, if he sent her back to England as soon as could be conveniently arranged.

Judy was astonished by her reception upon arriving back at Slyne. The servants ran into the hall, exclaiming and weeping by turn, joined mysteriously by some of the yard dogs which were forbidden in the house; the Colonel and Miss Botley vied with each other in prescribing remedies for shock, broken limbs and an assortment of misfortunes which had not come to pass, and even Noel expressed a concern which, judging by Raff's expression, was a trifle overdone. Only Marcia remained aloof, her eyes darting from one to another of them while she herself made no attempt to join in the chorus of commiseration. Judy was aware that she must present a comic appearance with Raff's old mackintosh clutched round her hips in lieu of a skirt, but there was no amusement in Marcia's glance, only a watchful impatience and, when she looked at Raff, a slightly incredulous expression, as if she were seeing him for the first time.

"Hadn't you better go straight to bed, Judy?" she said when the first commotion had died down. "Since it's you who requires an immediate hot bath, Timsy, I'm sure, has stoked the furnace. Go back to the kitchen, all of you, please—there's no need to make such a fuss—and take those dogs with you and turn them out."

"Yes, get them out, Timsy,' Raff said quietly, and soon the hall was still again and Marcia repeated her advice to Judy, adding an indifferently polite inquiry as to whether she wanted any help in undressing.

"That ankle needs strapping properly," Raff said. "When you've had you bath, Judy, I'll come up and do it. Shall I carry you upstairs?"

"I'm expert at carrying maidens up to bed. Go and get yourself a drink, my dear chap, you look all in," Noel said, and swung Judy up into his arms. "No need for the physician act, either. I'm a very pretty hand with the first-aid box. I'll bandage her up and tuck her into bed with an aspirin and a nice bedtime story."

"Yes, come and sit down and have a drink. You look tired, darling," Marcia said, linking an arm with his.

He hesitated, rubbing the bridge of his nose and frowning at Noel, who was already mounting the stairs with his burden.

"Very well," he said, "Goodnight, Judy."

"Goodnight, Raff," she replied, chilled by his sudden indifference, and gave a little wriggle as Noel murmured softly above her head:

"You'd rather it was him than me, wouldn't you, my sweet? What fairytales have you and Raff been exchanging by the light of the silvery moon? Marcia didn't like it, you know."

"Marcia might have offered a little more sympathy, for the look of things. Raff mightn't like *that!*" she retorted sharply, and he grinned.

"O-ho! Is there rivalry between you two? I shouldn't try telling tales, if I were you."

"Are you afraid, Noel?"

"Afraid for Marcia? Well, hardly."

"No, for yourself."

He had reached the nursery now and had deposited her on the bed. Mary Kate or, more probably, Rosie, had banked the fire up well with turf and the room looked warm and comfortably shabby as it had, no doubt, when Raff and his brothers had occupied it and chalked their drawings on the faded wallpaper.

"What's all this about?" Noel asked.

"I overheard you and Grogan quarrelling this afternoon," she said. "You were going to exchange the tallboy, weren't you?"

He sat down on the side of the bed and grinned at her impudently.

"So you think you know all, as the novelettes say, do you?" he replied. "And have you passed on your unworthy suspicions to friend Raff?"

"I tried to warn him, but I was rather mixed up with other things at the time and he thought I was light-headed," she said, too honest herself to try and match him at his own game.

"And that's what you were, of course. It was foolish to try and get me the push when you'd had the sack yourself."

127

"I haven't been sacked."

"I understood it was Marcia who got you a reprieve," he said a little mockingly.

"Because," replied Judy tartly, "neither of you want to do the donkey-work now the place is beginning to fill up. Marcia doesn't want me here, but she'd sooner put up with me than have to hammer a typewriter all day."

"And when she's made use of you, she'll get you out of here, my dear. It's too late to try soft soap with Raff now. He's committed to Marcia."

"He hasn't said so."

"Not to you, possibly. He thinks, incidentally, that you've got a bit of a weakness for me. Silly, isn't it?"

"Very silly—Spongy!"

He laughed, but it was not a pleasant sound.

"You won't hurt my feelings with prep-school jibes," he said. "Neither will you convince our lord and master very easily, for I've said nothing to undeceive him, I assure you. Quite the contrary, in fact."

"You're just a spoilt, rather nasty child who only wants what it can't have," she said, and he dropped an unexpected and entirely meaningless kiss on the top of her head.

"I admit I'm perverse in that respect," he admitted a trifle maliciously. "I have to confess you didn't attract me at all at first, my sweet, but reluctance is always tempting when one's bored. Raff has the same effect on Marcia and, if she brings him up to scratch, I've no doubt the desire will pall. That's human nature for you, I suppose."

She looked at him with such plain disgust that the simulated merriment began to leave his eyes.

"You aren't thinking of repeating this little canard, when you can be presumed not to be lightheaded, are you?" he asked softly.

"Why not?"

"Because, my child, it would only boomerang on yourself. Do you think that Raff would want his future brother-in-law branded as a thief? No, my dear little Judy, if you try that line, you'll find you get very short shrift. He'll stand by Marcia, not by you."

It was, she supposed, only too true. He would be bitterly hurt, but if he was already committed to a future with Marcia, he would make the best of things rather than go back on his word.

Her ankle was beginning to throb painfully and she wished he would go. She had her proof at last, but she knew she could not use it and deliver such a blow to pride and friendship. Seeing the weariness and defeat in her face, he leaned over her and said persuasively:

"I see you're thinking better of your rashness. There's a very simple explanation, as I think I've hinted at before. Raff's pretty broke, compared to the old days, you know. I admit we went about our transactions in rather a cloak-and-dagger fashion, sneaking things in and out of the house when no one was about, but we didn't want the servants talking."

"And doesn't Miss Doyle talk?"

"Oh, no one pays any attention to her, poor soul — besides, she thought Grogan did repairs to the furniture as an excuse to see her. Raff is proud, you know. He wouldn't like it known that he was selling the family stuff; that's why it was always done through me."

She did not believe him, but she remembered that when she had asked Raff if he had known about the dealings with Grogan he had only replied by saying that she appeared to be incoherent; another word for lightheadedness, perhaps.

"Grogan said the money went into your own pocket," she said, still trying to fight what she felt to be a fabric of half-truths.

"Grogan was simply trying to air knowledge he doesn't possess—nasty, blackmailing little spiv!" he replied. "I bank everything in my own name. When a worthwhile sum has accumulated I hand it over, that's all."

"You must," said Judy very wearily, "take me for a fool."

"Oh, no!" he retorted, patting her lightly on the shoulder, "I take you for quite an astute young woman who knows which side her bread's buttered. Don't play tricks with me, my sweet, and I won't play tricks with you."

It was a merciful relief when Mary Kate came bursting into the room to demand to know why Judy had not been in a hot bath long ago.

Tucked up in bed, Judy knew again that comforting return to childhood. The well-worn furniture, the fairy-tale pictures repeating themselves round the walls, the criss-cross pattern the fireguard made on the ceiling, brought familiarity, and protection from the world out-side.

"You're so kind to me, Mary Kate," she said. "You must have been a nice nanny. I'd like to feel there were children here again in the nursery, wouldn't you?"

Mary Kate looked about her, her hands on her hips, and there was reminiscence in her eyes, a slow recaptur-ing of the essence of a room long since forgotten.

"Childer . . ." she said softly. "Aye, doty, the place needs that . . . will you be stayin' here awhile?"

"I don't think so," Judy replied sadly. "But I shall stop in Ireland, if I can find another job. I would like to feel my roots were here."

"Roots, is it? Well, I'd be thinkin' an English young miss had that much sense!" said Mary Kate, her eyes brooding on the bed. "Are you ready, now, Miss Judy? Will I alarrum the master?"

Judy was still not quite used to this descriptive Irish-ism, and her forehead puckered.

"Alarm?" she echoed, thinking there had been enough alarms for one day.

"Advise him that you're waitin'," Mary Kate translated patiently, and Judy smiled.

"Oh, yes," she said. "I'm waiting—but I could go to sleep any minute."

"You'll not sleep without me good broth inside you," Mary Kate observed severely. "When himself has finished with you, I'll bring it up."

Judy waited in drowsy anticipation, glad that it was Raff and not Noel who would come to bandage her ankle. She could tell him again, perhaps, the strange thoughts that had been chasing around in her mind and, even if she could not prove her suspicions a certainty, she could somehow warn him to be careful. But when he came, Marcia came with him, carrying the first-aid box, and although she inquired solicitously enough for Judy's comfort, she stood by the bed, her dark eyes bright and watchful on Raff's hands bandaging and strapping with swift impersonality.

"Is that comfortable?" he asked, straightening his long back.

"Yes, thank you," she said. "I'm sorry, Raff, to have caused so much trouble."

"So you should be," Marcia observed with dulcet reproach.

"Well, Judy, now that your adventures seems to have had a happy ending, we had better leave you to sleep. Do you want to say goodnight to Noel?"

"No, why should I?" Judy replied, with difficulty preventing her eyelids from closing with the fatigue that had settled upon them.

Marcia shrugged, and her eyes met Raff's with amusement.

"I only thought you might like that bedtime story he promised you earlier," she said. "He would have come up to bandage your ankle, you know, only—well, he thought you were a little overwrought and emotional and might expect too much of him—isn't that so, Raff?"

Raff's face seemed to be a frozen mask in the shadows, but exhaustion lay too heavily upon Judy for her to care any more.

"You," she said with untroubled clarity, "are a bitch . . ." and closed her eyes.

III

She spent the next day in bed, glad that Raff has issued the order, but disappointed that he never came himself to inquire for her. The events of the day before were a little confused in her mind now, though she dimly remembered calling Marcia by a rude name before she went to sleep.

Noel looked in on her after luncheon, but she pretended to be asleep, and presently Marcia came with a basket of fruit which she said Raff had brought back from Knockferry.

"Did he go especially to get them?" Judy asked her, feeling soothed by the fact that he had thought of her even though he had not come to inquire.

"Naturally not. He had to make arrangements for the car you so successfully ditched, and he wanted to see his lawyer, I believe," replied Marcia coldly. Then she smiled as if remembering she wished to be pleasant and settled herself by the bed with cigarettes and a box of chocolates.

"He didn't forget me either, you see," she said, offering the chocolates. "Have one."

"I'm afraid," said Judy, accepting a chocolate gravely, "that I wasn't very polite to you last night."

"No, you called me a bitch, darling, but no doubt I deserved it."

Judy was puzzled. Of late Marcia had not troubled very much to make herself charming, and she mistrusted the change from yesterday.

"I'm sorry," she said. "Whatever I thought, I shouldn't have said it aloud."

"Excellent for releasing the subconscious, my dear," Marcia replied cosily. "It never does to bottle things up —that's why I'm often unpleasant, I expect. By the same token, did you do some unbottling to Raff last night after he'd pulled you out of the ditch?"

So that explained it, thought Judy, with a faint smile. Marcia, just as her brother had, wanted to find out what Raff had been told.

"You mean about the furniture?" she said with a clear, level look.

"I know nothing about the furniture," Marcia snapped. "And if Noel's been up to anything tricky I don't want to know anything about it."

"Then what did you want to know?" Judy inquired politely. It was, she supposed reluctantly, very possible that Marcia herself had had no direct part in her brother's dealings with Grogan, that with her own ends in view she would have taken care not to be involved in anything questionable.

Marcia ate another chocolate, forgetting to share the box this time, then lit a cigarette and leaned back comfortably.

"Oh, just idle curiosity," she said. "You have your attractions, Judy, I'll give you that. I just thought—well, men are susceptible creatures, aren't they?"

"Are you imagining Raff is?"

"I wouldn't know, except where I'm concerned. I thought you could tell me."

"If you're sure of a man yourself, Marcia, the question shouldn't arise," Judy said gently, and the older girl gave an impatient flip to her cigarette, scattering the ash over the sheet.

"I'm not, damn it!" she said unexpectedly. "Raff admires me—I can even rouse sparks if I set my mind to it—but all this Kathy business has me confused."

It brought her down to a human level to admit to confusion, Judy thought, and said prosaically:

"That was all a long time ago and she was very young. A man doesn't mourn the dead for ever if he's normal."

"Haven"t you ever heard of wish fulfilments, father fixations, and what have you?"

"Of course. But I don't see——"

"Oh, Judy, be your age! You must know by now that you remind him of the wretched girl—he even took a dislike to you at first for that reason."

"You're going to marry him, aren't you?" At last she could ask the question that teased them all.

"I don't know . . . yes, of course—of course I am. I'm just talking nonsense." Marcia fell silent, suddenly brooding.

"Be pleasant to the girl for a change. She can be dangerous to us both," Noel had counselled earlier in the day, but she was not concerned with her brother's peccadilloes; she had things to find out for herself.

"I bet he made love to you, for all that," she said, with her sophisticated little smile of worldly tolerance.

Judy considered the question, untroubled by the older woman's curiosity. Could that brief little interlude at the crossroads be described as making love? She would like to think so, but honesty forbade it. He had taken her in his arms to warm her; he had even kissed her with a tenderness which still lingered in her thoughts, but she had been

133

distressed at the time and not very discreet; he would have done as much for a child.

"No, I don't think you could call it that," she said slowly, and Marcia's eyes narrowed.

"But he made a pass—kissed you, perhaps?" she said.

Judy looked at her and to her surprise, felt compassion. Marcia's standards were like her brother's, bound up with clichès and the more obvious reactions; there was little depth in either of them, she thought, and they looked for none in others.

"Yes, he kissed me," she admitted. "One kisses a hurt child, you know, to take away the tears."

"Were you crying then?"

"I expect so."

"And the good, puritanical O'Rafferty dried your tears!"

"Oh, Marcia!" Judy felt she wanted to laugh and weep at the same moment. "Can't you understand that there can be tenderness between two people without passion, without tricks on one side or the other? There must be so many different expressions of affection."

"I only know one," Marcia replied. "Men are all alike, whatever excuse they like to wrap around their primitive urges. Your maiden-aunt notions of affection and hurt children and what have you all boil down to one thing in the end."

"I don't think you can understand Raff very well," Judy said gently, and Marcia laughed with the old assurance.

"I don't need to, darling," she said. "Under that apparently indifferent manner he's just a man like the others, as perhaps you've found out for yourself. Don't think I grudge you your little interlude, my sweet, you probably haven't had much fun in that direction—but lay off this Kathy stuff in future, will you?"

"I don't understand."

"I think you do. I'm paying you a compliment, really, by recognising you as a possible danger to my own plans. I'll admit I hadn't given you a thought until lately as a serious rival, but Raff's a queer one—I don't want any slip-up now."

Judy eased her bandaged ankle under the bedclothes and stretched her thin body back on the pillows. It was very strange, she thought, that Marcia, so lovely and poised, so much older in experience, should be offering equality of standing, however grudging.

"Marcia—what do you really feel for Raff?" she asked. "Do you love him?"

"Of course I love him. I want him!" Marcia said arrogantly.

"It's not the same thing—loving and wanting."

"How should you know?"

"I don't know, but I do. To want and not be prepared to give is surely a denial of something fundamental."

"Claptrap!" Marcia said, and lit another cigarette. "Where have you learnt such corny ideas, darling? Every woman gives—herself, if nothing else."

"But you wouldn't be giving yourself," Judy replied, her eyes on a shaft of sunlight, watching the dancing motes. "Your body, of course, but not yourself."

"What the hell do you mean?"

"I mean, I suppose, that one's real self has to merge to an extent in the other person's. You don't care for Slyne and it's Raff's life. How will you adjust yourself?"

"I shan't try, my dear. Slyne has little marketable value these days, I suppose, but sell up the contents and we'd be in clover for a time."

"Raff would never sell."

"I think he would—to please a wife who expected something a little more from life than being buried alive in the mouldering ancestral home."

"If he did," said Judy, "he'd be selling his birthright—and that would be a very foolish demand to put upon him."

Marcia got up and stretched luxuriously like a cat, reassured by the reflection of her own lovely body in the mirror.

"Well," she said, "you've read me your little lecture, now I'll deliver mine. I don't go in for sermons, darling, so just take it as a friendly warning. Because you're being kept on here for a time, don't try to make trouble for any of us. We could make some for you, too."

"You've done that already, haven't you?" Judy replied wearily, "making out that Noel and I were having an affair."

"And weren't you?"

"You know very well we weren't. You've told me often enough that I wasn't your brother's cup of tea, and so, from time to time, has he."

"True," said Marcia carelessly. "But what other distraction was there for him? Miss Botley's a little long in the tooth for fun and games!"

"I don't care," said Judy, suddenly disdainful, "to be taken for one of those girls Noel's always talking about. I don't care at all for the fact that Raff was given the wrong impression."

"You can hardly blame him. I gather he surprised you at some awkward moments," Marcia said lightly, and then looked thoughtful, remembering that the only time she had seen anything approaching jealousy in Raff's eyes had been on Judy's account.

"Perhaps it wasn't such a good idea to try to cast doubts on your high moral standards, after all," she said, and Judy looked at her with eyes that seemed suddenly very green.

"Did you do it deliberately?" she asked, and Marcia gave her a conciliatory smile.

"Not really," she said. "Noel can't resist making mischief, of course, and he likes to take a rise out of Raff sometimes."

"And you?"

"I? Well, I wasn't going to have you putting a spoke in my wheel without putting one in yours, was I?"

"I never tried to do that, Marcia."

"Didn't you? Well, all's fair in love and war, so they say, and you *are* a bit in love with him, aren't you?"

Judy regarded her gravely.

"If I am, then that's my own private cross," she said, and Marcia raised sceptical eyebrows.

"I suppose, at your age, you would talk about bearing crosses," she observed with a yawn. "Just a schoolgirl crush, my dear. You'll get over it."

"Marcia—don't hurt him," Judy said softly.

Marcia smiled a little mockingly and picked up her cigarettes.

136

"I'll leave you what's left of the chocolates," she said, and went out of the room.

CHAPTER SEVEN

I

IT seemed to Judy that after this episode the relations between them all seemed subtly to alter. Raff was withdrawn and detached from them all, and was much away from home, visiting his lawyers in Knockferry, or concerning himself with his tenants to the exclusion of his business with the affairs of the house.

Judy's ankle was almost well now, for it had after all been no more than a severe wrench, but, on Raff's orders, she kept her feet up in the afternoons, and was lying now on a sofa in the Grand Saloon, where Noel found her.

"Still feeling like a dog with a bone?" he teased. "And why do you spend your afternoons in here? To be sure we don't make away with your precious tallboy?"

"No," she replied, refusing to rise, "but I have to sit somewhere, and the sofa's comfortable in here. Doesn't it strike you that Raff is worried?"

"Not particularly. More annoyed, I should say, by the impression that his artless little secretary has a weakness for his manager. Dog-in-the-manger, wouldn't you think, since his intentions are fixed on Marcia?"

"How you love to make mischief. Noel. Why can't you leave me alone, if you're so sure that Marcia's getting what she wants?"

He shrugged.

"Force of habit, I suppose. You used to rise so beautifully at one time. Getting back, though, to these visits to the lawyers, which seem to disturb you unduly—hasn't it occurred to you that it might be a matter of marriage settlements?"

"No," she said, and wondered then why such an obvious explanation had not struck her. "But there's nothing definite between them, is there?"

"I wouldn't know—Marcia's very cagey—but Raff's the type of man who would approach his nuptials with old-fashioned correctness, don't you think? Dowry for the bride, trust funds for the hypothetical brats; I only hope he doesn't tie things up too tightly, for poor Marcia's sake."

Judy's eyes travelled instinctively over the room, assessing the beautiful furniture, the tapestries and period panelling in terms of cash value.

"Will she really try to get him to sell up, once she's married to him?" she asked a little wistfully.

"She'll have a jolly good shot, if I know my sister. Permanent stagnation amongst the pigs and praties won't suit her at all!" Noel replied, and gave her a glance of mingled mockery and conciliation. "Pity he couldn't have fallen for you, isn't it, my sweet? You'd be quite happy bowing to the claims of house and tenants alike for the rest of your life, wouldn't you?"

"I haven't thought about it," she said a little stiffly, and he grinned and pulled her hair.

"Liar!" he retorted amiably, and went out of the room.

The Maules too had altered, she thought uneasily. Marcia's tongue was less sharp and her manner more conciliatory, as if she knew she could afford to bide her time before ridding herself of Judy, when the suitable moment offered. Noel, whose idle attentions had become a habit, she thought, was pleasant enough on the surface, but between all three of them there lay the unspoken knowledge that they shared a secret which only Judy's affection for Raff kept her from revealing.

It seemed that their two regular residents were also aware of impending changes. The Colonel and Miss Botley took it in turns to visit the Grand Saloon while Judy was still lying up, and although Miss Botley asked inquisitive and often impertinent questions, the old soldier was too conventional to pry directly, though he doubtless acquired his information by other means.

Miss Botley was more difficult to remain on terms of mutual respect with, for she probed shamelessly, and no amount of polite snubbing could deflect her.

"I shall not, of course, stop on here," she said. "And a little bird tells me that you too will be leaving shortly."

"What little bird?" asked Judy innocently, but she wondered whether it was Marcia or Raff who had intimated that her services were about to be dispensed with.

"Never mind!" Miss Botley replied archly, patting her blue curls.

"I have a little suggestion to make, my dear. When I leave, how would you like to come with me as my companion?"

Judy stared at her in fresh astonishment.

"But I'm trained as a secretary, not a companion," she said a little helplessly. "Besides, I would like to get another post in Ireland if I *do* leave."

"What does it matter what you're trained for?" Miss Botley said sweepingly. "As to remaining in Ireland, I should be quite agreeable for a time—but somewhere with more modern comforts than this place. Dublin, perhaps, or a good hotel, if it's to be found, in one of those beauty spots like Killarney. Think it over, my dear."

"I'll do that, of course," said Judy politely and, touched by the unexpectedly eager light which came into the inquisitive, rather prominent eyes, added gently: "Why have you stayed so long, if you don't care for the place, Miss Botley? It must be lonely living by yourself in hotels."

Miss Botley sighed, and fidgeted with the floating scarves she always wore.

"Yes, it's lonely," she confessed, without any of her usual aggressiveness. "But when you get to my age, Judy nobody particularly wants you. This place seemed as good as any other until I discovered how extraordinarily feckless the Irish can be in managing their affairs and the comforts of others, and I stayed on, perhaps, because you came here and I liked you, and I could see at once that you were not going to be happy here."

"But I've been very happy here," Judy said. "It's just that —well, there may be changes at Slyne, as I don't doubt you have guessed, and—well, I'd just be redundant, that's all."

Miss Botley tossed her head.

"Oh, it's been obvious that Miss Maule means to catch Mr O'Rafferty—more fool he! Men never see beyond the length of their own noses! If they're not being deceived themselves, they're deceiving others, so I suppose there's no need to be sorry for them."

She and Miss Doyle evidently shared a point in common, thought Judy, beginning to feel a litle hysterical, and it was a relief when Raff walked in unexpectedly, and Miss Botley, with a slightly heightened colour, hastily withdrew.

"Who's been deceiving who?" he inquired. "From the glare she gave me I imagine she must have meant me."

"I'm the recipient of everybody's confidences while I'm lying here," Judy answered, evading the question. "She's not a bad old thing really, Raff—just lonely."

"Well, I'll take your word for it. Who else has been confiding? Colonel Frazer?"

"Yes, he comes in, and that funny little man who came a few days ago and says he's writing a book."

"Probably making up to you for free typing services!"

"Probably, only he's going tomorrow. He says the vibrations are wrong here."

He sat down on the sofa beside her and she moved her legs to make room for him. He looked a little harassed, she thought, but he seemed for the moment to have forgotten the courteous remoteness he had shown towards her since the night of her accident.

"You have a decided way with you, haven't you, Judy?" he said. "You're probably wasted as a secretary."

"I can take a job as companion to Miss Botley when she leaves here,'" Judy said demurely.

"*Is* she leaving? What incredible good fortune!" he exclaimed with much satisfaction, then frowned. "What do you mean—you could take a job as her companion? Has she asked you?"

"Yes."

"Good grief! Had you told her you were leaving, then?"

"No, but things get around'. I thought you probably had."

"I've told no one anything of the sort," he said. "I thought, in any case, that subject had been left for future discussion."

"But you *did* give me notice provisionally," she reminded him gently.

"I did nothing of the kind! And don't you go tying yourself up to that old battle-axe without due thought! I can find you something better than that if you really want to leave."

"I never wanted to leave, Raff. It was your idea—when you were being avuncular," she said with the ghost of a grin, and he smiled reluctantly.

"There seems to have been a great deal of confusion of surmise and reaction of late," he said.

"Yes, I've noticed it too."

"Have you, Judy? And have you, like me, sometimes put the wrong construction on certain things?"

"I've put no construction that could distress you on anything that concerns you," she answered carefully, and he gave a sharp little sigh of frustration.

"And that's a pretty ambiguous answer," he said.

"Perhaps it was an ambiguous question."

"Yes, perhaps it was. Judy—often I want to talk to you seriously, but you put up funny little barriers."

"You put up your own barriers, too," she said. "Lately you've been miles away, and—so often you treat me like a child."

"Do I? A form of defence, perhaps." He paused, hesitating. "You once told me that I had the gifts most women want. I wonder if you understood what you meant."

"Oh, yes, dear Raff, I understood very well."

He was silent, mulling over some fresh problem of his own, and she wondered if he had heard her reply, or whether, indeed, he knew what had prompted his question. There seemed to be a latent anxiety about him, a weary suggestion of something that was not quite unhappiness at the back of his eyes. Did he talk to Marcia like this?

"You're worried, aren't you?" she said, and he smiled at her as if apologising for a weakness that was unfamiliar to him.

"Yes, I am a little," he replied. "I had another not very encouraging session with the lawyers today—also with the bank."

"The bank?" Banks surely could have little to do with marriage settlements and trust funds. "Are money affairs bothering you, then?"

"I suppose they bother most people from time to time," he answered evasively, "but this place has run into a great deal more expense than I'd allowed for. I've been slack, I suppose, not seeing where the overheads were going, and I'm beginning to think Noel is a bit too slapdash for careful management."

"You should have accountants," she said with slight asperity. "They'd soon demand explanations for unaccounted-for items in the books. Why don't you suggest it to Noel?"

"I think I will, but it's a little late now to be crying over errors in the past. Do the sort of guests who come here really expect out-of-season food and luxury appointments when the main attractions of the place should be the fishing and rough shooting and plain if plentiful fare, and a comfortable bed to sleep in?"

She observed him curiously. It was, as he had admitted, a little late in the day to become conscious of the shortcomings of the management, but it was encouraging, she supposed, that he had at last emerged from his dependence on his subordinates.

"I tried to tell you that not long after I came here," she said. "But you just went king-of-the-castle on me."

"Marcia's phrase seems to have stuck," he said, a little curtly. "Am I so high and mighty?"

"No, Raff, no," she said quickly. "You are, I think, what your forebears have always been, and refuse to alter with the times. You thought, didn't you, that when Noel took over there was nothing you need do but remain in the background as a figurehead?"

His eyes, watching her with sudden intentness, had an alertness behind the cool grey.

"You think the fault is mine, then?" he said with unexpected humility.

"The fault was yours only to the extent that you allowed your own feelings to be overruled," she said. "Noel's idea was good, but he never took the background into consideration. This place could have been a paying concern now if you hadn't tried to cater for the sort of guests who expect caviare at every meal."

"A flash establishment for rich tycoons," he said, and she laughed, looking surprised.

"So you remember that? But it's true, Raff. Slyne was never meant for that kind of place. How did Noel persuade you to his way of thinking?"

"He didn't in so many words," he said. "He'd had experience of hotel work before and seemed full of ideas, whereas I was a child in such matters. He'd been ill and was broke. If I could give him a job and keep Slyne going at the same time, it seemed the answer to both problems. And then Marcia joined us. . . ."

They both fell silent and when, presently, Judy asked her next question, she felt that already the crux of the matter had been reached.

"And Marcia blinded you to more prosaic things?" she said, tentatively, ready for his displeasure. It was never, she knew, safe to skate on such thin ice because for the moment his mood was relaxed and receptive, but he did not immediately freeze up on her.

"Marcia is a very beautiful woman," he said slowly. "To me, I suppose, she was also a new experience—we have simple, and probably undemanding tastes in our womenkind in these parts."

"And?"

"What do you want me to tell you?" He began to sound impatient and suddenly wary. "A woman's touch was needed here and Marcia filled the bill excellently. We were, I suppose, a well assorted trio, none of us interfering with the others."

"And to you, as you said, she was a new experience," Judy prompted, and saw the chill beginning to come back into his eyes.

"Yes . . . well . . ." he answered vaguely, and began to run a hand over her damaged ankle. "How is it today? Shall I bandage it again for you?"

"It's not necessary," she replied, accepting his change of mood with the knowledge that the time had passed for confidences if, indeed, he had intended to make any. "I hardly limp at all now. I can quite well do a full day's work instead of just mornings."

"Let's see you walk," he said, and she eased herself off the sofa and paraded obediently before him across the polished floor. As she had said, she scarcely limped now, and he watched her sombrely, observing the way her wide skirt swung out from her slender waist, the gentle curve of her breasts beneath the tight sweater, and the free fall of her red hair about her neck.

"Yes," he said absently. "It seems almost mended. You are very young, aren't you, Judy?"

She paused to stand and look at him.

"No younger than Kathy was," she replied gently, and saw him frown.

"No, I suppose not," he said, and got to his feet. "We've had one cancellation," he remarked casually, as he made for the door. "Friends of that American couple who made a fuss about their bill. Noel's efforts at making a bit on the side have got around, I imagine."

"That's never good," she said, ignoring the obvious opening. "Was it a long booking?"

"I forget. Marcia seems annoyed, but I tell her we can do without the Yanks."

"She's thinking of the dollars, and I suppose one has to —still, there are some very nice Americans," Judy said hopefully. "They don't all want to sample poteen and buy up your antiques. What exactly *is* poteen?"

"Something to be avoided by young ladies who boast of strong heads!" he retorted, reverting to his usual manner with her. "Well, we'll be full again by the end of the month, I suppose. Tomorrow's the first of May."

II

The first of May . . . "It's summer," Judy stated firmly as Marcia, and even Raff, raised quizzical eyebrows at the cotton dress she had put on, in defiance of the rain that was falling.

144

"Not so that you'd notice," Marcia retorted dryly. "Does it never do anything else but rain in this country, Raff?"

"Oh, yes," he replied with a faint smile. "You must have forgotten last summer—and we call this a soft day."

"I can't see the distinction between a soft day and a good old downpour myself," she said a little crossly. "Judy, there's another cancellation to be dealt with this morning and that family from Manchester now want a private bathroom and are bringing their dogs."

"Ours will probably fight them, and we haven't got any private bathrooms," said Judy cheerfully.

"Then we should have, as I'm always saying. Two of the dressing-rooms could easily be converted, Raff. We haven't nearly enough bathrooms."

"We have four apart from the servants' quarters. That should be enough when we can only accommodate a dozen guests at the outside," Raff protested mildly, and she gave an exclamation of impatience.

"Two bathrooms in a great barracks of a house like this is archaic!" she said. "You skimped on the job when it was done, Raff, and now you've made Noel cancel the extra plumbing we were having put in which could easily have been extended to the dressing-rooms if they were converted. And that rag-bag collection of dogs outside ought to go. Apart from the annoyance to visitors' pets, the wretched creatures get into the house and bring dirt and fleas, if nothing worse."

"Once and for all, Marcia, will you please understand that this is my home, whatever you've chosen to make of it," Raff said with a complete change of manner. "The dogs belong mostly to the farm-workers and are not for disposal, as you very well know, and in regard to the bathrooms, I'm not prepared to spend any more money than I've done already. If visitors find our accommodation insufficient they can go elsewhere."

It was so unusual for him to assert his authority in such blunt terms that Judy jumped and glanced nervously at Marcia, whose colour was slowly rising.

"Well, really!" she said. "I think you must be out of your mind to speak to me like that—and in front of your secretary, too."

"I'm sorry if you don't like plain speaking, my dear, but you and Noel don't seem to understand that there's a limit to one's capital. The profits of the place, so far, have been swallowed up in quite unnecessary expenditure, and it's got to stop," he replied, then added on a milder note: "And the fact that Judy is employed as my secretary doesn't place her in the position of a servant, you know."

"Very evidently not!" Marcia snapped back. "And I imagine I've her to thank for this charming little outburst. Why don't you put her on to running your guest house for you and see how she makes out?"

They were still sitting over a late breakfast in the deserted dining-room, and Raff got to his feet.

"Come along, Judy . . . we'd better get down to some work," he said. "Has Noel gone over to Casey's again?"

"Yes," said Marcia with sulky venom. "We need fresh supplies again, which I suppose you consider further bad management. Your precious staff account for half of it in the kitchen. I don't mind betting."

Raff paused behind her chair and bent over her with that curiously intimate little gesture Judy remembered observing before.

"Don't be cross, Marcia," he said softly. "I didn't mean to bite your head off. I'm a bit worried, that's all."

"Lay off work, then, darling, and take me gallivanting somewhere," she said, but he shook his head.

"Another time," he said. "Judy and I have a lot of catching up to do as she's been out of action for a bit."

In the study, Judy stood turning to admire the crisp folds of her frock while Raff sharpened pencils for her.

"You shouldn't have said that about me being a servant," she observed.

"She shouldn't have implied it in the first place," he replied equably. "I'm sorry about our bickering, though."

"You don't bicker enough—not with Marcia."

"What on earth do you mean?"

"I don't know—but when two people are——"

"Are what?"

"Oh, nothing," she said. "I'm afraid my speech sometimes runs away with my discretion."

"Yes, I've noticed that. But you were going to say, I think, that if two people care enough it's natural to bicker. Is that what you had in mind?"

He was still standing by the desk, looking down at her, and she raised her eyes to his and gave him the clear, untroubled look with which he had become so familiar.

"Something like that," she said, and he smiled.

"And you were thinking, perhaps, that you and I had several times crossed swords."

Her eyes widened with surprised inquiry, then she looked away.

"That was different," she said. "You were mostly ticking me off."

"And you, I seem to remember, frequently replied with a show of temper not usual between secretary and boss," he retorted.

"It's my hair," she said. "You told me that very first evening that you suspected my temper matched my hair."

"So I did. Well, Miss Judy Ware, on your reckoning, it all goes to show that we're scarcely indifferent to one another."

"Hadn't we," she said, lowering her eyes suddenly, "better be getting on with some work? There seems to be an enormous pile of unchecked correspondence here."

They worked together each morning in a companionable impersonality, which checked any thoughts that might stray, but often in the afternoons Raff would leave her to finish off letters, and go out after duck or such game as could be found on the moors. The Maules too would take one of the cars and drive to the town for shopping or such gaiety as could be found, leaving Judy to hold the fort, since Slyne was virtually empty of visitors.

The weather had turned suddenly to the false promise of a summer not yet to be taken seriously, and Judy was able to cling to her cotton frocks. One day she would wear the green, the next a blue, and on another a daffodil yellow, until the whole of her meagre wardrobe had been exhausted. She preened artlessly for Raff before they settled down to work each morning, for the invisible thread between them had strengthened into an unspoken intimacy. It was no longer difficult to evade his questions

147

or dissemble when he talked in riddles. She did not flatter herself that he had anything but polite admiration for her cheap summer finery, but had he not implied that first day of May that he was not indifferent to her? Whether he was to marry Marcia or not, he did not, she thought, love her, and even Marcia could not grudge those brief moments of pleasure which soon she must learn to do without.

The Maules were too busy preparing for the imminent American invasion to pay much attention to Judy just now, so that provided she kept her mouth shut when extravagant plans were discussed in front of her, she avoided their label of busy-body. Marcia, who usually favoured the decorative role of hostess, delegating the more tedious of a receptionist's duties to others when she could, was tireless in her efforts to create an illusion of luxury for the transatlantic visitors she considered so important.

"You must order one of those cocktail cabinets for the Sarsfield Suite, Noel, they will want to throw private parties, of course," she said, consulting a list. "And they can have those Georgian glasses, from the cabinet in the Grand Saloon—they're never used."

"My best Waterford is certainly not going to be given over to strangers who probably don't know the difference between bourbon and good Irish whisky," Raff observed mildly, and she made a small face at him.

"If you never use them, why don't you sell them?" she pouted. "You'd get a wonderful price in the States for genuine Georgian Waterford."

"I dare say, but I like to look at them," he replied.

"In that case we must buy others, for the bar takes all our spares, and that will mean more of the needless expense you're always carping at," she said triumphantly. "I must see what Knockferry can produce in the way of coloured sheets to cheer up that gloomy four-poster, and chocolates, Noel—you must order a lavish weekly supply. Americans adore candy."

"Can't they buy their own?" Raff asked with innocent inquiry, but Marcia did not even smile.

"It's a *gesture*, darling," she explained, as if to a child. "These people are stinking rich and say they have Irish ancestors. They'll prove invaluable contacts when they go back if we've made a fuss of them."

"They all have Irish ancestors," Raff remarked with resignation. "Look at those two tiresome women who were here in March and claimed relationship with Timsy, and didn't tip him when they left because they said it would be insulting a relative."

"Oh, they were a couple of cranks!" said Noel airily, then his eyes slid away from Raff's as he remembered that it was this same couple of cranks over whose bill he had so badly blundered, making the same error with the Lucases who had nearly caught him out. Come to think of it, he reflected uneasily, he never had been quite sure whether he had got away with it. Judy had taken the blame for the last occasion, with a little quick thinking on his part, but old Raff was a deep one. It didn't do to take that absent-minded act of his too much for granted. . . . Marcia was still issuing instructions, and he had to admit that she was a damned good-looker, even if she was his sister, and, he saw, getting herself into fine trim for her future role of *châtelainè*, but Raff suddenly got to his feet as if he had lost interest in the whole affair, and said:

"Come on, Judy, we're superfluous here, I think. I've got some business to attend to in Knockferry. You might as well come with me."

"Why not take me instead?" said Marcia quickly. "I can see about those coloured sheets."

"You hate market day—remember? And I really think, in view of the large supply of ancient but excellent Irish linen we still possess, that coloured sheets are redundant, even though they may relieve the gloom of the four-poster," he replied with a faint twinkle and, taking Judy by the hand, swung her out of the room with him.

While Raff attended to his business he left Judy to wander round the town with its stalls and pens erected in the streets, blocking any traffic whose drivers were ill-informed enough to try to get through. She had been to Knockferry on market day only that once with Noel,

149

and the noise and bustle and the gaudy colours of the cheapjack wares on the stalls were still a novelty.

When she tired of the market she looked in shop windows. There was not a great deal that Knockferry could offer to excite more extravagant tastes, despite Marcia's assumption that coloured sheets could be obtained there, but in a draper's window Judy saw a long cotton house-coat invitingly draped on a stand, and went in to inquire. It was cheap and badly made on closer inspection, but the effect was good, even tried over her dress and cardigan, and she could afford the price of something that might last the summer and then be thrown away. She bought it with a slight feeling of defiance.

She arrived at her meeting-place with Raff breathless and a little dishevelled, her bag and parcel clutched tightly under her arm. The new housecoat had several times been in danger of being knocked into the mud by passers-by intent on more serious business, and the crowded streets, besides offering further distractions, had proved difficult to negotiate.

"Am I late?" she asked, and he raised his eyebrows at the childish anxiety in her voice.

"What matter if you are?" he replied, taking her arm to pilot her back to the car. "It's a holiday, my dear, and I hope you've enjoyed yourself. You look a little as though you'd met the tougher portion of the crowd!"

She put up a hand to smooth her hair and dropped her parcel. He stooped to pick up and smiled indulgently as he tucked it under his own arm. She would not know, he supposed, that in her yellow dress, with her red hair flying, and the tiny freckles standing out on her white skin, she presented a picture which touched and warmed him after his unsatisfactory dealings with bank and solicitors. Just so had Kathy come to Knockferry on market days and enjoyed the familiar sights of the little town while she waited to meet him and drive home in the evening, chattering of the day's delights until she fell silent under the spell of his gentle love-making.

"What have you been buying?" he asked, tapping the parcel.

"A housecoat," she said, trotting beside him to keep up with his long stride. "A dressing-gown, really, only long and sort of fluttery, like that thing Marcia wears—only, of course, not at all grand, like hers."

"I've never thought of you as a person who was conscious of clothes," he said, amusement in his voice, and she replied with slight asperity:

"That's because you like to think of me as a child. Don't you realise, Raff, that in these days young girls grow up very early? Why, look at the child brides, and the eloping teenagers the papers are full of! Besides . . ." she added, because she felt that to herself at any rate she owed an explanation for a flippant extravagance, ". . . I couldn't bear that old red dressing-gown any longer! It did nothing for me, except to cover me and keep me warm, and supposing the house caught fire!"

"How absurd you are!" he said, and when they had reached the car, he tossed the parcel into the back and held the door for her while she settled herself in the passenger's seat.

"I don't think of you as a child, Judy," he said, taking his place behind the wheel. "You have the enviable gift of combining youth with wisdom—and a queer sort of understanding, too."

"Queer?"

"Well, new to me, perhaps. I haven't much experience of young girls, you see. One expects them to be callow, without much thought for the future, I suppose."

"That's just your avuncular complex! Kathy wasn't callow, was she?"

He smiled.

"Compared with you, I think she might have been," he said. "But I was very much younger then. I didn't look for hidden depths and worldly knowledge."

She was suddenly silent, twisting her fingers in her lap, aware that her hands were dirty and probably smelt of the farmyard. Was that Marcia's hold on him, then, she wondered, the hidden depths of astute femininity, the worldly knowledge of a bored sophisticate; qualities which were new to him and, like all fresh experiences, disturbing in their novelty?

"Shall we go back by Lough Creagh and visit the inn again?" he said, watching her downcast profile, and thinking that in some way he must have blundered.

"Oh, *yes!*" she cried, her face immediately alight with pleasure, and he smiled again as he started the engine and began to edge the car out from the haphazardly parked vehicles that blocked the road.

III

All the way back she chattered excitedly about the things she had seen; the irresistible fairings decking the stalls, the inconsequent babble, the beasts, the smells and the hats.

"Oh, the hats!" she exclaimed. "Is there anywhere else where you see such hats, Raff?"

"Probably not. We're used to them, of course, and don't think they're so funny," he said, but remembered that even Kathy, born and bred to the peculiarities of her countrymen, had found the hats funny.

"Timsy wears one of yours. It's like an apple dumpling turned up all round!"

"Most likely my father's, or even my grandfather's. O'Rafferty headgear is handed down for generations among the tenants. What would you do in an office, Judy? I can't see you there with your love of the soil, and sense of the ridiculous."

It was as udden and uncomfortable reminder that she was, after all, only a subordinate to whom he had given an unexpected treat.

"You've forgotten that I want to remain in Ireland," she said in a rather flat voice. "There must be work for secretaries—or even just typists—in racing stables, or the big farms, or—or even another guest house."

He did not reply. They had reached the Plain of Cluny, that desolate stretch of moorland which had disquieted her the first time. It was more kindly now, with its softer hues of early summer, but there were still great patches of stony ground which yielded nothing from the soil, and the rocks and boulders stubbornly resisted moss and lichen alike. Judy shivered, as she had before, and as before, he asked if she was cold.

"No," she said, and thought, as then, that it was a coldness of the spirit that blew in from the Plain of Cluny.

But at Lough Creagh the warmth returned; the little lough was more beautiful than ever with the changing season, and the water seemed an even deeper blue.

"Let's stay out here," she cried, and without waiting for an answer kicked off the sandals she wore without stockings and ran down to the rim of silvery sand at the water's edge.

Raff followed more slowly, conscious that he had, by some remark, disturbed the simple pattern of her enjoyment. He sat down on a sun-warmed rock to wait until she was ready to offer him again the confidence and companionship he had come to expect of her, and lazily filled a pipe while he watched her dig her toes in the sand, letting it run through them as he remembered he used to do himself, as a boy; then she tried the water, but withdrew her foot hastily, letting out a small scream, and ran, laughing, back to him.

"Ooh, it's cold!" she complained, and sat down at his feet in the heather.

"Lake water is always deceptive. It has to be very hot to bathe with any enjoyment," he said. "Have you recovered now?"

"Recovered?"

"Something I said upset you, I think. This is the second time you've shivered coming over the plain and it's a good deal warmer today. What was it?"

"Something about the place, I suppose. It's so desolate and bleak," she answered evasively, and, leaning back on her hands, stretched her legs out to dry her feet in the sun.

"Better use this," he said, tossing her his handkerchief, and when she made no move to use it he got up and knelt down beside her and began to dry them himself.

"This is the second time I've dirtied a handkerchief for you," she said, and he looked up quickly, meeting her eyes with a long, grave look.

"Judy . . ." he said ". . . that nice clean heart you talked about on that other occasion—did you know what you were saying, or were you really a little lightheaded?"

"You said I was."

"Well, there seemed to be several unexplained matters mixed up in your mind just then. Something about Grogan and Noel and calling in the Garda. Is it a wonder I thought you lightheaded?"

"No, I suppose not."

"Would you like to tell me the rather incoherent story of the two tallboys again?" he asked with such sudden directness that she wondered if he already suspected something of the truth of what she had tried to warn him. But Noel had tied her hands now. She could not, because of Marcia, bring an accusation which would not only hurt Raff but brand herself as a troublemaker who told tales for spite.

"Forget it," she answered briefly. "I'd got mixed up in the first place, I expect, and anyway, Raff, you shouldn't throw my unguarded remarks at me when you know very well I'd had a nasty fright and Granny Malone had put the 'fluence on me."

"Very well," he said, gravely studying her face. "If you're going to evade me by talking nonsense about poor Granny, we'd better leave it for the moment. You've become quite good at answering in riddles, haven't you?"

"Self-defence," she retorted. "You often talk in riddles."

"Do I?" He sounded surprised, and resumed his seat on the rock and took up his pipe again. "If I do, then perhaps mine is a form of defence, too."

"From me?" It was her turn to sound surprised, and he nodded unsmilingly.

"From myself too, perhaps. At my age one becomes wary of impulses, of mistaken hopes and desires."

"Riddles again," she said, and added a little crossly: "Old Uncle O'Rafferty and all!"

He laughed, but there was now a faint weariness in his eyes.

"One of my defences, most likely," he said. "I assure you, Judy, I don't always feel avuncular, despite your accusations."

"Raff——" she began hesitantly, "there's so much about you I don't understand."

"Yes, I expect there is," he replied, and it could have been a warning that she had misunderstood him. "You upset a good many things for me when you came here, you see."

"Because I reminded you of Kathy, you mean?"

"No, that was only to begin with. You are not alike at all, really, except for your youth and simplicity. But Kathy had the simplicity of a guarded childhood and no very great desire to explore outside her own appointed sphere. Yours, I think, is the true simplicity that springs from a humble heart and loving kindness. You have the enviable qualities, Judy—don't hanker after the meretricious gifts of others."

It was a strange little speech for him to have made, she thought, pledged as he was to a future with a woman who could give him none of these things, and seeing the faint disillusionment in his eyes, she said gently:

"If you're in—in any sort of mess, Raff, it's not too late. I mean, it's better to make a clean break than get further involved."

"I'm involved with my financial affairs at present—not quite a mess as yet, but pretty near it," he answered, deliberately ignoring her meaning.

"Oh!" She sounded disappointed, but glancing at him quickly, she saw the sudden lines of worry and tiredness in his face.

"Your interviews with the bank and the lawyers didn't go well?" she asked.

"They went damn badly and I'm already in the red," he replied a little grimly, and she drew her bare knees up to her chin, clasping her arms round them, and leaned forward to listen.

"How badly are you in the red?" she asked with practical unconcern. Her father, when he had been alive, was frequently in that state; it just took adjustment and rigorous cutting down to get clear again.

"Nothing that can't be rectified with care," he said, "but it means I have no margin to work on as I had when we first started this business. I've already sold out what capital my solicitors will let me lay hands on, and unless we cut down very considerably on expenditure for the guest house, I'm broke."

Judy felt her anger beginning to rise.

"It's Noel!" she exclaimed. "All these wild schemes for turning Slyne into an imitation of any flashy road-house! That lighting plant, and all the wiring, for instance—supposed to be done more cheaply because Grogan provided the contact. I came across the receipt in Noel's file the other day and it seemed a needless extravagance to me when lamps are much nicer." She mentioned a figure that made him raise his eyebrows.

"Are you sure of that amount?" he asked sharply, and she stared.

"Perfectly. I can show you when we get home, if you like. Why?"

"Simply that I remember writing a cheque for considerably more than that. Grogan must have made a mistake in sending the receipt."

She rested her cheek on her knees, letting the hair fall across her face, hiding it from him.

"Didn't you keep your own receipts until I came here?" she asked.

"Not those kind of things. I simply wrote the cheques. It was Noel's job as manager to file the receipts."

"I see. So you never saw the receipts."

"No. Once the bills were paid I had no further interest in them."

"Oh, Raff! Can't you see?" she exclaimed, suddenly flinging back her head. "He must have done this every time there was some large outgoing. He's only got to persuade Grogan or some not very scrupulous tradesman to fiddle the statement, and when you've paid up they share the perks and produce the correct receipt."

The skin seemed to tighten over the bones of his ugly face and she remembered the same illusion the night he had found her in the wrecked car.

"Why don't you get rid of him?" she demanded, too angry and upset to watch her words any longer. "I know —or at least I'm told—that perks are legitimate pilfering among hotel staff, but at this rate you can't hope to run a small guest house with any profit. Why not get rid of him, or at least have a showdown and tell him it's got to stop?"

His eyes as they rested on her distressed face were curiously gentle.

"You think I'm a weak fool who has just let things slide, don't you, Judy?" he said.

"Neither weak nor a fool—just too trusting. You can't deal with matters you know nothing about."

"But I did know," he said gently, and saw her eyes widen. "Not about things like that cheque to Grogan, perhaps, but I guessed there was some sort of fiddle going on between them. Grogan was the contact man for too many introductions to fresh trade for my liking. That's why I object to him coming to the house."

"But why did you put up with it?"

He shrugged.

"A certain amount of commission is to be winked at, I imagine, besides——"

"Besides, there was Marcia," she finished for him.

"Yes, there was Marcia," he replied gravely, and got to his feet. "Come along, my dear, we might as well go home. It hasn't been a very happy ending to our stolen holiday, I'm afraid. Put your shoes on."

"What are you going to do?" she asked, struggling with the buckles of her sandals.

"Nothing very spectacular, I'm afraid. Just acquaint them with the fact that I'm nearly cleaned out, and then it's up to them."

"Marcia wouldn't have anything to do with shabby little deals," Judy said trying valiantly to ease his disillusion, even though she might have her own doubts in the matter.

"How nice you are, Judy," he replied, tenderness touching his mouth. "No, I'm sure she wouldn't."

They drove back to Slyne in comparative silence, and as they reached the bit of road which bounded the shores of the lough, she said suddenly:

"If you were up to Noel's tricks, didn't it occur to you that he and I——" she broke off, and he said gently:

"Were not amusing yourselves as I thought?"

"Yes."

"Perhaps I didn't really believe it."

"You *behaved* as if you did."

"Yes, well—jealousy does strange things to one's reasoning powers, Judy."

"*You*—jealous of *me!*"

"Does that surprise you?"

"Yes—yes, it does rather," she replied, hugging her arms about her thin body, and then they were at the gates, and the dogs ran, barking, to meet them, and Marcia came out under the stone portico and stood leaning gracefully against one of the slender doric columns which supported it. She looked, thought Judy, the perfect picture of the lady of the house welcoming home her husband. She even reached up and kissed Raff lightly on the cheek as he went into the house.

He called a conference after dinner and they all repaired to the study where privacy could be assured.

"Why the solemn conclave?" Noel asked, sulky at being expected to discuss business after dinner. "And shall I order the cocktail cabinet through Grogan? He can always guarantee quick delivery—and Marcia was thinking it would be better if she sent to Dublin for the sheets. Knockferry's hardly likely to run to fancy bed-linen."

Raff had been wandering absently round the room, gazing at the stuffed trophies as if uncertain how to begin, but as Noel finished speaking he sat down suddenly behind his desk and leaned forward, resting his arms upon it.

"There will be no more ordering of anything that isn't strictly essential, so put right out of your mind cocktail cabinets, fancy sheets and all the rest of the phoney humbug you've planned for visitors who could doubtless buy us all up and not even notice it," he said, and there was a note in his voice which made the Maules, brother and sister, turn to regard him with puzzled uncertainty.

"What do you mean, old boy? It may seem like humbug to you, but all these extra frills are sprats to catch mackerel. I know from past experience," Noel said, beginning to bluster.

"I dare say you do, Noel," Raff replied quietly. "But Slyne was never designed for the sort of place you have in mind. And my intention, since you ask, is that things must be put on a very different footing if we are to survive as a going concern. This extravagance has got to stop, and if you don't like more humble methods of running the place—well, then, you have your own remedy."

"What do you mean?" said Noel again, his eyes shifting uneasily.

"I mean," Raff said quite pleasantly, "that I'm broke—cleaned out."

There was a sudden silence. Only Judy, sitting in the window embrasure away from them all, moved sharply, wishing that Raff had not insisted that she should be present; then Noel laughed.

"Is this meant to be a joke, old chap?" he asked.

"Certainly not. One hardly takes threatened bankruptcy as a joke."

"As bad as that?"

"Well, not quite, but if things go on like this it might end that way. I don't think you've quite realised, Noel, that you've been drawing on funds that weren't your own all this time, and they won't last for ever."

Noel began to bluster again.

"You know I couldn't put money into the business—you agreed to leave everything in my hands. You couldn't care less, you said, how the place was run providing the lodgers didn't get in your hair!"

"Did I? Well, I dare say you're right, only—I'd hardly bargained for the scale on which you proposed to run it. You aren't content with a simple guest house, my dear chap; you're trying to build the sort of business which needs unlimited capital behind it, and I haven't got it."

Noel wheeled round suddenly to observe Judy, sitting quietly by the window. She was, it seemed, staring out into the falling twilight and paying no attention.

"I suppose we've Miss Snake-in-the-grass Ware to thank for this," he remarked unpleasantly, and she jumped and turned her head to look at him questioningly. "Don't try to look so innocent, my sweet—we've all known your views for some time. What do you hope to get out of this—the sympathetic ear of the management and a small reward at the end of it?"

"Leave Judy out of this, please. She has nothing to do with my own findings," Raff said in a voice that was

159

suddenly harsh, and Marcia, who had not so far spoken, laid a hand on her brother's arm.

"Don't let's lose our sense of proportion," she said, her calm voice soft and quite unperturbed. "If Judy has been a little indiscreet and—shall we say—over-imaginative—that was perhaps to be expected in the circumstances. But Raff has a perfect right to call the tune—after all, he pays the piper."

"Thank you, Marcia," Raff said. "Now perhaps we can arrive at some conclusion. Any extras in the way of stores, wine, and these proposed additions to the ordinary comforts of the house must be cancelled immediately unless they've already been passed by me, and furthermore, all future orders must have my sanction before they go out. Judy will bring all receipted bills to me for my own files, and this rather overdone habit of dispensing drinks on the house must be modified. Do you understand, Noel?"

Even in the shadows the ugly sneer could be seen on Noel's face.

"I understand one thing," he said. "You, inspired by that gossiping little secretary of yours, are making it pretty clear you don't trust me. Judy must bring you the files, you must check all orders—nothing, in fact, is to be left in my hands. What do you imagine I've been doing—chiselling you out of the proceeds?"

"My dear Noel," Raff replied wearily, "I'm perfectly aware that you've been putting away perks and commission —that, I suppose, is a legitimate supplement to the fairly handsome salary I pay you. But there are limits even to that, and since you might quite justifiably accuse me of slackness in the past, it seems only reasonable that I should adopt a firmer stand in the future if we're to keep the place going, don't you think?"

Noel's manner suddenly changed.

"You're taking it all too seriously, me boyo!" he said with a swift return of his old, easy impudence. "What's it matter being in the red these days? Everyone is—not to worry!"

"You say that a little too often," Raff observed rather curtly. "It's very easy to shrug off worries when they don't happen to be your own. Now, this is the position. I've been into the matter very carefully with my bank manager and the lawyers, and I gather we can just hold out for the summer with the bookings we already have if, during that time, we manage to save money. I can sell out no more capital, so it's obvious we must draw our horns in. If, after the summer, our overheads haven't been reduced, then we must start running the place on quite different lines or close down altogether. Have I made myself clear?"

"Very," snapped Noel, his boyish manner vanishing. "And if you imagine I'm going to work under those conditions in a dead-and-alive hole like this, you can think again."

"Very well," Raff replied quietly. "Perhaps you've rather lost sight of the fact that you were grateful for this dead-and-alive hole when you were sick and out of a job, but if that's how you feel you'd better go."

"Rats leaving the sinking ship, I suppose you mean to imply."

"Well, it might look a little like that, mightn't it?"

"It can look any darn way you please! You were the boss—why did you leave your affairs to a paid employee, without looking into them yourself? Because you were too damn king-of-the-castle to bother!"

"You've got something there, I'll admit," Raff said rather wearily. "But it was my ignorance that kept me in the background rather than a sense of superiority, as I thought you understood. And I regarded you as a friend, Noel, rather than as a paid employee. You might remember that."

Noel began to shuffle his feet uncomfortably without answering, and Marcia slid an arm across Raff's shoulders.

"You're both getting hot under the collar for no reason," she said, a little undertone of amusement in her voice. "Even if you are sailing rather near the wind, darling, you have the answer right here under your roof—and *I* won't desert the sinking ship."

"Thank you, Marcia," he replied gravely, and reached up a hand to touch hers in response. "I'd hardly expect you to stop on without Noel, however."

"But, dar-*ling*!" she protested with fond indulgence, and now the laughter was uppermost in her voice, gently persuading. "I wasn't thinking of your silly old guest house. You had other plans for us, I thought."

Judy, anonymous now in the shadows, watched them motionlessly from her place in the window. Marcia was leaning over him, her soft hair brushing his cheek, her beauty and utter self-confidence exposed in the lamplight like a challenge. Raff seemed to stiffen for a moment, then he said very gently:

"Such plans as I may have imagined for anyone, myself included, could hardly be said to have crystallised, could they? Shall we say we've all of us suffered a sea-change?"

"You," she said, still sure of her power, "had only to ask for what you wanted. I threw myself at you pretty shamelessly, didn't I, darling? Well, perhaps the time has come to take stock and be sensible."

"I'm nearly broke, my dear," he said patiently, as if he was unable to make her understand, and she threw back her head and began to laugh.

"Broke!" she echoed. "Why, you could make your fortune if you'd only listen to me! The house is falling to pieces and not worth restoring, for all your high hopes that the lodgers would take care of that—but the treasures inside! I've had schemes for months as to how and where we would get the best prices—once we were married."

CHAPTER EIGHT

I

JUDY sat frozen into immobility on her low stool. She had watched with helpless fascination the rich colour flood Marcia's lovely face as her assurance and excitement rose. She wanted to cry out and implore her not to speak the very words that must destroy her ambitions, and even Noel had taken a step forward, gesturing feebly, as if to warn her to be silent. But they were both of them forgotten, she knew, and only the dreadful little silence which followed seemed at last to penetrate.

When Raff finally spoke, however, it was with such soft quietness that even Judy was deceived.

"I see your plans have rather outstripped mine," he said. "This is my home, Marcia, and all that goes with it. If I decide to carry on the business on more simple lines or, alternatively, just live on here quietly as I used to do and cut down rigorously until debts are cleared—would you still be prepared to stand by me?"

Marcia looked puzzled. She knew now that she had spoken too soon and brought about a double crisis instead of allowing one to follow naturally on the other, as she had planned, but he was taking it calmly enough.

"Well, naturally, darling—what a curious question," she replied glibly. "But of *course* you'll sell—you'd be mad not to. What do you care about all this mouldy stuff you've lived with all your life without ever appreciating its commercial value?"

"It's familiar, and I'm old-fashioned in my habits—not at all the sort of man you'd care for as a husband."

"How do you know? How do you know what you mightn't become once I got you away from this decaying mansion you've allowed yourself to become obsessed with? I can teach you to live, Raff."

"Do you think so? But supposing I don't care to live the kind of life you have in mind?"

"Oh, Raff, think of the fun you've been missing!" she cried, rushing obliviously into recklessness. "Think of what we both could do on the proceeds of what all this junk would fetch! Why, apart from the furniture and glass and china, Grogan says the panelling and the Adam fireplaces would fetch a fortune in America."

"So you'd strip my house and leave it a shell?" His voice was gentle with the soft cadences of his race.

"Why not? The place isn't marketable as it stands, and Grogan says——"

"Oh, God!" groaned Noel, turning his back, and Judy, although she had been expecting an outburst, jumped as Raff got to his feet with a suddenness that nearly threw Marcia off her balance, and began to speak.

"Very well, Marcia. Since you choose to discuss such matters in public, we'll carry it on to a conclusion," he said, and Judy had never heard such bitterness and distaste in his voice. "You don't care for me—you only want to get

163

your greedy little hands on the money you could raise from my possessions. You're a beautiful woman, my dear, but life hasn't taught you yet that there are some things a man won't barter his birthright for. I thought of marrying you once, yes, but you took too much for granted. I never made you an offer of marriage, and if I've misled you in any way as to our future, I apologise. Had you really cared, I might have seen things differently."

Marcia was very white, but it was the whiteness of temper rather than of humiliation. She said, staring up at him and still trying to quench the ugly words that were clamouring to be spoken:

"You're wrong, Raff, and rather cruel. I did care—I wanted you."

"And want is the word you really understand," he said more quietly. "You wanted me because I was a new experience, just as you were to me, but love and plain animal desire are two very different things. You can live with one but not with the other. Once you'd satisfied your natural urge, you'd soon have tired of me, wouldn't you? Be honest for once—wouldn't you?"

She remained seated on the arm of the chair, graceful and indolent in the lamplight, but her breathing was suddenly rapid and she flicked her fingers impatiently at Noel to give her a cigarette.

"So our marriage was just a figment of my imagination, was it?" she said slowly. "Because I made all the running, you had nothing to offer in the end—except yourself and this barracks of a place you call a heritage. Yes, I wanted you, but did you imagine that was all I wanted? You asked me to be honest for once—well, I will be. You attracted me, damn you, because you were different—hard to get. I'd have had you for a lover, Raff, as I once told you, but I thought you were bent on chivalry at all costs. How wrong one can be about a person—how wrong about oneself."

Raff was silent while she leaned towards the lighter which Noel held for her, then she flung back her head, dispelling the smoke from her nostrils in a contemptuous, insolent stream, and when she again started speaking there was a vicious, deliberate bite to her words.

"Yes, you're quite right—I would have tired," she said maliciously. "What sort of lover would you have turned out to be, with your puritan streak and your roots bedded in the soil of a country which can never see beyond today? Yes, roots! Your precious Judy talked about that once, all dewy-eyed and simple. If the image of that blasted Kathy has always stood in my way, then take Judy to mould into your adolescent idea of what a wife should be—she's more than willing, I don't mind betting!"

Judy sprang up from her stool, searching for words with which to put an end to such crude revelations, and at the same moment, Raff gave Marcia a stinging slap across the cheek.

"You're hysterical," he said coldly. "You'd better go to your room. Tomorrow we can discuss your plans for leaving—yours and Noel's."

She got to her feet slowly and saw Judy standing on the edge of the circle of light, her yellow frock crumpled, and her eyes two startled points of green in her white face.

"Charming, Miss Judith Ware!" she drawled. "And have you thrown in Noel's other little deals with Grogan for good measure?"

"Marcia, for God's sake!" her brother exclaimed, and she turned to look at him without compassion.

"You never did have much guts, did you, darling?" she said. "I've come clean, so why shouldn't you, to make a job of it? Or hasn't dear little Judy told, after all?"

"I've told nothing," Judy said, ". . . not because of Noel's threats, but because I minded for Raff. Now, can't you rest on the damage you've done already, Marcia? There's nothing to add."

"Are you by any chance alluding to the deals over my furniture?" Raff asked, so casually that they all turned to look at him with varying degrees of surprise.

"So Judy did tell!" Noel exclaimed on a note of disgust.

"She tried to warn me on one occasion, yes," Raff replied, still with that strange air of disinterest, "but I'm afraid I didn't pay enough attention, owing to certain other things. I'm not, however, entirely gullible, Noel, however easily you've led yourself to believe I am. It wasn't very difficult in the end to put two and two together and guess what you'd been up to. How many pieces have you succeeded in substituting for the originals?"

"Only two," said Noel sullenly, then rallied a ghost of his old cocksureness to try to justify himself. "I did it to help you, damn it all, Raff. It seemed a justifiable swindle when you never knew one perishing antique from another, and I guessed things were a bit tight for you. The money's all banked, ready to hand over—not a fortune by a long chalk—but a tidy little sum."

"I wonder," said Raff reflectively, "if you would have handed it over if I hadn't found you out."

"That's coming it a bit strong! Actually there would have been more if we'd completed the last deal, only that rat Grogan's been holding out on me, trying a little black-mail because I said I'd finished with these transactions. Can't trust these wide boys!"

Raff's eyes hardened.

"Ah, yes, the mystery of the two tallboys is now explained. I didn't think, I must own, that I was taking a common swindler into my employ—even though I know Grogan's reputation."

"Are you going to prosecute?" Noel asked, and for the first time sounded scared.

Raff, who had been moving round the room as he spoke, came to a halt behind Judy, resting his hands on her shoulders. It was not, she thought, an conscious gesture of significance, but she felt his hands tremble slightly and covered them with her own as she had often seen Marcia do.

"No," he answered very wearily. "I don't care for the washing of dirty linen in public and—well, I once had a fondness for both of you. Let's leave it at that."

"That's decent of you," Noel said awkwardly. "I—I'll write a cheque for you before I go."

"No, keep it," Raff replied, and his hands under Judy's were steady again. "You'll need something to start off again—you and Marcia."

Marcia moved slowly away and ranged herself beside her brother.

"So we're being given the sack, are we?" she said, and her voice was light again and faintly amused. "How are you going to cope with your American visitors with no manager and no receptionist—or is watchdog Judy going to step into the breach and run this place single-handed?"

"I don't think that need concern either of you any longer," said Raff very courteously. "You will, no doubt, want to make your arrangements as soon as possible. It would be embarrassing for all of us if you were to linger on, don't you think?"

"Very tactfully put," she answered, sounding bored, then her eyes travelled with cool deliberation over the pair of them. Raff—tall and dark and a little untidy, with that provocative ugliness already softened into a look of release, Judy with her bright head resting in sudden weariness against his breast.

"*God,* how you would have bored me!" she exclaimed with callous cruelty. "I wanted a man, not an old-fashioned knight in armour with one foot in the grave of a lost love and another in the cradle of a fancied second best! Not quite such an innocent, either, if Noel is to be believed—I wish you joy of one another!"

"Shut up!" said Noel, suddenly shouting, and swinging her round roughly, pushed her from the room.

It seemed very quiet after they had gone, and only familiar small sounds disturbed the stillness; the slow ticking of the clock, one of the yard dogs whimpering in its sleep, and the gentle, timeless lapping of the water on the lough's shore. Judy spun round suddenly and, turning her face into Raff's breast, began to weep.

His arm went round her instantly and he held her close to his heart, the fingers of one hand running soothingly through the tangle of her hair.

"Don't, my darling . . . don't cry like that . . ." he said. "Her words can't touch you . . . just the final, spiteful outburst of a rather vulgar woman. . . ."

"I weep for you, not for myself," Judy sobbed.

"Why, then? Do you think she's hurt me?"

She nodded, and he smiled above her head, and for a moment his eyes were sad.

"Of the two, I think it was Noel who hurt me most," he said. "It's never pleasant to have one's kindness repaid with ingratitude, but I dare say I was a lot to blame."

"But Marcia—she must have hurt you."

"She hadn't that power. You have to be loved, Judy, before you can strike very deep with your claws."

"And did you never—love her, I mean?"

"I don't think so. She attracted me at first, as I apparently attracted her, because she was outside my experience and I had lived for a long time without any woman's company."

"But you would have married her," she said, and lifted her face, streaked with tears, and he wiped them away with a gentle finger.

"At one time, perhaps," he answered. "The time had come to marry and raise children, I thought, and Marcia was beautiful and seemed a fitting *châtelaine* for my home —I had never, you see, had a great deal to do with women. It would seem ungallant to say that she made the running if she hadn't already admitted it herself, but I never, believe me, gave her grounds for such a supposition once you were here."

"Me?" She looked puzzled, then the faint colour began to creep under her skin and he gave her a little shake.

"Oh, Judy!" he exclaimed, tenderness mixed with a hint of exasperation, touching his mouth. "Don't you know by now what I feel for you, or have all my tentative probings and hints gone for nothing?"

"Riddles," she said. "You always talked in riddles."

"But I remember telling you only this afternoon that you were pretty good at answering in riddles."

"Yes, you taught me how," she said a little bitterly, and suddenly pulled away from him.

"Judy——" he said tentatively, "I'd thought—but no matter—tomorrow will do as well."

"Tomorrow?" she faltered, plainly not having understood half the things he had been trying to say, then she spun round abruptly, with a whirl of yellow skirts and flying hair, and ran out of the room without another word.

She slept late the next morning, the deep, unrefreshing sleep of mental exhaustion, and awoke, heavy-eyed, to find Rosie Boyle setting down a tray by the bed.

"Sure, and I thought you were in a swound, Miss Judy," she said, her eyes bright with the excitement that prevailed in the kitchen.

"What's the time?" Judy asked, struggling to sit up and aware from the fullness of the light which streamed in at the windows that it was long past the hour for rising.

"Ten o'clock, no less, and that by the old granddad on the stairs, and he an hour slow," Rosie replied, and Judy, wide awake now, stared at her with dismay.

"Why didn't you call me at the usual time?" she demanded, reaching hurriedly for the teapot. "The morning's half gone and there's work to be done."

"The master said to leave you," Rosie replied. "He's gone to the other side to send telegrams, so you don't need to choke yourself. Is it true, Miss Judy, that there was fine shenanigans last night and them two was thrown out?"

"If you mean Mr and Miss Maule, they will be leaving shortly, I believe," Judy said reprovingly, wondering how much the servants already knew of last night's events.

"They've gone," announced Rosie with every evidence of satisfaction. "Had me brother Ned drive them to Knock-ferry in the master's cyar to catch the early train; never a word of farewell to any of us, either, and Timsy carryin' baggage to the cyar fit to sink a battleship! What will we be doin' now, Miss Judy, with visitors comin' from Americy and the elegant plans for them only just begun?"

"We'll manage," Judy said. She leaned back on her pillows, eating her buttered toast, while she recalled the happenings of the night before. It was both a shock and a relief to know that the Maules had already gone. They were rats, after all, she thought, not even waiting to tide over Raff's affairs before leaving the sinking ship; a couple of adventurers who, having squeezed the orange dry, had no further thought than their own skins. And what had Raff been trying to tell her afterwards when she had behaved like a child and refused to stay and listen?

169

When she was ready she spent what was left of the morning sorting out the files and correspondence in Noel's office, docketing bills and restoring some sort of order to the place. There was, she reflected, a queer feeling about the house. Miss Doyle was singing lugubrious hymns in the kitchen, doors banged without restraint, the dogs wandered through the hall unchecked, and presently Timsy's cornet could be heard as an inappropriate accompaniment to his niece's chant. *I will never,* Judy thought, *be able to induce order in this house as Marcia did,* then remembered that her own future in regard to Castle Slyne was still undetermined. She had deliberately thrust from her mind Raff's overtures of last night. He had turned to her, as at first she had turned to him, for comfort and reassurance after that humiliating scene, and if he had implied something more than a fondness for her, it was still mixed up with that old confusion with the happy ghost of the girl who had never hurt him as Marcia must have done. But at least her own defences had not weakened in a moment he might have regretted later.

She wandered down to the lough, followed by the dog which, true to its name, wheezed and snuffled at her heels, and saw Granny Malone picking up pebbles on the shore, as was her custom from time to time, no one knew why. Judy would have avoided her, never having quite rid herself of the local superstition which clung to the old woman, but Granny hailed her, and came shuffling over the stones to engage her in talk. It was evidently one of her more affable days.

"The saints be with you, young miss!" she began piously. "Would it be true what I'm hearin' that that fine pair have left the castle?"

"Mr and Miss Maule have gone, yes," Judy replied warily, and the old woman cackled with laughter.

"Sure, I saw it in the tea-leaves," she said. "Never good luck to Castle Slyne was them two, bad cess to 'em, and the bold lady with her two eyes fixed on the O'Rafferty, and he like to be caught by the black heart of her! Granny put the 'fluence on her, doty, that's why you're rid of her."

"Nonsense!" Judy replied briskly, feeling that she ought not to encourage such primitive notions, but Granny only cackled again, showing her toothless gums.

"Would you be fancyin' the O'Rafferty yourself, young miss?" she asked slyly, and suddenly seized one of Judy's hands. "I'll tell your fortune for you, doty . . . och, the disaster of it . . . the cruel fate to fall upon this place! I see ashes and ruins, and the tollin' of a bell. . . ."

Judy tried to pull her hand away, but the old woman gripped tightly, then suddenly flung it away, at the same time dropping the pebbles she had collected.

"You are bad luck to this place, too, with your red hair like that other wan and your child's body that would be comfort to no man. . . . The castle is doomed . . . doomed. . . .Och, bad cess to you, me pebbles are lost entirely!"

She began grovelling about on the shore to find the pebbles, muttering to herself, a dirty, rather pathetic old woman, with the sparse grey hair sticking out from under the old cloth cap, and Judy left her. She was used by now to Granny Malone's dire prophecies, but she returned to the house feeling slightly shaken, and it came as no surprise, after such forebodings, to find Grogan's van standing unattended in front of the portico.

II

She ran into the house, knowing the little dealer would be prying about in one of the rooms, assessing the amount that he hoped to make on his next deal, and wishing that Raff had returned. She had wondered several times if he had stopped away so long to avoid embarrassing himself by having to reopen a subject on which in the clear light of morning he might have had regrets, but although she had been grateful for his absence, she wished he was here now.

She found Grogan in the Grand Saloon, inspecting the tallboy, and wondered whether, with Miss Doyle's doubtful help, he had already managed to effect the exchange.

"Good afternoon, Mr Grogan—can I do something for you?" she asked, and he wheeled round from his inspection, and the frown on his swarthy face changed swiftly to an expression of sly ingratiation.

"Well now, Miss Judy, if it isn't yourself, poppin' up again when I least expect to see you, and me thinkin' the house was empty," he said, rubbing his hands together.

She looked him over coolly, then spared a quick glance for the tallboy, assuring herself with relief that it was still the original piece.

"Don't you ever ring the bell, Mr Grogan?" she asked. "One of the servants could have told you that no one was at home."

"Ah, sure, the place has always been liberty hall to me," he replied airily. "Besides, I knew the O'Rafferty had gone over to the other side and wouldn't be here to offer his usual hospitality. Would there be a drop of the crayture handy in the office, Miss Judy? Mr Maule, now, is very particular about showin' me a welcome when I come, God save him!"

"If you've heard Mr O'Rafferty went over to the other side, I'm surprised you haven't also heard that Mr Maule has gone, and I haven't the authority, I'm afraid, to offer you a drink," Judy said.

"Then I'll just help meself," Grogan replied jovially, then his face suddenly changed. "What's that you said? The young felly's gone—gone without the cash he thinks I owe him!"

"I don't think he had much choice," said Judy calmly. "Mr O'Rafferty knows all about your fiddle with the antiques, and if there's money owing on the deal I suggest you pay it to him since he's the owner of the stuff you switched. You've come again for the tallboy, haven't you?"

"You little she-cat! So you told, did you?" he exclaimed furiously. "What's the O'Rafferty doin' over in the other side—tell me that! Has he gone to the Garda?" He advanced upon her threatingly and she backed away.

"I don't know," she said, her confidence shaken. "Do the Garda have headquarters on the other side?"

"And you playin' the innocent, gettin' us prosecuted and sent to gaol! Wait till I get me hands on you! Wait till I get me hands on your scrawny little neck, me fine chicken!" he said, and seized her by the shoulders.

"*Grogan*!" Raff's voice from the doorway echoed round the room like a pistol shot, and the dealer dropped his hands as if he had been stung.

"Is it yourself, O'Rafferty?" he said, vainly trying to collect his lost *bonhomie*. "We was havin' a bit of an argument, Miss Judy and me—I had me temper mislaid for a minute or two."

Raff crossed the room with rapid strides and took the little man by the collar of his loud-checked coat.

"Get out of here!" he said, his face white with anger. "And if ever I find you laying hands on a woman again, there'll be more than the Garda for you to reckon with. I'll knock you silly, myself! Now get out."

"Aisy now, your honour," Grogan said, his eyes nervous but his boldness still making a fight for it. "We'd not be partin' till a little matter of cash is settled between us, would we, now?"

"Your cash dealings were strictly between yourself and my late manager, so I understand," Raff replied in what Marcia would have termed his king-of-the-castle voice.

"Ah, no! There's a small matter of payment on the last piece of work I had done for you, and Mr Maule never settled up. The piece is beyont in the van if you've a mind to see it sor—as fine a piece of gen-u-ine reproduction as ever I saw."

He glanced away as he spoke as if he expected Raff to hit him, but Raff merely looked down on him from his considerable height with a very unpleasant glint in his eyes, and Judy exclaimed with outraged indignation:

"I never *heard* such barefaced lies! I overheard that conversation you had with Mr Maule the day you tried to change the tallboys over, you horrid little man! You were holding out on him for the money you'd got for the desk and you taunted him with the fact that such prices that the stuff fetched went into his own pocket and Mr O'Rafferty knew nothing about it. Blackmail, he called it—and so it was—and you laughed in his face and said he wouldn't dare to insist on his money. And now you have the nerve to suggest that Mr O'Rafferty should pay you for robbing him! Well, the Irish have me speechless for sheer audacity!"

"Oh, he's not Irish, are you, Grogan?" Raff said with deceptive casualness. "Just a nasty little mongrel from the slums of some Latin quarter somewhere, overlaid with a brogue too good to be true. The Garda might be interested to see his papers, among other things."

Grogan's self-confidence began to ooze visibly. He could, thought Judy with interest, afford to bluff Noel, who was as cheap a crook as himself, but he could not for very long hold out against the master of Slyne, whose mildness of tone matched so ill the hard expression in his chilly eyes.

"Now look, Mr O'Rafferty, sor, I'll say nothin' about the cruel slight you cast on me parentage, the saints forgive you—but we want no trouble with the Garda, do we?" he said ingratiatingly.

"I want no trouble, if it can be avoided, certainly," Raff answered coolly, then his voice suddenly changed. "Now listen to me, Grogan, you dirty little twister! I have no liking for my affairs being dragged into the open in order to teach you a lesson, and for that reason, and that reason only, I'll not prosecute you this time. But if ever I catch you round here again, or have any cause whatever to think you're practising your filthy trade in this district, I'll have you hounded out of the country and sent back to wherever it is you belong when the local gaol has done with you. Now get out!"

Grogan licked his dry lips and began to sidle towards the door.

"And what about me fine piece in the van?" he whined, hopeful to the last of making some sort of a deal.

"Drive it away and unload it on some poor mug who'll swallow your blarney before I fetch a chopper and break the ruddy thing up under your nose," Raff said, and turned his back.

Judy let out a long sigh and sat down rather heavily on the nearest chair.

"I'm beginning to think I can't keep pace with the natives of this country," she said, pushing an agitated hand through her hair. "No one reacts as you expect."

"Well, events have rather crowded one upon the other just of late," he replied, observing her thoughtfully. "I don't think you need trouble yourself at not being able to keep pace, though. You seem to tackle most things that come your way, including the unspeakable Grogan, with astonishing nonchalance. He didn't hurt you, did he, Judy?"

"Oh, no—only scared me a little on top of Granny Malone's dire predictions."

"Granny? What's she been up to?"

"Oh, telling my fortune again. She sees ashes and ruins and says I'm bad luck to the house with my red hair. Do you think I could be bad luck, Raff? An awful lot of unpleasant things have been happening lately."

He smiled, and the new tenderness was back in his face.

"For me you mean good luck, my dear, and for Slyne too, I think," he said softly. "You're accepted, you know, as Marcia never was."

"Except for Granny."

"Ah, the divil fly away with the old biddy and her evil eye!" he exclaimed, and she began to laugh. She laughed so long that Raff gave her an uneasy glance.

"You've had about enough, haven't you?" he said. "Why not go and lie down until teatime?"

She wiped her streaming eyes and got briskly to her feet.

"Certainly not!" she retorted severely. "There's masses of paper work to be got through yet. Noel's office is in a terrible muddle and I've been straightening things out. What are you going to do about the fabulous Yanks, Raff? Do you think we could manage between us?"

"I've cabled them not to come," he said. "That's what I went over to Casey's for. They may, on closer acquaintance, prove to be quite a reasonable family, but I thought we'd be better at present without the doubtful advantages of luxury-loving guests."

"Oh! Marcia always regarded that as a valuable booking leading to others," she said dubiously.

"Marcia's judgement might have been proved wrong, as in other matters," he returned dryly. "Are you willing to stop on, Judy, and keep me and the books straight? I

175

couldn't pay you the Maule's salary until times were better, but you'd make more than you would as a secretary."

She gave him a puzzled glance. Had those tender hints and half-formed declarations he had let fall last night only been leading up to this after all?

"I wouldn't want much salary. I'd be learning myself most of the time," she answered, lowering her lashes. "Yes, Raff, of course I'll stop on if you think I can make a go of it."

"Good!" he said briskly, as if he had concluded a satisfactory business deal. "Well, we'd better set to right away clearing up the mess Noel's left. Come on."

There was no time for the rest of the afternoon to indulge in personalities, or perhaps he saw to it that there should not be.

By seven o'clock Judy was aware that she was desperately tired. Raff prescribed a stiff drink for both of them, but she hardly touched hers, desiring only her bed and the blissfulness of unconsciousness.

"I've worn you out," he said remorsefully. "Would you like to skip dinner and have a tray upstairs?"

She shook her head and made an effort to sip her drink as if she enjoyed it. Miss Botley had already retired to bed with a migraine, and if they were short-handed in the kitchen, an extra tray would make more work. Raff looked tired himself, she thought, and wondered if it would seem strange dining alone with him instead of being one of the foursome they had always made with the Maules.

They did not, however, share a table together in the end, for with Miss Botley absent, Colonel Frazer was left marooned in the middle of the room, and Raff invited him, Judy thought, with a certain relief, to join them. The Colonel was not generally communicative, except in matters of complaint and his habitual sparring with Miss Botley, but he made a gallant effort to keep the conversation going when his two companions fell silent. It was true that his contributions mostly consisted of rather dull stories about the Regiment and life in India, but Judy was grateful to him. Being faced with the knowledge that she would, in the days to come, spend long hours in Raff's company with no one else to shift the focus from herself

176

had made her suddenly shy of him, and he, she thought, darting a surreptitious glance at his detached, rather weary expression, was possibly already regretting his unguarded remarks of last night.

"Will you advertise for another manager?" Colonel Frazer asked for the second time, and Raff smiled an apology for his absent-mindedness.

"No, Judy and I are going to try to tackle it on our own," he replied. "We shall run the place on very different lines, of course, but there must still be people like yourself, Colonel, who want somewhere quiet with a bit of fishing and shooting thrown in and the moderate comforts of a country house."

"Couldn't agree more," the Colonel barked. "Wouldn't have stayed on meself, I don't mind telling you, if that couple had jazzed the place up any more. Miss Botley's going, of course. Rather took a shiner to that no-good young manager of yours. Flattered her; gave her ideas, silly old bag!"

"She's lonely," said Judy gently, remembering her conversation with Miss Botley. "She says when you're old nobody really wants you. That's dreadful."

"Yes, well—that's true enough, I suppose, and one ought to remember . . ." the Colonel cleared his throat in some embarrassment and finished dictatorially: ". . . I shall stop on, of course, if you'll get that lazy feller of yours to stoke the furnace properly, O'Rafferty. Only needs discipline and a little dragooning—might take him on meself and knock a little stuffing into him."

"Thank you, Colonel, that's very kind," Raff said courteously, and Judy surprised the old soldier by leaning across to kiss him and inform him that he was a perfect dear.

"God bless my soul!" he observed, turning brick-red. "Don't you worry, Miss Judy! We'll soon get this place going, and if I may say so, a little organisation on military lines wouldn't come amiss, what? Call on me, m'dear, call on me any time."

He rose to take his leave of them and went off delighted with the alluring prospect ahead, and Raff observed with a crooked smile:

177

"Another lonely one, do you suppose? You mustn't go turning the heads of our elderly guests in such a flagrant fashion, Judy!"

"He was so sweet, trying to lend his support," she said. "Wouldn't you love to see him organising Timsy into a smart recruit?"

"Well, thank goodness we're going to get rid of the old biddy, after all. I thought we'd got her for life," Raff said, and cocked an eyebrow at her. "If you become so successful as manageress-cum-everything else, running my modest guest house for me, I shall have to think about a new secretary."

But she was not listening. Her gaze wandered round the high room, imagining it as it once was.

"What did you say?" she asked, aware that Raff had spoken to her.

"Merely a frivolous comment," he answered, watching her withdrawn expression. "What were you thinking of?"

"Slyne as it used to be," she said. "Don't you ever see ghosts, Raff?"

"Ghosts?" His bony features creased into lines of wry remembrance. "Not of the eighteenth century, which I think you had in mind."

"I wasn't thinking in terms of any century," she said, surprised.

"Possibly not, but Ireland is very eighteenth century in character still, you know. Dublin's Georgian houses, the old, decaying mansions such as this—the dust of that century still blows over us," he said, and she thought that, like Timsy, he could speak sometimes with a poet's tongue, and wondered if this might be an unconscious characteristic of the Irish.

"Is that why you say your feet are in the past?" she asked, remembering how she too had fallen into the trick of thinking backwards.

He smiled.

"I don't know. Probably it's merely an excuse for insufficient interest in the future. Are you falling into the habit yourself, Judy? You were such a direct, uncomplicated young creature when you came here. Wolves were wolves, you once told me, and nice men were nice men

178

—both easily defined. You used to make me a little envious by your simple approach to life."

"Did I? But then, you see, I didn't know very much about life."

"And do you now?"

"No. . . ." She sighed and folded up her napkin with absent-minded deliberation, and he said, with a change of tone:

"You're tired, my dear. Why don't you nip up to bed?"

"I think I will," she said. "Goodnight, Raff."

"Goodnight," he replied, rising as she pushed back her chair.

"And don't slip away from me altogether in your concern for my country's past. We live in the twentieth century, as you used to be fond of telling me. You and I must meet halfway."

"Halfway? Is it riddles again?"

"Not really. Go to bed, Judy, and tomorrow perhaps we'll sort the riddles out."

She went through the hall, pausing to sniff the malodorous smell of Timsy's paraffin stove which, more than usual, seemed to pervade the house. It was probably smoking again, but she could not be bothered to go to the pantry and turn it down, and Timsy most likely was there, sleeping off the effects of his private celebrations. She switched off the lights to save what current was left and went upstairs to the nursery.

III

No one had turned down her bed or drawn the curtains, and the light of a full moon flooded into the room from the open window. She stood for a long time looking out at the lough and the dark shape of Slieve Rury, and listening to the small sounds of the still May night. A light went out in old Paddy's cabin down the boreen, but in Granny's none burned, and soon the tiny gleams from the few scattered homesteads would be doused too, for the country folk went early to bed here. Judy wondered if they had looked across to the castle, missing the lighted windows and the sound of laughter from the bar, and the noisy arrival and departure of cars disturbing the peace of the south road, and been glad that in the space of one day the place had slipped back to its gentle decay. And the Maules? Had they gone back to England, or stopped in Dublin to live riotously for a while in the plush hotels of their ambition; and had Marcia no regrets for the bounty she had thrown away? And had Raff?

Presently she saw him walk down to the jetty and stand there for a long time, staring out across the lough as she was doing, his tall, loose-limbed frame outlined against the path of moonlight across the water. He turned then and began to walk slowly along the shore, and soon she lost him in the shadows. Dear Raff, she thought, leaving the window and beginning to undress; he had been disturbed all day, and now he was seeking the solitude which had become habitual to him as an escape from his guests, and was tonight, perhaps, an escape from something else. . . .

She put her new housecoat on, tying it snugly round her narrow waist, and turned and twisted dreamily before the mirror. In the moonlight it no longer looked cheap; the colour which had seemed a little crude had paled to the green of lake water, and the long, full skirt brushing her bare legs made her feel feminine and frail. *Illusion,* she thought rather crossly, and became aware that she had lost the desire for sleep, or even for the doubtful comfort of her bed with the broken spring. She decided to sit by the window and watch for Raff's return.

She realised vaguely, after a time, that it must be getting late, for she remembered hearing the Colonel come up to bed, and the faint sounds of the servants moving about in the upstairs rooms had long ago ceased. Raff must have gone for a very long walk, she thought, discovering that she was beginning to feel stiff sitting so long by an open window, and at the same moment became conscious that the pungent smell of Timsy's stove had penetrated even to her bedroom. For a moment she sat there, wondering sleepily how the smell of paraffin could possibly reach this wing of the house, then became suddenly wide awake as her senses recognised something more ominous, the unmistakable smell of burning.

180

"Oh, lord! Oh, goodness! The silly old idiot must have set light to something!" she exclaimed, and flung open her door.

The smell of burning was stronger in the corridor, and she thought she saw a faint haze of smoke drifting through the shafts of moonlight, but Timsy's pantry was in the other wing and something down there must be well ablaze if smoke had already reached this part of the house. She pressed one of the light switches, but the current had been completely exhausted by now, and as she ran along passages, banging on doors, she was thankful for the brilliant moonlight and the servant's careless habit of never drawing the curtains. As she ran, she had time to think of Granny Malone's prophecies . . . *ashes and ruins . . . ashes and ruins.* . . . "Oh, *no*!" cried Judy, flying down the stairs, but it seemed only too true. As she reached the hall great clouds of smoke billowed to meet her, and now she could hear the sinister roar and crackle of flames. The pantry was ablaze, and the panelling had already caught in the Small Saloon next door.

"Raff! Raff!" she shouted, running to the study, where he would most likely be if he was still up, then she remembered that he had not returned from his walk, and when he did . . . when he did . . . he would find his home in ashes as that horrible old witch had predicted.

"I'm bad luck to the house like she said . . . she's put the 'fluence on me, on Slyne, perhaps on Raff himself . . ." she cried distractedly, and became aware that someone had her by the shoulders and was shaking her none too gently.

"Don't panic, don't panic! Pull yourself together, girl, and tell me where the fire-extinguishers are," Colonel Frazer was barking at her.

"Where's O'Rafferty?" he barked at Judy, and snorted when he was told. "Have you rung the fire brigade? No? Then do so now, though God knows what degree of efficiency they may have in this disgracefully run country!"

Judy got on to the fire station at Knockferry, after the usual arguments with the erratic exchange, but it seemed that someone had seen the fire from across the lough and already notified them.

"Sure, there's no need to disturb yourself, miss, no need at all!" a cheerful voice the other end assured her. "The boys have been spoilin' for a good fire, and they with the tarrible monotony on them for want of an elegant blaze! The boys will be with you in the wink of a pig's eye—if Micky Doolan doesn't drive the contraption right off that tarrible road of yours, that is."

The Colonel had managed to organise pails and buckets of water from somewhere by the time she returned, and it was only then, seeing them all trying to tackle the flames without much success, that she missed Timsy. He had not come down with the others, she remembered, and suddenly the beating of her own heart sounded louder in her ears than the roar of the flames. The old man had been slightly drunk for most of the day; he could have fallen asleep in his pantry to which he retired indefinitely upon these occasions with his bottles and his cornet; he might even have knocked the stove over in his unsteadiness.

"Timsy!" she cried in terror, and ran across the hall and through the smoke before the Colonel could stop her.

The bar was blazing in earnest now, the dry old panelling in the Small Saloon acting like tinder, and at the door of the pantry she was beaten back by the heat.

"Timsy . . . Timsy . . ." she screamed, and felt the pain in her hands as she tore at the burning wood which was obstructing the doorway. She had managed to force an entry when she felt herself lifted from behind and Raff's furious voice shouted:

"Are you crazy, you little fool? You can't get in there, the place is an inferno!"

"Timsy's in there!" she sobbed, and never knew that she was crying. She could only remember that Timsy had been her friend, offering strange comfort when she needed it, making her laugh, teaching her to love this feckless country of his birth. She fought Raff with all the strength she had left, but he simply pinioned her hands in a grip that made her cry out with the pain of her burns, and carried her back into the hall.

"You idiotic, gallant, bloody-minded little loon!" he shouted at her, and shook her hard. "There's your poor charred victim coming down the stairs! Sleeping it off in comfort in his bed, so Agnes says, having done his best to burn the place down first,"

"Oh, *Timsy*. . . ." Judy wept with relief and reproach and a hint of laughter in her tears.

The old man was sober now and he looked round him with mild astonishment, then his rheumy eyes found the blazing doorway of his pantry and he said in a quavering voice:

"Me cornet . . . merciful heavens, me cornet is in there! Destroyed it'll be . . . destroyed entirely . . . whirra . . . whirra. . . ."

"And a good job too," said Raff heartlessly. "Pull yourself together, Timsy, and go and join the bucket-chain outside. You'll all do more good there till the brigade arrives than fighting the flames from inside. Come on!"

"Can't we get the furniture out?" Judy asked, rubbing away the tears from her smarting eyes. "If the Grand Saloon catches, all that lovely stuff will go up like matchwood."

Raff merely seized her hand and pulled her after him to the front door.

"We've had enough trouble with those ruddy antiques as it is. Let the damn things burn!" he said.

The cool night air was a blessed relief after the heat and smoke and confusion, and at first she just stood and stared. The place seemed like Fair Day in Knockferry, for people had come from far and near, from across the lough in boats, and even, it was said, from the mountains, to lend a hand in saving Castle Slyne. Men in various aspects of the national hat argued and gesticulated excitedly in groups; some ran hither and thither, shouting to their friends, with little purpose it appeared except to render more confusion; the bucket-chain worked tirelessly from the lough to the house, and Judy recognised familiar faces: Mick and Pat and the entire Boyle family, including Rosie; Casey from the other side, and a couple of the Garda; Willie-the-Post, with a fine tale to spread tomorrow. Even old Paddy had taken his turn to pass the buckets and now sat on the terrace steps for a good ringside view in company with Granny Malone. Glare from the flames lighted the gesticulating figures like the demon effects in a pantomine, and the noise was indescribable.

"It's fantastic. Where do they all come from?" Judy exclaimed, uncertain whether to laugh or cry again, and Raff's smile was a little grim.

"Any occasion's a beanfeast in Ireland," he said, "but they'd all want to help. Slyne has been a landmark in these parts for a very long time."

"Don't take alarrum, O'Rafferty, we'll have the castle saved for you!" they shouted as Raff and Judy hurried among them to relieve a couple in the bucket-chain, and suddenly a great shout went up, and amidst wild cheering the fire brigade arrived taking the bends in the south road in magnificent style with screaming tyres and a clanging bell, and driving over Raff's lawns without stopping once to inquire their direction. When they came to a violent standstill and the men jumped off and started unwinding their hoses, it could be seen that the engine had collected two flat tyres.

The buckets were hastily dumped as the willing workers surged towards the house for a fresh diversion, and Judy half expected that the fire-fighting appliances, like the household extinguishers, would be out of date and inadequate, but the little force of men were well trained, and soon powerful jets of water were playing on the flames, and orders were issued and obeyed with heartening speed.

Judy had lost Raff in the crowd, and she slipped down alone to the water's edge to watch, away from the crowd. The house was unbearably beautiful in the moonlight, the shadows of its moulded stone and gracious abutments etched sharp and clear; even the burning wing had a strange, fierce beauty against the night sky. Just so must it have looked once before, she thought, when another wing had blazed in the angry darkness of Ireland's "troubles" and still not been destroyed. Watching from the solitude of the shore, Judy knew a tightening of the throat. Was, she thought in sudden anguish, her castle in the clouds to vanish in smoke like the burning of Valhalla in *The Twilight of the Gods?* Were the old gods to be driven once again from their peace in this land of so

much unrest? *I'm slipping back, as Raff warned me* . . .
she told herself, suddenly shy of the emotions the night
had brought her, and as a cheer went up from the
milling mass of humanity round the house she saw that
the flames had died and the smoky glow which hung over
Slyne was fading into the soft radiance of the May moon.

In a little while the crowd began to disperse, and she
watched them leaving in the divers ways they had come,
by ancient car and bicycle, by farm wagon and weedy
hack, by the humble ass-drawn carts, all pressed into the
work of salvage. Only the fire-engine remained, shining and
magnificent, on the trampled grass, and Judy went slowly
back to the house, her long skirt trailing in the dew.

Men were still hacking away at bar and pantry, and
water seeped into the hall in black, evil-smelling pools, but
the fire was out. It had not, one of the men was cheerfully
assuring Raff, done as much damage as might have been
expected, and wouldn't that old sinner, Timsy Sullivan,
be havin' a skelpin' for leavin' his pants to dry on the
stove and he away in his bed, not mindful that the stuff
would scorch?

"Me cornet . . ." Timsy himself was still muttering un-
happily, picking about amidst the blackened remains of his
pantry, and two of the firemen were surveying the bar
and scratching their heads sorrowfully.

"Would you credit it, Murphy, all that good liquor
wasted, and never a wan of us to save a bottle or two?" one
said to the other.

"Ah, sure, 'tis the bad luck that's been on us these
days past," Murphy agreed mournfully. "Would you think,
now, the O'Rafferty would be havin' a drap of the crayture
stored away beyont?"

"There's some still left in the cellars," Raff reassured
them, with a grin. "Timsy will see to you. Mary Kate, take
them all to the dining-room and do what you can for them.
The kitchen, I think, is still too choked with smoke to
prove a comfortable spot for entertaining. You might bring
something to the study for the rest of us, Agnes, when
your uncle has taken his pick from the cellar. Come along,
Judy, and the rest of you. We can all do with a pick-me-up

before spending what's left of the rest of the night in our beds."

But it was only Judy and the Colonel who followed him to his study. Miss Botley, remembering her chin-strap too late, removed it hurriedly and, not liking to look in Colonel Frazer's choleric eye, observed crushingly that since she did not drink, even in an emergency, she would retire again to her bed if she could be assured she would be safe for the night.

"I shall leave in the morning, however, Mr O'Rafferty," she said. "I'm sorry for your misfortune, but really I cannot be expected to stop on here any longer with the house in this state of turmoil. Will you kindly have my bill made out in the morning, and I shall expect, of course, a small reduction in terms for this week's inconvenience."

She swept upstairs, coughing as she inhaled the smoke which was still hanging about, and Judy wanted for a moment to run after her, offering apologies for the shortcomings of the house, but she was too tired. A burst of merriment came from the dining-room where the firemen were evidently well on the way to being entertained by the kitchen staff, and the Colonel closed the study door and cleared his throat.

"Might have been worse!" he said. "Might have been a lot worse. I remember when I was in Simla——"

She could not bear it, Judy thought, if the old soldier were to embark on one of his deadly reminiscences now, and she curled up on the hearth, surprised to see that the turves were still a glowing heap of white ash, and examined her burnt hands.

"Gad! You're hurt, Miss Judy, what?" the Colonel interrupted himself to exclaim, and Raff, who had been foraging for candles, looked down at her sharply.

"Let me see," he said, kneeling beside her, and taking her hands gently in his to examine the palms.

"Yes, you are," he said, frowning. "Quite nasty burns, in fact. I'll get the first-aid box—these must be painful."

"Plucky, though, by jove! Damn plucky little filly," the Colonel observed admiringly, and Miss Doyle came in with a tray bearing glasses, a magnum of champagne,

186

and a many-branched silver candelabrum which gently touched the room with light.

The pop the cork made was a heartening sound and Judy watched the bubbles rising to the surface of each glass with sleepy interest. The Colonel raised his own glass with the appropriate vague noises to accompany a toast and observed optimistically:

"Insurance—make quite a thing out of that, O'Rafferty —only those two rooms and the one above badly damaged. I should let 'em go to ruin to match the other wing and concentrate on the rest of the house, what? Still room enough for P.G.s, and that damn bar's no loss."

"Yes . . ." Raff said, absently sipping his champagne while his eyes brooded on Judy's bent head, bright in the candlelight. Miss Doyle brought the first-aid box and put it on the desk with some stringent observation which received no answer, and went away again, and Colonel Frazer, finding that he too was receiving scant attention at the hands of his host, downed his champagne and did not wait to be offered a second glass.

"Get those burns fixed up. Painful thing, burns. Girl's probably in pain, what?" he remarked from the doorway, and was gone, congratulating himself on his tact.

Raff put down his glass with an exclamation of remorse.

"What am I thinking of! Here, come to the light and let me see to your hands," he said, setting out such remedies as he needed with swift efficiency, but a great lassitude had fallen upon Judy. Her hands were throbbing, but no more noticeably than the uneven tempo of her heart, and the champagne was going a little to her head.

"You come to me," she said in the provocative tones she had sometimes heard Marcia use, and wondered a little lightheadedly if the trick would work for her.

He gave her a quick glance, then, setting the candelabrum on the floor, knelt down again beside her and started dressing her hands. She watched him closely, observing all the small familiar details which she had come to know so well; the flecks of grey in his hair, the sharp, irregular outline of his bony features, and that endearing suggestion of a break in the high bridge of his nose. He was so close to her that she could trace each line and idiosyncrasy in his face with loving attention, and only looked away when he glanced up suddenly, and caught her at it.

"Isn't it queer," she said, beginning to talk very fast, "that I bought this housecoat in case the house caught fire? Do you remember—it was only yesterday?" He did not answer, but pushing the first-aid box aside, sat down on a low stool to regard her steadily. "Granny Malone saw ashes and ruin in my fortune . . . she said I was bad luck to the house because of my hair. . . . Do you think I'm bad luck? Raff . . . do answer me. . . ."

"Are you ready to sort out those riddles now, I wonder?" he asked, and his grey eyes were grave and questioning. Her answering gaze was as grave as his, but the first faint flicker of alarm changed to a look of untroubled acceptance, and she smiled at him.

"Yes . . ." she said on a long sigh. "Yes, Raff—perhaps I had the answer all the time. . . ."

"I think you had. I think, perhaps, you just refused to let that part of your mind grow up."

"Oh, yes, I did. It was your fault if you didn't understand what I felt about you. Everyone else did—even Timsy and the Colonel—but you were too busy being avuncular."

"You mustn't grudge me my defence," he said, and his smile was tender and a little rueful. "Lovers are humble creatures, I think, my dearest dear, and I, with only one love of long ago to show me the way, had forgotten, perhaps, that one must be bold in order to conquer."

"I wouldn't like," she said, suddenly sitting up very straight and stiff with her long skirt spread about her, and her bandaged hands folded primly in her lap, "to be confused with Kathy."

"Meaning just what?"

"Meaning, I suppose, that I wouldn't care to be part of a fixation—a sort of Kathy-symbol, or whatever the right jargon is."

He moved so abruptly that he nearly knocked the candelabrum over, and it was she who stretched out and moved it, holding it between them like a bright shield.

"Jargon is right!" he exclaimed, and was on his feet. "Where did you learn such nonsense—from Marcia? Here,

188

give me that thing!" He snatched the candelabrum from her and set it on the desk, seeing as he did so the new challenge in her green eyes and the brief unsteadiness of her mouth. "Come here! The time for riddles between us is past, and I can be tough, my dear, if that's an approach you'd understand better."

He pulled her up into his arms and kissed her, as she had once seen him kiss Marcia, with angry exasperation, and knew then that provocation, even though unwilling and freshly learnt, was a woman's easy weapon. But as she offered herself willingly for whatever he should choose to bestow, no longer caring if she did not please him as Kathy had done, the quality of his passion changed and the warmth and gentleness that flowed from him took her without words, into his keeping and into his heart. . . .

"Don't you understand that one love is an echo of another?" he said, his cheek against hers. "My love for Kathy was a young, untried thing; my love for you is a mature completion of what might have grown between us, because with her you share that quality of innocence and loving kindness which I must need for my own fulfilment. But I have never confused you, my darling. You are you, and love for you has grown into my very bones, just as my love for Slyne, and can have no uprooting. Will you share me with that and that alone?"

"You and Timsy both speak with the poet's tongue when you are moved," she said wonderingly. "Is it an Irish trait?"

"I don't know. Eloquence is supposed to be attributed to our race, but mine, perhaps, has not been much tested until now. Do I have to plead further with you, Judy, or shall I summon Timsy from his revels to do it for me?"

"Timsy would do it no better, and you've no need to plead, dear Raff, with someone whose nice clean heart you took long ago and squeezed dry."

"This time," he told her with mock severity, "I refuse to give you the benefit of the doubt on the score of light-headedness—unless the fire has been too much for you!" He caught sight of her bandaged hands and brought them to his lips. "Oh, Judy, my child, you'll never know the fear you put on me when I saw you trying to force your

189

way into that inferno—and all for the sake of that miserable old sinner who ought to be shot. . . ."

"He was my friend," said Judy gently. "With Timsy I never had to pretend, and he could make me laugh, and sometimes he could make me cry, too. Can we go out, Raff?"

"Out? Haven't you had enough for one night, you astonishing child?"

"Avuncular again—you must learn to stop it if you're thinking of making me your wife," she said sedately.

"I beg your pardon! And I was certainly thinking of making you my wife, so don't let there be any more misunderstandings between us on that score. We'll go out."

They walked through the dark, silent hall, the light from the candles through the open doorway making a dim path for them. The acrid smell of charred wood still hung on the air, and Raff opened the great front door to the fresh stillness of the hours before dawn. She took his hand and led him down to the shore where she had stood and watched the castle burning, and, still hand in hand, they turned to look back.

There it lay, the sleeping house, as it had lain for centuries, with the same moon keeping watch and the same stars looking down so impersonally on the slow passage of a decay that would never be absolute until the place like its two burnt-out wings should become, in some distant decade, a heap of stones too long forgotten to be mourned.

"Satisfied?" Raff asked very softly. "You wanted to make sure it was still there, didn't you?"

"How did you know?"

"Oh—because for me, as well as for you, perhaps, its had a kind of magic."

"But for you it was never a castle in the clouds—something out of reach and not quite real," she said, and he looked down at her with tenderness.

"Not out of reach any more, Judy. Sometimes one finds one's cloud castle, like the leprechauns' crock of gold at the end of the rainbow," he said, and as he spoke she saw the first light of dawn begin to break in the sky behind Slieve Rury.

A new day, she thought, a day different from all the others and one to be remembered for a lifetime, because it was the beginning. . . . She lifted her face to his, closing her eyes for a moment in a silent vow, and the dawn breeze blew a strand of her hair across his lips.

Somewhere a cock crowed, and down the boreen Paddy-the-Sheep's dog woke from its slumbers and began to bark. Soon it would be answered by Mulligan or Holy Joe or Wheezy, and pails would clatter in the milking sheds, and sleepy voices would call a greeting or, more likely, a good-tempered curse, and the pattern of their lives would begin again.

Judy's bright head, heavy with long-denied sleep, began to drop against his shoulder.

"Raff—who *was* Finn MacCoul?" she murmured drowsily.

"A legendary hero, my bemused sweetheart, a myth—and no possible relative of any of us," he said, and picked her up and carried her back to the house.

THE END

INFORMATION PLEASE

Would you like to learn a little more about Harlequin, the services offered, the publications available and a host of other things which could mean a great deal more reading pleasure for you — it's very simple to find out all about us — without any obligation of course. All you have to do is send your name and address to us on the coupon below, and we'll be happy to tell you all you need to know about some of the things we do for Harlequin Readers.

In addition to some valuable information, we will also forward to you the very special "Collector's Edition" of LUCIFER'S ANGEL by Violet Winspear, **ABSOLUTELY FREE**. It's our way of saying "Thank you" for your interest in us, and in our novels.

You'll enjoy reading Violet Winspear's explosive story of the fast-moving, hard-living world of Hollywood in the 50's. It's an unforgettable tale of an innocent young girl who meets and marries a dynamic but ruthless movie producer. It's a gripping novel combining excitement, intrigue, mystery and romance.

LUCIFER'S ANGEL, Violet Winspear's first Harlequin novel has been newly printed in a special "Collector's Edition" with a new, exciting and distinctive cover design, and a complimentary copy is waiting for you — just fill out the coupon and mail it to us, to-day. SEND TO:—